CW00971976

SMOKE

30127085125966

santiago dargallo

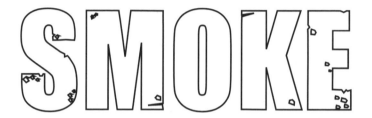

Copyright © 2008 Santiago Dargallo

The moral right of the author has been asserted.

Apart from any fair dealing for the purposes of research or private study,
or criticism or review, as permitted under the Copyright, Designs and Patents
Act 1988, this publication may only be reproduced, stored or transmitted, in
any form or by any means, with the prior permission in writing of the
publishers, or in the case of reprographic reproduction in accordance with
the terms of licences issued by the Copyright Licensing Agency. Enquiries
concerning reproduction outside those terms should be sent to the publishers.

Matador
9 De Montfort Mews
Leicester LE1 7FW, UK
Tel: (+44) 116 255 9311 / 9312
Email: books@troubador.co.uk
Web: www.troubador.co.uk/matador

COVER DESIGN
© 2008   Chris Gibson
© 2008 Santiago Dargallo Nieto

ISBN 978-1906510-961

A Cataloguing-in-Publication (CIP) catalogue record for this book
is available from the British Library.

SUFFOLK COUNTY LIBRARIES & HERITAGE	
07277851	
HJ	11/12/2008
F	£7.99

Typeset in 11pt Stempel Garamond by Troubador Publishing Ltd, Leicester, UK
Printed in the UK by The Cromwell Press Ltd, Trowbridge, Wilts, UK

Matador is an imprint of Troubador Publishing Ltd

To my wife Samantha and all our children:
Laura, Holly, Lucy, Felix and Carmen.

FOREWORD

This is a work of fiction. It is based on an entirely surreal case-scenario, which could nevertheless have occurred. Some of the peripheral characters are real (including Lord Leweson-Gore who is real and worked in the

LIGHT UP

Chapter 1

Smoke rings floated lazily in Buckingham Palace's courtyard. Their source was enjoying their flight as he broke the rules, yet again. He had, after all, devoted years of practice to both! Barry Smith was a junior footman in the palace. One of the many staff whose main role at Buckingham Palace seems to be that of opening and closing doors for passing dignitaries and the royal family. He was enjoying a crafty cigarette outside the kitchens of the palace. Standing at five eleven (and a half as he always insisted when being measured) he was enviably slim with a mop of clean wavy dark hair. His eyes, a warm hazel colour, were darting left and right constantly. This might have been interpreted as anxiousness at being caught but his languid posture, reclining against the wall almost like a stretched bow, with his cigarette hanging loosely between his index and middle finger conveyed an image of confident relaxation. Next to him, sitting on a crate of laundry waiting to be washed sat Melanie Hatton, a maid.

The contrast between Barry and Melanie, couldn't have been more striking as she stood at five foot two was quite tubby and her short legs in regulation thick dark stockings and lace-up flat shoes were dangling above the ground.

'You'll get caught again and will have to report to Conns again' squeaked Melanie in her broad Shires accent. 'You aren't exactly the flavour of the month with him you know.'

'Don't worry yourself "Quota",' drawled Brian, 'Conns is looking more towards his retirement than to anything else and is too busy planning a graceful look when he receives his retirement plaudits and farewell do's not to mention his ringing Moss Bros to Hire his morning coat when he gets his peerage "for services to the country" he added in a slight fake plummy voice.

Melanie frowned slightly. She didn't like the nickname of quota. This had been unkindly bestowed by an unpleasant supercilious senior footman who cruelly said she had only got the position as palace maid because she had been the only applicant from Rutland, the smallest county in England, and it was policy in Buckingham Palace to have employees from every county in Britain "however poor their standards may be". This was a total fallacy. Melanie was a hard working, conscientious house maid with impeccable references. She was deeply loyal and much liked by staff and the Royal family alike who found her habit of giving a little squeak of excitement whenever she came across a member of the Royal family quite endearing. This habit had not gone away despite having worked at the palace for over three years.

Barry Smith, on the other hand, was not in Melanie's league. In fact you would have struggled to find a less likely candidate to get his photograph taken for the employee of the month photo frame. He had only started working at Buckingham Palace (or Buck house as he liked to call it) three months ago and had already managed to receive two verbal warnings from Sir Ian Connaught (a.k.a Conns by the rest of the staff) a fierce Ulsterman in charge of personnel. Brian had managed to get very quickly into the cross hairs of Sir Ian's pet dislike with remarkable speed. To be fair to Sir Ian, Brian had unwittingly ticked the boxes appertaining to most of his personal cardinal sins with remarkable speed. He was unpunctual (that was a top three cardinal sin) lackadaisical (a top ten) and managed to convey the impression he was just making time until something better came along thus being suspect of lack of loyalty (top of the list!)

'Anyway Barry, you will soon not be able to smoke in the Palace anymore. The smoking ban starts soon.'

'Don't be silly, it only applies to working places including pubs,' he added wistfully, 'this isn't a working place, it is a private residence, with the best location in town, home to queen Bessie Mark II Gawd Bless 'er' he added in a mock cockney accent.

'Only Ma'am's private apartments count as a private residence, the rest of the palace isn't' she retorted disapprovingly. Barry's lack of respect towards the Royal family always managed to annoy her.

'Anyway it isn't your home since you feel you are too grand to use the servants quarters.'

'Why should I? I have a perfectly nice flat in Kensington where I don't have to queue for the toilet or a lukewarm shower.'

Brian sighed and stretched out his arm ready to flick his smouldering stub into the courtyard. He caught Melanie's censorious expression with the corner of his eye. He smiled and walked towards a puddle in a corner, bent over and extinguished it. He carried the now soggy dog end almost ceremoniously between his thumb and forefinger and dropped it in a small rubbish bin next to the servant's entrance which was set there for that purpose.

Melanie's posture relaxed perceptibly and she stopped drumming her heels against the side of the laundry crate. Barry offered his hand and she jumped off.

'What are you duties now?'

'I don't know. Probably summoned to patrol the corridors so any flunkey marginally senior to me can torment my feet sending me from one side of Buck house to the other carrying a note when a phone call or e-mail would have been just as useful. Have you guys never heard of intranet? It would halve your cobbler's bills!'

Melanie gave him a wry look. 'Well Bill Gates when you're in charge of running this place you can set up the electronic revolution. In the meantime trot along and tone those nice calves of yours.'

'Yes modom' Brian gave her a brief curtsey and sauntered into the palace.

Melanie giggled and shook her head. Despite his many defects and lackadaisical approach to work she couldn't help liking him. Perhaps it was his insouciance or, in her view, his reckless disregard for rules. It was a source of wonderment among the staff how two people with such different backgrounds and approach to life could still rub along so well. There might have been an element of infatuation on Melanie's side even if she was well aware that Brian's raffish behaviour and trendy apparel would never fit the expectations she had of a boyfriend. She also knew, because he had never tried to hide it, that he had a girlfriend who worked in the real estate business.

Later in the evening Barry left work through a side gate in the palace. He weaved past the tourists taking photographs of the poor Grenadier guards (Irish today) and gave the less than martial token punks, who eked a meagre existence out of having their photograph taken for some money, a wide berth.

For some obscure reason they hated palace staff and could sniff one at twenty paces. As he walked down the Mall at a leisurely pace he enjoyed the rare sunshine and eyed the pretty secretaries leaving the government buildings. His relaxed mood was rudely interrupted by a text message offering cheaper Internet broadband to all sabscribars (sic). He looked at it briefly and sighed, as he pulled out a different, cheaper, pay as you go mobile. He then keyed in a well-memorised mobile phone number. It only rang once.

'Well?' Barked a voice on the other end. That single syllable managed to convey arrogance, impatience and a Scottish burr.

'No news yet I'm afraid Jock' he replied.

'What do you mean no news yet laddie? Three months you've been there. I do not pay you a handsome salary to swan around in knee length stockings, velvet breeches pocketing a second salary and enjoying all the perks. I cannot believe you have not unearthed even the slightest whiff of scandal among those cretinous inbreed leeches who call themselves the royal family or that bunch of spineless sycophants who positively orgasm at the thought of bowing and scraping to an outmoded concept while clinging to their privileges.'

'Even the most casual reader will have easily deduced that the Scottish grouch at the other end of Barry's phone didn't have fond feelings for the British royal family.'

'I can see you clearly harbour strong feelings about the lodgers and staff at Buck house boss but I'm afraid there is not a lot to report. The Queen and her worse half have been touring a fair bit lately and Andy Pandy, the last resource of the desperate gossip columnist has been on secondment to NATO HQ since shortly before I started so not even a chance of sniffing out a scandal there either. The staff are wary about blabbing to a complete newcomer like me so frankly, I see no point in blowing my cover to "sensationally" reveal that Her Majesty actually prefers PG tips to Fortnum and Masons finest Lapsang Souchong!'

'Is that a fact?' Jock's voice betrayed the excitement at the possibility of ridiculing or smearing his favourite Bete Noire.

'No! It's a Joke.' He adopted a more conciliatory tone. 'Listen Jock, I know you called in a few favours to get me into the inner sanct….'

'Too right I did laddie, I had to keep shtum about a particularly juicy scandal at…'

'Jock, I know, I know and I am very grateful for the opportunity you've given me. I just don't see the point in revealing some bloody trivial suburbia style tit bit at the top or some sorry sordid shagging story downstairs. It just isn't going to get the punters rushing to the newsstand to buy the Daily Herald. The Mirror got in there ages ago with the Tupperware gate. I don't think we should offer a reheated old story with slightly different garnish.'

Jock appeared to relent at this argument. 'I suppose you have a point,' he added gruffly, 'but I don't need one of my reporters hanging around while everyone else has to work harder. You come up with something good soon or I'm pulling the plug and you will go down!'

'OK Jock I'll speak to you soon.'

'With news laddie, with a scoop!'

Barry groaned as he switched his mobile off. Bloody, bloody Jock! He thought. "Handsome salary" indeed! It was a pittance; he worked on a retainer most sweatshop workers would turn their noses up at. This had been halved when he started working at Buckingham Palace, something Jock had conveniently forgotten to mention. He only earned any real money if he had a story or an article published. The amount then varied on the length of the story and how close it was to being front page news. It was a 19th century attitude, with a matching stipend.

Jock's paranoia on the other hand was very much 21st Century. So as not to be traced or tracked he used a Pay as you go mobile to speak to him and only when he received a misspelled text message. He had provided inaccurate personal details (his half blind, half deaf and totally mad great aunt in Wales was the registered owner). If he ever got caught he would get a 3 year holiday in Guantanamo under the prevention of terrorism act!

Jock Robertson, the Managing Director of the Daily Herald

reclined on his wooden chair while tugging at his lower lip. This was a familiar habit whenever he was deep in thought. His change of editorial slant since taking over 4 years ago was losing him readers in droves. His rabid anti-royalist stand had alienated many of his paper's regular readers while failing to recruit new ones. The major shareholders and loan guarantors were beginning to ask questions.

He flicked a switch on his phone control and barked 'Norman! My room, now!'

While he waited for his chief editor he got off the chair and paced around his plush office. Short and squat, with a ruddy complexion anyone could have easily mistaken him for a jovial Jane Austen country squire, until they looked at his eyes: a very pale grey although this seldom showed as his pupils were more or less permanently dilated by his bilious temperament. Jock's mood had two major settings: irate and incandescent. He could be obsequiously charming if he wanted but only the rich or powerful would see this rare side to him!

Norman Sewell, the diffident chief editor walked into the room. His recruitment (or poaching according to the owner of the Guardian) six months ago had been one of Jock's greatest triumphs. He was a crucial part of Jock's plan to stop the Daily Herald's financial and readership haemorrhage.

'You called Jock?' He was slightly out of breath, having just run from his office. He was not used to this behaviour. He was polite to the point of timidity. He would have normally been overlooked for promotion bar for one aspect. He had finest nose in the country when it came to detecting what was newsworthy. He could sense which way the politico-economical wind was blowing, way before any other hack could feel the slightest zephyr. If he was on the chase as he called it he would not accept any interference, not even from Jock, with his modus operandi. On those occasions he showed steely resolve and determination and his list of news achievements ensured his editorial independence remained.

'So Norman, any major news brewing?'

'Nothing much I'm afraid Jock. Maybe…'

'What?'

'Well I was reading the news about the purchase of 5% of Rolls Royce Aero engines as well as 5% of BAe by a consortium.'

'Not quite the catchy headline I was expecting.'

'Indeed no. It is the way it was done.'

'Quit it with your bloody riddles!'

Norman didn't rise to the bait. He seldom did, certainly not for this megalomaniac cretin; he had only accepted the position as chief editor because it allowed him to pay for his mother's nursing home fees. He was beginning to seriously loathe Jock and he wondered, once again, if the penny was worth the candle.

'From what I could glean in the FT it appears that a group of 9 or 10 private individuals have been steadily purchasing shares in these two companies over the last 18 months. About two months a go they decided to form a Limited Liability Partnership, which is similar to a PLC, but not subject to the exact same company rules. A Far East consortium has just acquired this LLP for 20% more than its true value…'

'Right so some foreign Johnny wants to buy the pride and joy of British industry. We shall expose them and stop them right now!'

Norman sighed inwardly, bloody Jock he thought, never waiting for the full picture always jumping both feet first. He let him rant briefly, took a deep breath and stopped him.

'Jock.'

'What?' Jock didn't like being interrupted while ha was having one of his tirades.

'I'm afraid you may not be aware of all the facts. BAe and RR aero *are* already partially owned by various foreign consortia to the tune of 23, sorry 28% now. These are high tech companies who deliver reasonable yields and add prestige to any industrial portfolio. Moreover, with aero industry all being so competitive and interlinked it is no uncommon for these companies to own bits of each other especially those involved in Airbus industries. Any way, I think this far eastern corporation is a front for the Chinese.'

'Most likely mainland then.'

Very good Jock thought Norman. More on the ball than I expected. ' Correct. The People's Republic of China's internal flight market is expanding brutally. They do manufacture some small planes but they are inefficient and not very reliable so they have been paying through the nose purchasing planes from the west: Boeing and Airbus mostly. It is beginning to become a problem for them. Not a big one at present but if their economy continues to expand at the rate it is, a lot of people will be using more internal flights. They are already expanding their airport capacity especially runways'.

'What does this mean?'

'I believe the Chinese want to develop their own air industry big time and eventually join the big boys at the high table. If they really wanted they could eventually swallow us in 20-30 years.'

'Not good for our aero industry then.'

'Hmm I'm not sure. I don't think they are limbering for confrontation or takeover, more like cooperation.'

'What makes you think that?' Jock's interest was definitely piqued; Norman could spin a yarn, on paper or speaking, like the best.

'Their premier.'

'Ma something or other.'

'Ma-Tsien-Zu. A very odd fish if you want my opinion. Raised through the ranks like a standard party apparatchick but is very keen on modernisation. He has been promoting foreign exchanges for the best students in technological or scientific disciplines for the last 20-25 years since he joined the central committee of the communist party of China. These students have been slowly but steadily promoted in the ranks, at least 300 are already in last but two tiers of the CPC and three or four are already assistant or deputy ministers. He is very patriotic, extremely subtle and as patient as drops of water drilling a hole in granite. He himself is no radical, he wants to improve the Chinese people's quality of life but from what I can gather he doesn't want to modernise society, he wants the party firmly in control but he also wants to improve China's financial and political influence. He wants China to be a proper financial and political superpower. If he plays to his strengths I think he could.'

'Where do we move from here?'

'I really am in a quandary as to what to do. Most of this is pure political and economical speculation with precious few leads. I would also like to see how the new government fares, their reaction to the South China sea incident should give us a fair idea of how on the ball they are.' (Especially Miss Stokes he thought to himself with a smile).

'Right, we'll hold fire until that nose of yours has got a bit more twitchy. Make no mistake though, if someone breaks the story first I'll have you guts for garters' he growled menacingly.

Norman left the room. Jock rang his broker and started ordering the purchase of RR and BAe shares. He also arranged for a call with the financial director of the Herald.

While this exchange took place Barry let himself into his girlfriend Pippa's tiny flat in one of the less salubrious parts of Kensington. It was reasonably convenient for him but it irked him that he was beholden to her from the lodging point of view, something she was quick to point out. He could have used the servant's quarters at the palace but he felt that with his double life it could only lead to disaster. Also he got a very welcome supplement from the long term lease of his flat (something he had been careful to keep quiet about) which not only paid his mortgage but also left him "something for weekend". All in all he was happy to let the current status quo even if it included the occasional henpecking by his very sexy (and sexual) harridan of a girlfriend.

'Hello darling, I'm home.'

A blur of a figure, topped by a glorious mane of blond hair, materialised in front of him, scarlet lips clamped around his mouth and eager hands pulled at his shirt buttons while an impossibly long leg clad in exquisite three inch Manolo's rubbed against his inner thigh eliciting an instant response.

Oh good thought Barry, she must have just sold a property, a good one too, as his hands softly caressed her inviting body. He could feel her wearing her sexiest garter and suspenders (a welcome Christmas gift) while his nostrils took in the unmistakeable sweet musky scent of Opium. He did some quick mental calculations before his lower brain definitely took over. It must have been at least £6 million property. Phillippa "Pippa" Coles, his voluptuous and mercurial girlfriend's sex drive and sexuality were always exactly mirrored by her success as an estate agent in fashionable Sloane Square. He sometimes wondered (and dreaded) what would happen if there ever was a property slump. At this very instant though, his mind and body were hell-bent on enjoying the nymphomaniac fringe benefits of London's property boom…

A very enjoyable hour later, tired but extremely satisfied Barry and Pippa were entwined together in *her* bed kissing and caressing softly.

'How was your day Pippa?' He asked this nonchalantly; he already knew it had been good but a mixture of betting and journalistic skills needed definite confirmation.

'It was fan-bloody-tastic she replied in her slightly nasal sloaney drawl. I have just sold two houses in Draycott Place, next to Sloane Square. They were side by side and this weird Russian billionaire went and bought them without batting an eyelid, £ 6.2 million!' she whooped.

Bingo! thought Barry, it pleased him absurdly when he got these little mind bets right. It also meant he and Pippa would be able to go and get some winter sun in the Maldives, largely at her expense. 'You must be the blue-eyed girl at the office' he added admiringly.'

'Too damn right I am!' She sat up in the bed her gloriously tanned body still glowing. 'The people of the office are mostly a bunch of chinless wonders who just don't get it! Can you believe that stupid cow Chantelle – she shuddered slightly at the naffness of the name- actually cancelled her appointment with Yevgeni because she didn't like his looks and would rather have her falsies redone? She will blow a fuse when she finds out just *how* expensive those falsies turned out to be' she said as she smugly admired her perfectly manicured nails, no need for false nails for her!

'Who, pray, is Yevgeni?'

'What?' she was still checking her nails and she had just noticed a little chip in her little fingernail polish which would need attending to. 'Oh Yevgeni Rudkin a Russian billionaire. I have to agree Chantelle did have a point, he *is* gross: short and fat, forever sweating. And hairy like you wouldn't believe it. Paid there and then though; I don't know why he bought the houses.'

'How come?' Brian's journalistic instincts prickling.'

'He has already got a lovely big house in Cadogan walk just up the road. Not one I sold though'

'Maybe as an investment?'

'No,' she shook her head 'too expensive to get a decent return, the rent would be stratospheric. Maybe he wants to set up offices for his business.

'What does he do? '

She shrugged her shoulders she was now losing interest in this subject, 'Oil I suppose that's what most of these guys deal in'.

Barry could sense she was no longer interested in the house sale so he wisely stopped trying to pump her for details. She could sometimes become quite suspicious.

'So how was your day at the palace?' There was a certain sneer in her tone which raised Barry's heckles.

'Ah well, you know the glamour of Buckingham Palace forever rubbing shoulders with the high and mighty of the land!' He decided not to rise to the bait and deflect things with humour

'Why did you take the job?'

'Sorry?'

'You heard me. Why did you take this dead end job? You appeared to be doing reasonably well at the Herald, moving steadily up the ranks, suddenly you jack it in and go to work in the Palace.' Pippa didn't have the full story of his resignation, Barry liked to leave as few loose ends as possible and she moved in circles where a slip of the tongue could end very badly for him.

He tried to sound as insouciant as possible, 'I guess I was bored of the rat race and the deadlines. Also it could be useful as a life experience. Maybe write a book.'

Pippa sniggered, 'Oh yes "The story of my life by Barry Smith" hold the press!'

You have no idea thought Barry as he started caressing her breasts and went for the next leg of his sexual triathlon much to her enjoyment, career prospects were forgotten in the delights of intercourse with her gorgeous boyfriend.

Chapter 2

Nr 10 Downing Street surely ranks as one of the most photographed doors in the world. It is uniformly black, bar the white 10 in the upper half. There was a policeman standing in front as usual. Today he was quite busy as the various Secretaries of State arrived for the weekly Cabinet meeting. Nearly all of them were enjoying high office for the first time and only a few had crossed the ultimate threshold anything more than a few times. They all had a spring in their step which still betrayed the excitement of their recent elevation. The worries and struggles attached to their job would soon quash that even if they didn't realise it yet.

Edward Faulkner, the new prime minister was sitting in his office finalising the details for today's agenda with Sir Norman Cressington the Cabinet Secretary and Wilfred Wilkes his private secretary. He had become PM almost unexpectedly. His predecessor called for a snap election so as to reinforce his mandate. Labour had read the signals very badly as it turned and the end result had been a hung parliament. The conservatives were the most voted party, so the liberal democrats chose to support them as did their traditional allies the Ulster Unionist Parties. Neither of them had chosen to enter into a formal coalition, instead they offered ad hoc support in exchange for a furthering of their policies. The liberal democrats had made no secret that the price to pay would be a reform of the electoral system. The general feeling was that this was going to be a brief government. Edward was treading very carefully trying to balance the interests of the country with those of his party. This resulted in his lack of formal commitment to anything until himself and his ministers had found their feet. As a result, the press had cruelly nicknamed him Flip-Flop Eddie an epithet that irritated him.

Edward turned to Sir Norman 'Which item should head the agenda?

Sir Norman leaned over, ' if I may be so bold PM the recent incident during the Sino-British naval exercise should top the list. As you are aware it affects several ministries and merits the utmost care in handling.' His voice was clipped and precise.

'Without making us look like complete pushovers it was partly their fault' interrupted Wilfred, the PS.

'Indeed Mr Wilkes we should not show weakness' conceded Sir Norman barely able to contain his disdain for this impudent and ambitious whippersnapper 'but arrogance and impulsiveness would not help at this juncture.'

'Very well, it comes first. What about the smoking ban? I know it isn't our baby but the timetable was already set and we must honour it; it is at the end of the month so this matter is becoming quite pressing.'

'Indeed PM but I feel it would be better placed as the 3rd item. I spoke with the DTI secretary who appears to have quite recent important information about our trade deficit with China and would like to tie it in with the first item.' Edward was slightly taken aback. 'Is that so Sir Norman?'

'Miss Steele contacted me about 30 minutes ago, you were in discussions with the Party Chairman and she asked me not to interrupt. She apologizes for not discussing it with you first.'

'Why didn't she try to speak with Edward anyway' blurted Wilfred.

Edward smiled gently, 'Wilfred, If Helen thinks that an item must be bumped up the agenda but doesn't warrant interrupting me, I am more than happy for Sir Norman to be appraised so he can inform me in good time. Do you have any more information Sir Norman?'

'I'm afraid not PM. She called to let me know there had been some recent developments in the stock market which she felt should be brought to our attention. She is gathering the final details but explained she might be five minutes late.'

Edward smiled. Helen Steele, the DTI secretary of State could sometimes be haphazard especially in keeping appointments but she was extremely focused and had become the master of her brief in the short time she had been in office, electrifying the DTI with her boundless energy and good cheer. He always had five minutes of tolerance for her.

'That will be fine Sir Norman. I am sure we can give Miss Steele five minutes of grace. I understand most ministers have arrived so I will be joining them shortly. I would be grateful if you could advise them of a slight delay.'

Sir Norman smiled. 'Certainly PM' as he gently closed the door.

No sooner than the door closed when Wilfred exploded. 'God what a git! Yes PM no PM three bags full PM' he mimicked in a slightly plumy voice. 'He is so smarmy!'

'Wilfred,' Edward said softly, 'Sir Norman Cresswell is the Cabinet secretary, the most senior civil servant in government a veritable mine of experience. His job entails the smooth running of cabinet meetings which means he receives no end of information and distributes it accordingly. I cannot fault his performance. Yes he is old-fashioned and likes things done in a certain way. So far he has not disappointed so I am more than happy to let him carry on with his ways.'

The object of this exchange appeared to glide towards the cabinet office. He was, by the nature of his job as Edward had pointed out, a quietly confident and supremely knowledgeable person. He had been described by other senior mandarins as a lethal combination of Sir Humphrey Appleby and a peregrine falcon. Occasionally self-serving, he would rarely plunge for the kill but when he did it was with ruthless efficiency and an unerring sense of timing most falcons would have given their talons for. His collection of political and administrative scalps was selectively small, almost bijou, especially once he had cemented his reputation, but it included high calibre specimens including two Secretaries of state and a cabinet secretary, his somewhat naïve predecessor. He enjoyed the intellectual challenges that his job provided and, despite his exalted status, was always ready to listen to a novel approach to doing things. He appreciated common sense and good manners he particularly disliked impetuousness and arrogance hence his approval of the new PM and his plans for his PS...

He walked into the room where most ministers were milling

around. ' Ladies and gentlemen,' he sounded like a genial master of ceremonies, 'the prime minister will be joining us shortly. If you would like to take a seat, refreshments will be arriving shortly'.

The people in the room availed themselves to a chair. There was a loose order of preference with the Chancellor of the Exchequer at the prime minister's right and the Lord chancellor on his left. The "star" cabinet post such as health, FO, education, health etc usually seated themselves either side of the PM while the less "glamorous" ministers sat where they wanted or they could find a chair. They tended to sit in cliques governed by friendship or pressure groups within the party. This also gave the prime minister a rough idea of how alliances worked within the cabinet. In this loose arrangement there was a slight exception: the chair directly opposite to the PM. Sir Norman could discreetly reserve it at the prime minister's request for any minister who had a major role in any meeting be it for explanation or for crucifixion. This had been an innovation of Tony Blair and Edward saw no reason to change it as it allowed him to focus his attention. Most ministers had mixed feelings about the "hot seat" where "cruel and unjust punishment" could be inflicted but it could also allow then to shine if they presented their case well, thus creating an opportunity for advancement. Today no buttocks would be clenched in anticipation, Sir Norman was chatting amiably with various cabinet ministers but not guiding any towards the chair.

Edward walked slowly into the room and nodded towards the gathering present. Helen Steele rushed in, close at his heels.

'So sorry I'm late Edward' she gasped while she clutched her red box.

'Don't worry Helen he replied we were just sitting down.'

'I would have thought the wretched woman could stick to a timetable like the rest of us' whispered Francine Weekes waspishly to no one in particular. She was a prim prudish women in her late 40s with a tendency to plumpness (or flabbiness as her many enemies would remark) who held the post of Health Secretary. She had worked as a middle ranking manager in a Northwest Health authority years ago. That and her husband's role as the clinical director of a small hospital had helped to push her ambitions towards this particular post. She knew Helen of old and disliked her intensely.

Edward looked at his papers and looked up again. ' Sir Norman, if you could please clarify the order of the items of the agenda.'

'Certainly Prime Minister. Ladies and gentlemen, in view of recent events the first three items will be as follows: firstly the South China Sea incident, followed by the trade deficit with China and thirdly the implementation of the smoking ban. The rest of the items will follow as planned.'

'Thank you Sir Norman. John I think you should give the basic outline of what happened with Rufus intervening when he deems it necessary.'

'Thank you Edward' said John Stokes, the FO secretary. He cleared his throat and took a sip of water. 'Dear colleagues, as you are all aware there was a tragedy three days ago in the South China Sea during the first joint naval exercise between the British and Chinese navies. The frigate HMS Suffolk accidentally rammed a Chinese fishing boat operating, illegally, within the temporary exclusion zone. Sadly three Chinese fishermen died this included the captain. Another fisherman was badly burnt while four others had severe shock but are recovering well.'

'How could this happen?' enquired Edward more for the benefit of less well informed ministers.

John looked at the defence secretary almost apologetically. 'Rufus, I think you should be able to shed more light on this.'

Rufus Compton harrumphed and took a deep breath as he started to explain in detail the embarrassing story.

'It would appear there was a chain of unfortunate events. At 0600, the time of impact there was a very thick fog, the principal radar system had become non-functional due to a minor electrical failure and the secondary radar system is not very good at detecting small non-metallic objects. I understand the Chinese fishing vessel was mostly wooden and no more than 30 feet long.'

'Surely there were lookouts?' asked the Lord Chancellor. He had served in the navy for several years in his youth.

'You are absolutely right. Unfortunately it was six bells and the handover was taking place. As I explained, the fog was extremely thick and although HMS Suffolk was travelling slowly, the ship appeared out of nowhere and she was hit amidships. She exploded almost instantly. That's how the deaths occurred. Our ship did stop immediately and the remaining fishermen as well as the corpses were rescued within 20 minutes.'

'Three dead fishermen,' said Edward, 'this is obviously a tragedy, bought on by an unfortunate chain of events, and yet… and yet, I understand the Chinese admiral was incandescent with rage, he threatened to pull out of the whole exercise. His reaction appears to be extremely disproportionate unless there was something else…'

Rufus Compton blushed as he spoke. 'Unfortunately there is something else Edward'.

'What is it?

'It would appear that the Boatswain made a very unpleasant comment at the bridge. This was what triggered the Chinese Navy's anger. There were two Chinese officers on the bridge acting as observers and as it happens they both spoke perfect English.'

Edward leant forward and looked to his left, directly at his defence secretary. He spoke very softly:' Rufus please tell me this wasn't a racist comment.'

Rufus was almost choking with embarrassment. 'Er.. strictly off the record he said Christ we've only gone and hit a load of fucking Chinky fish-gutters. Still no harm done eh lads! Loads more yellow bastards where they came from!'

There was an audible gasp around the table. This was the first time any of them had really heard the full story. Sir Norman, who had served in the British embassy in Beijing for several years and spoke passable mandarin covered his eyes with his right hand and shook his head in despair.

Edward took command again. 'Right Rufus what happened at the bridge then?'

'Here is where it starts getting a bit better. The duty C.O a Lieutenant-Commander Brookes reprimanded the Boatswain and sent him to his quarters. He did not arrest the Boatswain though. He offered profuse apologies to the Chinese officers and sent a discreet signal to Rear-admiral Sommerville. Regrettably the damage was done. The Chinese officers sent a coded message to their admiral and that's when all hell broke loose.'

Edward folded his arms on the table and bent over forwards gazing unseeingly at his papers. He then looked up to his right and asked John 'What is the present situation with the government of the People's Republic of China?'

'As you can imagine they are quite angry about the whole thing. I understand the Boatswain is still confined to quarters pending an investigation from the admiralty. Rear-admiral Sommerville requested an urgent meeting with the Chinese admiral where he offered profuse apologies on behalf of the Royal navy and HM government. The Chinese admiral acknowledged the gesture but warned he would have to inform Beijing and await further instructions. The naval exercise is now considered finished. The British ambassador in PRC is fully aware of the situation and has offered apologies to their government as well as requesting a meeting with the Chinese premier in two days time. He is, of course, awaiting further instructions from us but he has warned me that they are not pleased.'

Edward sighed. 'Well at least *some* people were quick off their mark. Rufus, anything more on your side?'

'We have instructed the naval attaché via the FO to request an interview with the governor of Kwang-Tung, the province in whose waters the incident happened. They are going to consult with their government before accepting or declining this meeting.'

'Right' Edward said he turned back slightly and looked at his Cabinet Secretary. 'Sir Norman, I understand you have lived in China for some time. I would be grateful if you could share with us what is, in your experience, the best way to deal with their government.'

Sir Norman had been expecting this. He rose from his chair and approached the table 'Prime Minister, with Mr Stoke's permission I took the liberty of contacting the head of the Chinese section at the F.O. with a view to implementing a damage limitation plan. If I may be blunt, we are in a phenomenal mess. Chinese people are extremely proud of their country, its culture and their achievements and rightly so. They are a phenomenally old civilisation. Historically they have been wary of external influence. They particularly dislike westerners, who they have previously described as ghosts or long noses. Historical events, such as the opium war or the Hong-Kong occupation reinforce their views. The fact Hong Kong it is a special administrative region still irks them. On the other hand they have developed a very pragmatic approach in recent years and understand the need of western technology and financial know-how. The do not like us any more for it in fact it could have heightened their resentment. They will expect an apology, financial compensation and maybe more.'

Sir Norman moved back discreetly and sat down. He hoped the message had got across loud and clear. He was certainly unwilling to be more explicit in his advice as this could be considered political interference; something he was always keen to avoid.

A little cough interrupted everybody's train of thought. Its owner was Francine Weekes, the health secretary. This was a particularly irritating way to draw attention to anything she had to say. She was astute enough not to use it at large public gatherings as it would be seized upon to ridicule her but in more intimate settings she allowed her innate smugness to use it.

'Edward if I may?'

'Yes Francine?'

'I cannot help but feel we may be overreacting a teensy bit here. I fully appreciate somebody made an insensitive comment as well as the tragedy of three deaths. Bearing in mind they should not have been there in the first place which is their navy's fault, should we be bowing and scraping all the way?'

Helen spoke: 'it isn't the deaths, tragic as they are, the Chinese are seething about. It is the fact some moron made a racist comment while we were guests in their territorial waters. Not exactly best behaviour in a region where we haven't exactly left many fond memories as Sir Norman pointed out. Matters are made worse by the fact that the shoe is clearly in the other foot now They are a damn sight more powerful than we are and the last thing we need is to get up their noses, however short or long they may be' she added with a wry smile.

Francine did not like one bit being rebuked in this way by Helen "Nell" Steele. There she goes again little Miss Perfect Prefect she thought resentfully. In her opinion it had been perfectly ghastly to be in the same party as Helen. Her memories of Cheltenham Ladies College boarding school came flooding back. After all those years always in her shadow she thought. Helen always appeared to achieve everything effortlessly. Hockey captain, prefect followed by head girl. Always with her clique of horsy girls sycophants, forever flying to exotic destinations for their holidays while she was lucky if she managed a fortnight in Benidorm. Her parents were nowhere as affluent as Helen's but had ambitions for her daughter and made all kinds of sacrifices to allow her to go to a boarding school. Matters were made worse by the fact Helen always got straight As and was offered a place in Cambridge while she barely managed to get into a former polytechnic where she got a 2nd in English. She had joined the party while at university and after working in the health authority for a few years had gained her parliamentary seat. She had been dutiful, always toeing the line but not really capable of great original thought except when it came to choosing the next leader of the party, a very frequent occurrence in the last 10 years! Her low cunning had been rewarded finally with one of the top 5 cabinet positions. Helen, on the other hand, had only been an MP for 9 years and she had joined the cabinet already albeit in a lower ranking position to her. She suspected that would not last for long and that rankled.

Helen, on the other hand, was unaware of the emotional turmoil she had caused. She remembered Francine and her memories were not fond either as Francine could be spiteful. She was too busy scribbling down on her pad, oblivious to the ongoing debate. It was a knack she had developed while at boarding school. She was intelligent and ambitious but also put in the hard work. Because of her social circle she developed the ability to while conversations went around her; it allowed her to keep up to speed with her coursework without behaving like a swot. The imaginary wall allowed her to work undisturbed.

At any rate Helen and Francine's exchange had been the starting point of a debate on the various courses of action available with everyone contributing with more or less fortune. Edward allowed this to carry on for a few minutes, he took some notes whenever a good point was made. Eventually he scribbled a few phrases on a piece of paper, which he passed on to John via the Lord Chancellor. John read it briefly and nodded.

Edward raised his voice marginally, enough to drown the increasing hubbub and gain everyone, even Helen's, attention.

'My dear colleagues, this has been an interesting debate but I feel we should try and reach some conclusions and take a course of action. He turned to his FO secretary, 'John, any suggestions?'

'Thank you Edward. I feel our response should be centred on offering maximum support to the families of the dead and injured fishermen. It is undisputable that the fishing boat shouldn't have been there but our warning systems weren't up to scratch and this was highlighted by the unfortunate chain of events. It ultimately falls down to Rufus and the Admiralty but the boatswain should have the most severe punishment without reaching the court martial level. This shouldn't be made public but the Chinese government would. of course. be made aware, discreetly, mind you. What are your views Rufus?'

Rufus pretended to study his notes while making some fast political calculations. He got on with John but he was damned if he was going to be outflanked so quickly!

'I thing my department and the admiralty could cope with this level of fallout as long as the press are fed a less truculent story. We will be analysing what went wrong and implementing new measures so this doesn't happen again. I think we should share our conclusions with the Chinese maybe even ask them to be part of a joint a subcommittee to analyse the incident and share any conclusions.'

'Excellent idea Rufus 'said Edward. 'May I suggest a two pronged offensive with our ambassador there discussing compensation of up to £500.000 in total for the families and the Naval attaché presenting further apologies, discussing this temporary subcommittee and informing them discreetly about the disciplinary measures implemented. I think it would show the Chinese we were treating the incident seriously enough without the need to lose too much face. Any other comments?'

There were general nods and murmurs of assent.

'Right, lets move on too the next item. Helen, I understand there have been recent developments in out trade balance with China.'

Helen leant forward and collected her thoughts briefly before starting to impart some very unpleasant news.

'Thank you Edward. I am afraid there is some serious trouble brewing in our commercial relations with China. I learnt recently that a consortia of investors had recently merged and were in control of 5% of both Rolls Royce acro and BAe. Said consortium has been recently absorbed by a far eastern conglomerate which, we are well aware, is acting as a front for the Chinese government. I have made some very discreet enquiries with a number of major shareholders and it appears they could very well end up controlling 10-15% of both firms within a couple of weeks, maybe sooner.'

'How on earth did you find this out' asked Edward voicing the question on everybody's mind.

'As you all know, I worked in banking and investments for many years before joining the conservative party. There I managed to create a rather useful network of people who can sometimes provide me with information. I have to admit that I have had to repay quite a few favours to obtain all this information. None of this is available to the general public I can assure you.'

There was a stunned silence around the table. Helen glanced around almost uninterestedly. It was unclear why she was there. She was the archetypical candidate to vote Tory. Her family being of the landed gentry and twin set pearl binomium which had been its backbone for many years. She had not been interested in politics to start with. After getting an economics degree with Honours she joined an old traditional style merchant bank through he family connections. This was the last time this happened. Her business acumen and her ability to think outside the box made her a vary sought after asset. She was aided in her rise through the glass ceiling of business by her reluctance to marry or start a family. This was not because of her looks; she was a slim attractive woman with patrician looks, She had had many admirers and even a couple of boyfriends but none of them seemed to be worth the loss of an independence she cherished greatly. Few in her social circle appeared to present enough of an intellectual or emotional challenge and she didn't venture outside her social circle, not through snobbishness but through the pragmatic view that different social and cultural backgrounds could put strains in even the most romantic relationship. In this aspect she had taken a very rational, almost materialistic point of view. As for wanting children, she had never had a very maternal instinct and even now, when there was no chance of her having children, did she ever regret having taken that course of action. After many successes in the city and abroad she felt she had no more challenges in the business world. Instead of trying to become an artist or live off the proceeds of her income she joined the ranks of the conservative party who had received her with wide open arms. She had been given a fairly safe seat at the end of John Major's administration, close to where she had been raised and encouraged to use her skills in the development of economic policy. Her rise through the ranks had been reasonably swift but not that meteoric that it generated sick jealousies and murmuring. Like Francine, the various changes of leadership had benefited her career. Unlike Francine she had seldom courted the good and the great in the party, merely accepting promotion when she felt the leader was in tune with what her gut instinct told her. She was, therefore not very politically minded hence the difference with the rest of her colleagues

The education secretary leant over. 'Are you absolutely sure about this Helen? I am sure you have researched this thoroughly and your sources are impeccable but the consequences, if you are right, do not bear thinking about especially from the research and development point of view. A lot of people will be less inclined to go into technical careers if they have nowhere to go afterwards except abroad.'

'I wish I had the slightest doubt about this Peter, I am afraid all this information is completely A-1 Kosher. I wish I knew how we should move forward'. She turned to her right. 'Any ideas no what kind of fish is this Ma-Tsien-Zu John?'

John shook himself from his reverie. His beloved wife Larissa had died over a year ago. She had suffered from ovarian cancer. The last few months had been horrible. Fortunately he and Larissa had married young and their children were fully grown up with their own careers and families blossoming when she eventually died peacefully. John had buried himself in his parliamentary and constituency work to block out the pain and longing. He missed her a lot and occasionally, without warning, her face, with her wonderful warm smile, would show up in his consciousness. It happened less and less now but it could make him appear absent minded, not on the ball. Edward Faulkner, one his oldest and certainly his dearest friends, had been a veritable rock of support in recent times despite mounting a challenge for the leadership and then running and winning the election. He had hesitated before offering him the post of foreign secretary but John who relished the position and still had the innate ambition of all politicians to rise to new challenges, had convinced him he could deliver without a problem.

'Sorry Helen, I was thinking about the trawler incident. Ma-Tsien-Zu. Hmm, difficult to read where he is going. He is a known pragmatist and a realist. He is keen on the modernisation of the country, especially from the high tech point of view. This of course isn't groundbreaking news; the CPC have long aimed for technological parity with the west, especially from the military hardware point of view, in the 50s and 60s especially. Russia cooperated with them with reservations but they kept the most important discoveries to themselves. That was one of the major reasons for the Sino-Soviet split. In the last twenty years they have been aiming at becoming an industrial and economic power of the highest magnitude. Their GDP is second only to the USA. They are currently specialising in producing low to medium quality goods imitating western ideas and technology, flooding the market with the products they produce at a much lower cost than us. The next, inevitable, step would be to become technologically advanced with the increased funds they have and move to the upper reaches of the consumer market. This was Japan's pattern in the 60s and 70s, it worked for them, China learned from it and they are going to do the same with a bigger, much much bigger impact.'

All the ministers digested this information. Britain was no longer a big manufacturing country. Their industrial output had moved from crude high quantity to small high quality. This, however was not the perception of the British public. Industry was still a very emotional issue. Any further losses would have serious political – and electoral – repercussions.

Christopher Ward, the Northern Ireland secretary interrupted everybody's train of thought by commenting loudly: 'Well, at last I can fulfil my lifetime ambition of purchasing a Rolls Royce…'

This drew several gasps and a few quizzical looks. Edward, who knew him well waited for him to finish.

'… leatherette upholstery and a the spirit of ecstasy replaced by a plastic figurine of Chairman Mao waving a red book may take the shine of it a bit but hey, at £15000 a pop with 3 years unlimited warranty you can't have everything!' He had raised his right arm and was moving it up an down with his diary in his hand.

This wry comment, delivered with a hint of scouse accent and impeccable timing,, raised a veritable gale of laughter. It relieved the mounting tension and anxiety in the room. Christopher had combined General Practice and politics until very recently and, like Patch Adams, he believed firmly that laughter was good for the body and the mind; it allowed you to think better. He leaned back on his chair and winked at Edward who winked back acknowledging what he had just done.

The release in tension permitted Helen to crystallise an idea that had been slowly accreting in her mind. 'John' she said

'Yes Helen?'

'How easy would it be to invite the Chinese premier for a state visit?'

'I'm not sure I follow' he replied warily. Was she trying to muscle into his remit?

'You just said Ma-Tsien-Zu is keen on modernising as well as being a pragmatist. I have read somewhere he is promoting foreign trained Chinese Nationals into positions of responsibility. This suggests he is not averse to western methods of doing things. If we invite him soon, we are sending the message that we wish to do business with China, discuss technology and industrial balance; we could potentially reach an agreement that is mutually beneficial. It would also make them more receptive in the future for further trade agreements with the EU where we would be the most valid associates.'

'It is an interesting way of looking at the problem. The question is how do we bring about this summit' said Edward.

Sir Norman moved again to the forefront. 'If I may be so bold prime minister' he said diffidently, I understand premier Ma is scheduled to meet president G W Bush at a Sino American summit between the 23rd and the 27th of June. He is then scheduled to meet with President Putin of Russia on the 3rd of July. The latter visit has been moved forward from the beginning of August. Your predecessor had extended an invitation to premier Ma in late December last year but with the election looming, it was felt prudent by both countries not to formalise any dates.'

Helen knew of Sir Norman's reputation as a smooth, behind the stage, operator but his latest intervention raised her respect and wonderment to hitherto unknown heights. You sly old fox she thought. I only gave you a 45 minute warning about this and you have all but set a date for Edward's first Sino-British summit without saying it. She could see Sir Norman was yet again trying to blend back into the background but she decided to enquire further. 'What about between those two dates. Is there anything major scheduled?' Her eyes sparkled with barely concealed mirth and she was grateful he could not see them.

'I understand there is a routine politburo meeting scheduled for July the 1st and 2nd. While he is expected to preside it is not unheard of that he is absent on foreign policy business' Sir Norman observed almost tonelessly. He understood perfectly well how Helen had read him and baited him gently. He felt he should observe her future career with extreme interest.

Helen curbed the cheeky impulse to enquire how was Sir Norman so au courant of premier Ma's business. She was aware of his scalp collection!

'Right' said Edward 'given the current situation perhaps we should take advantage of this potential window of opportunity and confirm the invitation for the Chinese premier if everyone is in agreement.'

He looked enquiringly around the table. There were no objections and several ministers were nodding their agreement.

'Does anyone want to add anything to this suggestion.'

'I just thought Edward, that we could blow a bit of a smokescreen if we described the summit as a commemoration of the 10th anniversary of the return of Hong-Kong to China. It would, hopefully, send a signal to the Chinese that this is a time to work as partners and not as a former colonial power dealing with a colony.'

'That is an excellent suggestion John. I will have to liaise with HM the queen to organise a formal state visit and banquet. Give it the full works of pomp and circumstance!'

Sir Norman winced internally at this dreadful joke; Edward Elgar was one of his favourite composers.

Christopher Ward muttered under his breath to the pensions minister sitting next to him: ' that should be fun for Ed, bearing in mind how he and "Brenda" haven't exactly hit it off!'

Edward checked his agenda again. 'Right, let's move on swiftly to the next item: the smoking ban in public places. How is it going Francine?'

Francine puffed herself like an overweight pastel pink pigeon. There was no need to cough now; everyone's attention was focused on her. ' Extremely well Edward' she gushed. 'We have news that over 30 million new no smoking signs have been delivered to restaurants, pubs and other places. The Department of Health has issued 10 million smoking cessation leaflets to be distributed in GP surgeries as well as expanding our quit line by 10% with the potential of a further 10% expansion. Hopefully, thanks to this government, smoking will be seen as a minority habit and frowned upon as much as drug-taking'. She beamed vacuously around the room.

Christopher groaned inwardly and pinched the bridge of his nose. What a stupid sanctimonious cow!. He found it hard to believe she had worked for the health service. Was she really that detached from reality? He had worked for nearly 15 years as a GP in one of the worst sink estates in Toxteth. For the people living there it was the one remaining pleasure and escapism of the horrors of their daily lives. He remembered going into patients homes which were freezing cold but there would be at least a packet of roll-ups. He himself had smoked for many years especially as a junior hospital doctor in Liverpool, where he had graduated. He knew how satisfying the first hit of hot air laced with carcinogens could be. He thanked them then, they had taken the edge of the urge to drink or worse, to remove the unpleasant memories of work and daily life. He had managed to quit 4 years 9 months and eleven days ago – not that he was counting – shortly after his father, a lifelong heavy smoker, had died from lung cancer. He agreed with the law in principle. He still had to watch himself almost daily and knew that banning cigarettes from pubs would make it harder for people to relapse. Bloody bloody lovely cigarettes!

'Please remind me of the penalties for breaching the ban' asked Edward.

'It will be £ 2000 for the owner or person responsible for the premises and the offender will be given a police caution as well as paying a £ 500 fine. I am scheduled to appear a week before the start of the ban and again the day after it starts. I do hope Edward you will help to endorse this worthwhile policy!'

She giggled kittenishly. She was, in fact positively orgasmic at the amount of attention she had already been receiving from the media and salivating at the prospect of more to come. She cared not a jot that most of the legwork had been done by the previous government. She had voted for it as she didn't like the smell it left on her clothes but this was the publicity kudos attached which made her such a relentless supporter of the new law.

Most people in the room cringed with embarrassment. Francine had always endeavoured to appear businesslike and devoted to the good of the Tory party and the country. Now she had let her true mask slip, however briefly, and shown her true narcissistic colours. Edward hadn't cringed, he had blinked perplexedly for a couple of times. Was Francine being serious? There was a lot of hard work ahead and there she was expecting him to jump through hoops like an obedient dog ad majorem gloria Francina? He would clip her wings right now!

'Well Francine, I am sure we can all try to find some time in our increasingly hectic schedules to help endorse this worthwhile causes even if was engineered by our unlamented predecessors!'

Several people noticed the irony in Edward's words and smiled, they realised Francine had dropped a brick of monumental proportions and Edward had just given everyone a free rein to support her as little as was decorously possible. Francine, who beamed vapidly and thanked him for his support, was clearly oblivious to this.

The rest of the Cabinet meeting proceeded smoothly. Edward

gave John a discreet signal and he nodded towards Helen and Rufus. This meant he wanted a private word will all three in his private office.

All four of them managed to linger in the office. Fortunately nobody wanted to catch Edward's ear in private so they were able to proceed into the office unnoticed. Sir Norman was already waiting, as was Wilfred as an "eyes only" minute taker. There was still little ceremony but people were a lot more apprehensive. Edward had an autocratic streak which he was able to curb most of the time and for good reason. He could, when the occasion demanded it, be extremely direct.

'Guys, thanks for staying. As you have realised we have a £2 billion trade deficit with China and I'm quite sure nothing would give them more pleasure than to pressurise us, EU quotas or not. Rufus' he growled, 'I want this fucking boatswain out of the Navy by the end of next month. It will be a dishonourable discharge and a police caution for inciting racial hatred. I want the three forces to include in their regulations the most severe penalties, including court martial and dismissal, for the next dickhead who thinks cracking racist jokes or comments is a bloody laugh. The Chinese will be informed about this, off the record, by tomorrow.' This wasn't a request; this was a direct order issued with a tone that broached no discussion.

Rufus was taken aback. He had leant backwards slightly as Edward confronted him. There was a satanic look to him, the white of his eyes was red, his complexion had taken a rich crimson hue and his normally grey blue eyes had become black, so dilated were his pupils. Rufus had heard about the less palatable side of Edward Faulkner but had never experienced it first hand. He was a brave man; he had trekked through the Australian desert as a youth. He felt the same sensation of unyielding vicious ruthlessness again. The hairs at the back of his neck stood out as if he had received an electric shock.

'Very well prime minister' he murmured.

'Good!'

Edward swung abruptly towards Helen and John They both flinched slightly. John had known Edward for longer and had seen a couple of his cold rages. It still unsettled him as it made him realise the enormous strains this normally kind and considerate man was going through. Helen had seen behaviour like this in the past. In her case what unsettled her most was the coldness of the rage and the sense of unremitting power it carried.

'Right. John and Helen. We need to handle this very carefully. As I explained before, our trade deficit with China is a source of concern. More worrying is the fact they are developing an increasingly powerful financial clout. I have heard they have earmarked nearly £ 50 billion for financial investment in the west. John, I need you to pour oil over the troubled waters as well as finding out as much as possible about them so as to best guide our next steps. Helen, I need you to use that magic diary of yours and find out all you can about the major areas of investment of the PRC in the UK, EU, USA, America and any other areas you can think of. Also assess where do you think they may be moving into. You will both have to work your butts off I'm afraid as I need this report within the next 72 hours. Once the reports are ready please contact Sir Norman.'

'I could also help' interjected Wilfred.

The atmosphere which had eased off and become almost business like tightened up again. Sir Norman, sensing this and wishing to expedite the end of the meeting intervened. This wasn't to protect Wilfred, whose pompous self-centeredness and lack of restraint irritated him exponentially every time he made a faux pas, but because he felt the current crisis needed solving.

'I am sure Mister Wilkes and I can liaise and we will ensure all the relevant information will reach you with the utmost expedience' he said smoothly.

'As I was saying we should meet as soon as possible and decide how we can best engage with the Chinese from a diplomatic and financial point of view. This means you will both have to work closely together. Is that going to be OK? I don't want any bullshit or platitudes just for my benefit. If you think you can't work together let me know now so I can nominate two deputies to do this.

John and Helen looked at each other carefully, as if for the first time. Their paths hadn't crossed much whilst in opposition. John had been more at ease in the legal and diplomatic areas whereas Helen, with her financial and business background had tended to gravitate towards the exchequer and industry, initially as a gifted technocrat, but had become more politically involved as her true skills and potential emerged.

John spoke first. Looking at Helen he said ' I do not foresee any problems from my point of view. I have no axe to grind with you Helen. I'm sure we can work well together.' Helen merely nodded while she checked her notes making sure she had all the necessary details.

'Very well. If it's OK I shall meet you in three days or earlier if possible. Let Sir Norman or Wilfred know. John, if you don't mind I would like to discuss something private with you.'

Everybody was aware of the close friendship between them so there were no questioning looks as they walked out.

A secretary rapped the door as it opened. It was clear she had been waiting for the meeting to end.

'Prime Minister, Lord Coe is about to arrive for your scheduled update on the 2012 Olympic games.'

'Very well Alison. This shouldn't take long. If Lord Coe arrives before I'm done please make sure he is comfortable. Can you also let my wife know I shall be joining her for lunch in 45 minutes.'

'Very well prime minister, I'll let her know'

Edward had been married to Sylvia for nearly twenty-five years. Theirs was one of the most solid marriages ever seen. She was the perfect politician's wife. Caring, supportive, extremely discreet and with an ever-ready sympathetic ear. He loved her very deeply and marvelled at his luck for being married to her. He made sure they always had one meal together in private every day. This was no mean feat at a time when working breakfasts had become a regular feature in most politicians' lives'.

As soon as the door closed Edward sat down next to John and clapped his shoulder.

'Everything all right "noodles"?'

John smiled. John was using his old university nickname. He was renowned for his fondness of pot noodles, a rather new fangled food at the time. It was a cheap source of calories in the days when deciding between three regular meals or a beer with friends always resulted in a trip to the Pig and Whistle. He was, however, a firm advocate of lining his stomach beforehand hence the ever-present rows of the plastic tubs in his kitchen cupboard. He was also reassured to see how quickly Edward's temper had settled and that even if he sometimes had to be a hard taskmaster the old links remained; the friendship was still deep and as solid as centuries old seasoned oak.

'I'm doing fine "squiffy".' Edward had never had a head for drink. He was known as the cheapest date in Oxford as two pints would have him under the table amid accusations he was dodging to pay his round.

'I shouldn't ask this but the stakes have suddenly become much higher. Can I count on you and your ability to cope?'

John wasn't offended by the question. Other than his immediate family, only Edward knew and understood the depth of his grief and devastation when Larissa died. At one point, shortly after her funeral, John had spent one evening with a bottle of vodka in one hand and a strip of sleeping tablets in the other. Edward, with the uncanny sixth sense that only comes with a long friendship, had turned up unannounced at his home. He had spent the whole night talking to him, consoling him and explaining the devastation his death would inflict upon his family and friends. That he had done this while he was running for the party leadership showed where his real priorities lied. Since then Edward had made sure they spoke almost every day and if he didn't Sylvia, who was also very fond of him, would. Slowly John had learned to overcome the pain of his loss and cope with the solitude. When the electoral victory came Edward had spent an hour talking him with him face to face. It had been an extremely frank conversation and in the end John had been offered the foreign office. There was a tacit understanding that if John felt he couldn't cope or Edward expressed concerns at his performance his resignation would be accepted unquestioningly.

'You have the right to ask. It would be disastrous if I plodded on without doing my duty properly. I feel strong enough to do this. I still miss Larissa dreadfully but I am learning to cope with the loneliness. Mind you the kids ring daily as do yourself or dear Sylvia. They also make sure I have lunch or dinner with one of them three or four times a week. Between that and the rushed snacks I'm piling up the pounds and beginning to wish for a quiet night in!' he laughed.

Both men smiled. They both stood up and hugged each other. John left, his mind already focused on the job in hand, his spirits lifted by the reaffirmation of Edwards friendship.

Chapter 3

Unlike John, Barry smith wasn't receiving any signs of friendship early in the morning. Pippa had insisted they went out last night to celebrate her latest real estate coup. The end result of their carousing had been their staggering into her flat at 3 am. They had fallen asleep immediately and he wouldn't have arisen until gone 10 at least had his very full bladder not woken him up just before 7 am. A quick glance at the clock on his bedside table alerted him that he had five minutes to be at the palace, a trip that normally took him half an hour not counting dressing up. To Barry's credit he managed to get there only ten minutes late. He enjoyed sleeping and cutting things fine so he always had a briefcase at the ready. It contained a clean pair of slacks and a shirt. It also held wet wipes an electric razor and some deodorant. He got dressed and smartened up inside a cab (an expense he could ill afford) on his way to the palace. He was going commando and only the fact that the cab driver had been distracted by a cyclist jumping the lights and spent several moments with his head out of the window hurling abuse had prevented Barry from being accused of indecent exposure!

Barry shoved a £10 note in the cabby's hand and rushed towards the servant's entrance. He could feel it was not going to be a good day. Despite looking reasonably presentable he felt bleary, the inside of his mouth tasting of mangy scouring pad. He was about 10 yards from the door when his particular nemesis, Sir Ian Connaught stepped into the courtyard. Barry screeched to a halt a mere five inches from Sir Ian, barely managing to keep his balance. There was a deathly silence only interrupted by birdsong and the distant roar of an airliner leaving from Heathrow. Sir Ian was standing straight as a ramrod his heels an inch apart while the tips of his gleaming black brogues were at an exact 60 degree angle. His left arm was folded behind his back while his right thumb was stuck in the waist pocket of his impeccable Marengo grey three piece suit. His black hair, peppered with grey, was cut with the military precision that 20 years in the Irish guards had instilled in him. This was confirmed by his regimental tie. He started rocking slowly on his heels describing a precise 15 degree arch between the extremes. Barry tried very hard not to flinch every time he came close to him. Without moving his head he slowly and deliberately pulled out his pocket watch (an old Ingersoll which was a farewell gift from the first company he had ever commanded). He stopped oscillating and tilted his head down slightly and to the right to look at the, exact, time. His head and eyes moved up again to face his victim who now was nearly paralysed with fear.

'And how about ye my lad?' He enquired. His Ulster accent had softened after many years of living in England.

Barry knew that trying to bullshit Conns was the one move that would end in complete disaster. His finely honed preservation instincts were sending a veritable carillon concert of alarm bells. He was certain Sir Ian was waiting for his next lame excuse and insincere apology so he could sack him on the spot. The repercussions with Jock didn't bear thinking of.

'I.. I am terribly sorry Sir Ian.' He felt that a contrite and afraid tone would show his awareness of the enormity of the infraction he had just committed. 'I'm afraid my girlfriend had a very successful day at work and insisted we went out to celebrate. We got a bit carried away and I'm afraid I overslept a bit and arrived 10 minutes late. I will of course work an extra half hour today and you can be sure I will definitely be on time tomorrow.' He could feel his tone had become slightly pleading but saw no point in holding back.

Sir Ian had slowly replaced his watch inside his waistcoat pocket. His pitiless steel grey eyes, which had inspired dread in Omani insurgents at his last foreign posting as well as any soldier unfortunate enough to incur his wrath in all the companies and battalions he had commanded, looked as cold and un-forbidding as the north face of the Eiger. He examined Barry slowly and deliberately from head to toes and upward again. He took in all the details of his attire. His sports jacket –slightly crumpled- his slacks and shirt (no tie) clean and pressed, the shoes were clean even if they wouldn't have stood up to his former RSM Seamus O'Flannaghan's standards. He tilted his head downwards and to the left examining Barry's expensive executive briefcase (it had been a gift from Pippa).

'Planning to do the Palace accounts today my lad?' His voice was silky soft, like the hiss of the finest rapier being slowly drawn out of its scabbard before it was plunged into its victim's heart.

Barry looked down to his right where his was holding the dark burgundy leather briefcase.

'Oh this!' Barry blurted out the first excuse that leapt into his mind, a fatal error. 'Oh no Sir Ian, I took with me a copy of the protocol for state banquets and made some notes so I could be prepared for next weeks review.' He attempted an ingratiating smile, a further error as Conns was not in an ingratiating mood.

'Is that so? Well I'm sure I would like to see what your "expert" point of view is on such a delicate and complex matter. Would you kindly open your lovely briefcase and get them out. I would dearly love to compare points of view.'

'What, now?'

'There is no time like the present my lad.'

Fuckety fuck and triple fuck thought Barry. He was aghast. He had made one minuscule mistake, he had exposed the tiniest sliver of a flank and Conns had expertly plunged his rapier into it without hesitation. Ah well he mused; it was good while it lasted. He hoped it wouldn't be too painful. He lilted the briefcase and put it horizontally and facing upwards. He flicked the clasps open and closed is eyes waiting for the explosion.

Sir Ian opened the lid carefully between his right thumb and index. As he did so he leant forward to inspect the contents. This obscured the view for the many footmen and maids who were watching events with undisguised interest. His nostrils were attacked by the rank smell of alcohol impregnated old sweat. His eyes took in the pyjama bottoms and the crumpled novelty T-shirt (Barry didn't like to sleep naked). He examined the packet of wet wipes the electric razor and roll-on stick of deodorant with the lid only half closed. He became upright again, closing the lid gently as he did so and clicked the clasps close. His countenance relaxed a fraction. His eyes, two blocks of ice ten seconds ago, warmed up by a few degrees. His right eyebrow raised slowly with a smooth deliberateness Roger Moore would have killed for and the right corner of his mouth twitched briefly and almost imperceptibly into a smile. He had been in a similar situation as a young second lieutenant arriving late for parade many years ago. His CO had given him a punishment he still remembered. The little bugger! Two minutes ago he was ready to sack this slacker on the spot but he had shown courage and resourcefulness. The night clothes and toiletries told a story with no need for words. The lad had a talent for improvisation and split second decision taking. Barry didn't know it but he had just achieved two of the three top cardinal virtues in Sir Ian's very personal bible. He would be reprieved if he took his punishment well.

'I see Mr Smith. Very interesting. I particularly enjoyed your point of view on the level of cleanliness of silverware.'

Barry's eyes became wide open. 'What the..' he thought.

'I think you should lead by example.' Sir Ian continued. 'Queen Margaret of Denmark is due to visit us in a month's time for an informal visit. I think it would be a lovely touch if she could dine with her great-great-grandmother's dinner service. I would like to see the entire Queen Alexandra's dinner service polished to your exacting standards and we should do a formal inspection tomorrow at, oh I don't know. shall we say 0630 hours? You will ask miss Hatton to assist you with collecting the silverware and the final inspection. There will be no need to get changed, again.'

Barry's relief at his temporary reprieve was swiftly overtaken by the dread of his punishment. Queen Alexandra's dinner service was a 50 placing, devilishly intricate, silver set. It was seldom used due to the pain it was to clean. At eight pieces per table setting it totalled 400 pieces of cutlery not counting serving utensils, salvers and a huge soup tureen. He would be lucky if he got off before midnight! He also knew there was no point in complaining. He would have to accept and execute the punishment without a murmur.

'Very well Sir Ian, as you wish.'

Sir Ian nodded curtly, turned around with military precision and went back into his office.

Barry rushed into the kitchen and sought out Melanie's help.

'Mel, I have just been given the "lovely" task of polishing the QA dinner service. And you have been given the role of supervisor by Sir Ian.'

Melanie gasped. She was aware only too well about the service. It was a legendary form of punishment for errant footmen and maids. The severity of the infraction determined how many pieces would be polished.

'How much do you have to do?'

'What do you mean how much? All of it of course' said Barry in exasperated tones.

Melanie whistled. Conns *was* mad at Barry. He was playing by the rules though since she had been detailed to monitor and supervise him.

All large organisations have several tiers of management with a pyramidal structure. The troops at the bottom invariably were the most put upon. This creates an unwritten code of conduct where the victim of a punishment will receive support from his fellow workers. Buckingham palace is a large organisation and extremely keen on tradition. Polishing the QA service was a traditional form of discipline. All the new footmen and maids were swiftly appraised of the existence of this legendary punishment. If you went down you could expect, at least some sympathy and moral support as a typical example of corporate behaviour, unless you had been sent to Coventry in which case you were on your own.

Melanie went to a cupboard and opened it with a key. She took out an old fashioned key with a plastic tag attached which read: CEREM SILVER. She signed the book. She walked purposefully towards the door that led into the cellars. With out speaking she grabbed Barry's jacket sleeve and forced him to follow him. They walked silently down the stairs, their steps echoing eerily, into a dimly lit corridor with a row of well spaced doors either side. Melanie stopped at the first door on the left and opened it silently with out a key.

'Wait here' she said dryly she then walked into a room flicking a switch as she did so.

Barry could hear the clanking of tins and boxes as they landed into some metallic container. Eventually Melanie came out pushing a small shopping trolley. She closed the door behind her and flicked the light off. She gestured to Barry to follow her. One of the trolley wheels had a squeak, Barry couldn't help noticing the ratio of two steps for every squeak. Twenty squeaks later they stopped in front of an old fashioned –looking door. Melanie turned the old key, swiped her card and punched in her exclusive seven-digit code. This code, by palace security regulations couldn't be a date of birth or a personal telephone number. In Melanie's case she had chosen the three numbers of her first car's registration plate followed by the age she was when she started working here and the grandmother's street number. It was easy enough to remember. The door clicked, she pushed the trolley inwards.

As soon as they entered, motion sensor lights became activated. They both blinked in the bright light. The room they were in was enormous: 30 by 60 feet, lined with glass fronted cupboards in which silver and gold gleamed. Along the centre there was a long pine table with coarse felt tacked crudely on. There were ten chairs along each side.

'Welcome to the 5th circle of hell Barry.' Melanie murmured to herself. She was an avid reader and enjoyed Dante's Divine Comedy; she had correctly identified Barry as guilty of sloth. He was about to experience the correct punishment.

She walked towards a cupboard and opened it. It had no key. There were two columns of drawers in the lower half of it with five drawers per column. In the upper half there were three shelves, laden with salvers, bowls and a huge, intricately carved, soup tureen. They were all slightly tarnished. Nobody had been punished for some time it would appear. She opened the top left drawer and grunted slightly as she lifted the heavy object. Inside it were fifty solid silver spoons. There was a slight thud as it landed on top of the table. She repeated the action two more times. She closed the door and swung round glaring at Barry.

'How did you get away with it?' She demanded.

'Excuse me?'

'How on earth did you get away with it?' She repeated more emphatically.

'You call this getting away with it?'

Melanie took a deep breath and armed herself with patience. 'Barry, this morning Conns was in the kitchen at ten to seven. You were due you three-month review today. He asked after you regarding punctuality, diligence and commitment to the job. We all gave as non-committal answers as we possibly could but anyone with two ounces of common sense could see your ass was on the line. You turned up, today of all days, late. Conns had started tut-tutting and scribbling on his pad, a sure sign that someone is going to get fired.' She paused to draw breath. 'And yet, you didn't, you are still working here! What on earth happened on that courtyard? We could see your eyes were closed while he was inspecting your briefcase.'

Barry was quite taken aback. Even though he suspected he was in dire straits he wasn't aware of how desperate his situation had been or indeed still was. Mindful of the clock ticking away he explained last night and that morning's events as succinctly as possible.

Melanie smiled. She could see why Conns had granted him a reprieve. Barry had clearly shown courage and panache, trying to make the best of a self-inflicted crisis and almost pulled it off. She was glad for Barry and she mentally added an unexpected gold star on Sir Ian's sense of humour column.

'OK then. Have you ever polished silver?'

Barry nodded. 'My grandmother insisted I polished all the portrait holders every month to earn a few pennies.'

'Right. Here is all the necessary equipment. Always use the cotton gloves. The stuff they use here is quite irritant to the skin. Use the hard cotton arrow tips to deal with the fiddly bits. There's a loo at the end of the room. It's the only place without smoke detectors' she added as an afterthought. 'I'll come and check on you in an hour or so. I'll bring a coffee and a snack to keep you going.'

As she walked out Barry sighed and donned some gloves. He dipped a cloth in the silver polish and started rubbing.

Melanie rushed out of the room barely able to contain her

laughter. She ran as quick as she could up the stairs and into the servant's dining room where twenty or so staff were having their early coffee. They were expecting her to tell and she didn't disappoint them. The story, vividly narrated raised quite a few laughs. Nobody disliked Barry intensely, it was just the gallows humour shown by the palace staff; it was a good story, one worth re-telling with suitable embellishments. Melanie looked around the table and raised her eyebrows to draw the attention of several maids and footmen. They all nodded silently. Many pulled out their mobile phones and started texting. The QARS was being summoned into action.

As promised, Melanie went downstairs about an hour later. Barry, to his credit had not been slacking and was finishing his 30th spoon, 29 others were already gleaming on the table.

'Not bad she observed and you seem to be getting on with it.'

'Oh yes' he retorted sarcastically, only 470 to go plus extras and the bloody tureen!'

'No point in my distracting' you she replied brightly. 'I'll be back in a while to replace the trays and will bring you another drink and a snack.'

Barry grunted and merely increased the rate of polishing. At this rate Conns would find him here in the morning up to his elbows in flaming silverware!

Melanie walked silently down the corridor. Jeremy, one of the older footmen was waiting at the bottom of the stairs. He looked enquiringly, she nodded briefly and went up the stairs. Jeremy walked as soundlessly as possible down the corridor until he reached the room where Barry was. He walked into the room as Barry was completing his 31st spoon. He sat down, donned some gloves and started polishing furiously.

'What the..!' Barry exclaimed.

Jeremy raised a gloved hand to his lips as he smiled and winked. After 20 minutes or so with eleven spoons under his belt Jeremy took off his gloves and walked away acknowledging with a wave Barry's mouthed thank you as he polished a knife. And so, throughout the day, a veritable procession of junior staff walked into the ceremonial silver room and sat down to polish ten or twelve items of silverware at a time. Melanie would come every two hours or so to inspect the progress and the quality of the workmanship and replace the canteen drawers silently. At one point she donned some gloves on and gave one of the larger salvers a superb polish. It was late in the afternoon when she walked in and spoke again.

'Archie' she asked another footman who was busy polishing a ladle, 'I'm taking this bozo out to get some fresh air before he dies from the fumes. Can you hang on until he returns?'

Archie nodded briefly, his mind occupied with a particularly stubborn bit of tarnish.

She jerked her head in the direction of the door and raised her eyebrows menacingly when he tried to talk.

They both walked into a small courtyard. Melanie waited for Barry to light up. He sucked greedily at only the second cigarette of the day. He was trying to rub some life into his wrists and elbows, the cigarette dangling from one side of the mouth. Melanie eyed him critically. The punishment was legendary. He was only the second person in living memory to polish the entire QA silver service. (Incidentally the other was Fergus Leveson-Gower, a nephew to the queen on the Glamis side, he had gotten very drunk in one of the garden parties and dropped a tray of canapés on the Lady Mayor of Birmingham's lap.) The gallows humour of the palace junior staff forbade warning the condemned person of the impending relief of his punishment. They were expected to sweat a bit. Barry's relief had arrived earlier than usual. No-one was quite sure how long would it take. She pulled the cigarette from his lips and took a deep drag and let the smoke come out through her mouth. She inspected the smoke curlicues as they played against the sunlight.

'How are you getting along?' She asked almost tonelessly.

Barry looked at her, holding his cigarette and leaning against a wall. She looked weary and experienced beyond her years. This was not the mental image of Mel he had composed in his mind. 'I'm doing very well as you know. There is only one drawer left as well as some salvers and the tureen. What was that all about, the silent help? Not that I'm not very grateful of course.'

Melanie sighed and shook her head. Despite his obvious cleverness

Barry could sometimes be quite obtuse. 'You have just become a member of QARS, the Queen Alexandra Rescue Service. It is quite a select club at the palace and one that only admits staff who have been punished by having to polish the QA silver service. Whenever a staff member goes "down on the silver" as it is known, when this punishment is meted out, all the club members on duty will go and help out during their break. No words are exchanged, no payment is expected BUT, whenever a new club member, such as your good self, joins you *will* help out when someone else is in the soup. You rat out on the deal, you get sent to Coventry, you blab about this to anyone you get sent to Coventry. The new member will suffer and then know the pleasure of relief from others. It's no Zen shit, it just *is*. You don't like it? Tough banana. No one outside the club knows, except Conns, he tried to stop it and we had to get "persuasive". By the way there is no tie or Christmas meal or badges, just the knowledge that when you were down people helped out as you will when others…'

'..go down on the silver' Barry completed the phrase.

'Correct.'

'So everyone here has cleaned the QA service?'

'No, only parts of it. You have become a legend already.'

'So Jezza?'

'Three drawers.'

'Archie?'

'Five drawers and two salvers.'

'Lottie?

'All the salvers.'

'What about Bernard?'

'No-one knows, he is the doyen of the QARS. He won't say and we don't ask.'

'How much longer do you reckon I have to go?'

'Well what with people still due to come and judging by how much you have left I reckon about three hours. Most of it will be taken up by that bloody tureen and, let me tell you, she's a bitch and she's your bitch. Trust me.' She winked.

It suddenly struck Barry. Mel had helped; she was a member of QARS!

'What did *you* go down for?'

'You're not very fast on the uptake are you?' She gave a wry smile. 'I was stupid enough to pinch a minute slice of the queen's favourite chocolate cake. She has the eyes of an eagle when it comes to that cake. Put me off chocolate for life' she laughed. She became pensive for a moment but soon snapped out of it. 'Right, this won't get the baby a new bonnet. I'm off and Archie will be taking over as supervisor.'

From the window in his office Sir Ian had watched, though not heard the exchange. He allowed himself a brief smile and he buried himself in his paperwork.

Barry returned to his polishing. Mel had been absolutely right. It took him the best part of three hours to finish with the tureen being the stuff nightmares are made of. Archie arrived as he was giving it the final buff. Together they checked all the pieces were accounted for and signed the book. They walked in silence up the stairs and into the hallway. Once there, rather formally, one veteran to another, they shook hands and went their own way.

Barry arrived home exhausted and with a headache from the fumes. He had walked most of the way home trying to clear his head and reflecting on today's experience. He had bought some paracetamol and it was beginning to kick in. His conscience, never a major force to contend with, was prickling him. This was a good story, how punishment was meted out at the palace. Maybe not front page but surely good enough for page three (at least he wouldn't have to compete with the "charms" of lovely Joanna from Basingstoke as the poor hacks at the Sun did!). That and other titbits of gossip would make for a great story which would raise his stock at the paper. On the other hand, he was struck by the level of support he had received from a group of people whom he barely knew. They were obeying a code of conduct set many decades ago. In the end he decided to keep quiet. This was partly because the story didn't warrant blowing his cover and partly out of loyalty to the members of his club.

Pippa was on the sofa painting her nails with half an eye on an old episode of friends showing on Sky. There was a half full glass of white wine on the coffee table. She was wearing a faded blue bathrobe and her hair was in curlers. Despite her homely appearance she still managed to look quite gorgeous even with her eyes slightly crossed as she applied a final layer of coral pink to her toenails which matched the colour of her hands and the lipstick on her generous mouth. Brian groaned inwardly, partly out of lust and partly in despair at the thought of having to go out tonight.

Once she had finished the task to her satisfaction she looked up and smiled.

'Hi sweetie!' She lifted her face so Barry could kiss her gently on the lips, he was careful not to smudge her latest work of art.

'Hi darling!' he replied after kissing her. She smelled lovely, of lavender and lemon. Barry felt a lustful surge in his nether regions, which his exhausted brain swiftly overrode, obeying orders from the rest of the body. You are looking lovely. What time did you get up this morning?'

'About ten o'clock. Ugh! I felt ghastly. Fortunately I didn't have any appointments till noon so I rang the office and told them I was finalising my paperwork at home. Bearing in mind my recent form they were only too happy to oblige. What time did you get up?'

'Just before seven'

'You poor thing! You must be exhausted. Well, go and have a bath and get into bed. I'm going out with Clar and Chessie. There's some pizza left by the way she added as she started pulling out her rollers.

Barry's mind did a triple somersault with a backward flip at the end. Pippa was going out with her oldest and closest friends. That explained the extra care in her appearance. She wouldn't be back till late so he could hog the bed and catch up on some badly needed sleep. He yawned somewhat ostentatiously and said 'sure love, you have fun. Shall we try and go out for a quiet meal tomorrow night?' He didn't want to sound too delighted at his quiet night in; Pippa could be quite neurotic if she felt she wasn't the end all and be all if his life!

'That will be nice. Try and surprise me.'

'I will.'

Barry padded into the kitchen. He put the remainder of the half congealed pizza in the oven and switched it on. He poured himself a glass of wine and took some sips while he waited for the pizza to heat up. He lit a cigarette up. He toyed with the idea of going back into the sitting room but Pippa wouldn't be there and he felt if he sat down comfortably he would never get up. He massaged his right elbow absentmindedly. It still ached. It served as a reminder of today's events. Pippa walked into the kitchen. Her strappy high heeled sandals clicking on the tiles. She looked gorgeous in the proverbial little black dress, with the emphasis on little; she was showing as much well toned thigh as possible without becoming sluttish. The rest of the wisely applied makeup had transformed her face into a veritable symphony of sexiness in G (spot). He wolf whistled. 'Wow!'

'Why, thank you.' She gave a little twirl, the dress hugged her figure beautifully showing her wonderful curves at their best. 'Right, I'm off. She kissed Barry. 'Ugh!' her nose wrinkled in disgust. 'You reek of polish. What on earth have you been up to? Have you been demoted even further?'

'No, I was late this morning, which was the icing on the cake of a sequence of misdemeanours'.

'Polishing silver? For being late?' She arched her perfectly plucked eyebrows in wonder. 'It sounds a bit antiquated doesn't it? What happens at the next infraction? Do you get put in the stocks or ducked in the palace pond?' She was being ironic but she had a point.

'Ha, ha! Very funny! It was that or the sack. Today I wasn't in the mood to scan the help wanted section' he added flippantly.

She shrugged. 'Suit yourself. By the way, do you know anyone in Derby?'

'What?'

She tutted and repeated more slowly:' do-you-know-anyone-in-Derby?'

'No. I-do-not-know-any-one-in-Derby. Why-do-you-ask?' If she was in the mood to be sarcastic, he wasn't in the mood to put up with it.

'Yevgeni.'

'The ugsome Russian billionaire?'

'The one and only. He wants a three bedroom house, nothing fancy in the south of the city.'

'Talk about downsizing. Sounds like an odd purchase after blowing £ 6 million in two townhouses. What's his full name?'

'Yevgeni Rudkin. Why do you ask?'

Barry had this excuse at the ready. No more fiascos. 'Well I'm a bit worried. Some of these Russian oligarchs can be a bit shady so I would like to ask around in case it becomes unpleasant.'

Pippa's expression softened visibly. 'You are so sweet sometimes Barry.' She kissed him again softly on the lips and withdrew before it developed into something more passionate. 'Get into bed, you look like death warmed up.' She walked out and cried over her shoulder: 'I'll be back in a couple of hours.'

Barry opened the oven, got the reheated pizza out and put it on a plate. He stood in the middle of the tiny kitchen blinking like a barn owl. Boy did he feel tired! He had only slept 3 hours and just completed the ultimate marathon on silver polishing with the worst ramps at the end. He had been running on coffee and adrenaline all day. His exhausted body and mind had declared bankruptcy an hour ago. He managed to bring himself to the kitchen stool and write down Yevgeni Rudkin's name and past and future purchasing record and he put it in his pocket. He toyed with the idea of ringing the Herald but the thought of listening to one of Jock's diatribes put him off. He would speak with Norman Sewell tomorrow, a much better bet. Norman allowed people time and space to think rather than shouting them to do it. Also the newspaper's final edition would be in its early stages. No, Norman, patient as he was would not appreciate the interruption at this time; especially if he couldn't make sense. He finished eating, with very little enjoyment, and downed the rest of the wine in one gulp. He staggered, zombie-like into the bedroom. He selected a shirt and tie as well as a decent looking jacket. He hung everything in the bathroom. He set his alarm for 5 am, no way was he getting dressed again in a cab, and fell asleep instantly.

Pippa was in a black cab on her way to the trendy wine bar in Covent Garden. She was deep in thought and ignored all the cabbies attempts at chatting her up. Barry's last comment had touched her. He obviously cared for her but the question was how much? She felt frustrated at his lack of direction. At the age of 28 he had moved from being a jobbing journalist with limited, but at least some, career prospects to this pointless job in the palace. She just couldn't understand it!. One day he turned up and told her he had jacked in his post at the Daily Herald and gone to work in the palace "for a change of air". She on the other hand had gone from one success to another in the last two years. She was seriously being considered as a manager in another branch. She had a degree in sociology and was working on her MBA. At 26 though, she was beginning to feel the ticking of her biological clock. She wanted a stable loving relationship first, and then a good wedding followed by a nice house with a big garden and children. She was beginning to feel that Barry, like his new job, was a dead end.

'We're here love.'

The cabby's voice snapped her out of her reverie. He was disappointed she didn't want to chew the fat but at least he'd managed to have a good look at her through the rear view mirror.

She got out and paid him. She walked into the smoky atmosphere of Tony's, the latest "must be seen at spot". She saw her friends Chessie and Clar already sitting at a table and trying very hard to avoid the attentions of two fat young bankers who weren't taking a "no" for an answer. She barged right in and started greeting them loudly and effusively kissing air while discreetly excluding the two uninvited guest who, finally, took the hint and retreated.

They eyed each other critically comparing outfits, accessories and figures. Women, however hard they try to disguise it, do not try to dress to impress or attract men. They dress to show other women, who is top bitch! If, in the process of achieving this, a rich, handsome and generous man fell in their clutches it was considered nothing more than a pleasant by-product of their efforts. Pippa won the first round easily. Clar was short and dumpy with a very limited dress sense. Chessie, whose tall, elegant frame and jet black hair usually offered stiffer competition had clearly arrived directly from work. She was wearing a dark, crumpled linen trouser suit, minimal make-up and her hair tied back on a pony tail.

Pippa moved swiftly into the second round: success at work, by commenting on this fact.

'Tough day at the office Chessie?'

Francesca –Chessie- who had just lit a Marlboro light and was exhaling nodded. She was a rising star in the stock market section of Goldman-Sachs. She was a veritable workhorse and extremely ambitious but the suspicion of wrinkles in her forehead and the slightly pasty complexion revealed that the stress was beginning to get to her.

'It's been vile. They have just appointed me deputy VP in charge of the far east markets and my immediate boss, a lazy prick if there ever was one, keeps piling the work on me as fast as he can. Matters aren't made any easier with our latest big clients: a group of Chinese who are trying to get hold of as many air industry shares as possible. They want everything under wraps though, so I'm spending fucking ages on the computer locating the sodding shares and even more fucking ages trying to get people to sell them to me at a price where we make a profit.'

'Surely your team are doing all the legwork?' observed Clarissa, Clar, who worked as a PA to a barrister and was aware of all the unrewarding slog galley slaves are expected to do.

Chessie snorted with derision. 'Huh! Team. I have Tim "nice but dim" who has the intellect of a lobotomised Labrador and whose only objective is to get inside my PA's knickers and she is a complete dolt; the current holder of the self-centred air-headed bimbo award 2006-07. So there you have it Clar, I do not exactly have a great supporting cast!' She chewed furiously on an olive from the plate on the table. 'How about you Pippa?' She looked at her in a calculating fashion.

'Doing nicely' she said nonchalantly. ' I managed to sell about £10 million in real estate since the last time we met and they're thinking about promoting me to manager of the Kensington branch.' Compared to Chessie's recent promotion it was not exactly groundbreaking however much positive spin she attempted to give.

They both looked at Clar enquiringly. She shrugged her shoulders good-naturedly. She knew the rules of the game well enough and even if she seldom scored it was a way of passing time. ' Business as usual with me, being ordered around.' She switched seamlessly into the third and final stage of the competition. Here things could get interesting sometimes. 'How are you and the lovely Barry doing? I think he's so funny with all those celeb stories he always has.'

'I'm afraid the source has dried up since his latest career lurch' she replied bitterly. 'It really annoys me. He's gone to work as a footman in Buckingham palace and is getting nowhere fast. He keeps banging on about "accumulating life experience to write a novel". A novel I tell you. About what? How I opened the door for the queen and she said thank you?' She almost spat out the last words.

The two other women shook their heads in sympathy. They had known each other since starting together in an exclusive secondary day school. They had fantasised together about prince charming and blissful love. As they had grown older and more realistic they had readjusted their expectations and aimed for a handsome man without too many unpleasant habits who would keep them in the comfortable style they had been brought up with and was now considered a natural entitlement. A rudderless boyfriend with no sense of direction or purpose and limited career prospects ticked very few boxes nowadays, no matter how handsome and charming.

Pippa blushed slightly. She didn't want her friend's pity. She deflected their attention by turning to Chessie: 'how are things between you and Howard?' He was a work colleague who was working his way in the hedge fund management section.

'I don't know. He seems to be more interested in how well I'm doing than how well I'm feeling. I am beginning to get the distinct impression he is trying to advance his career by hanging onto my tailcoat.'

'Or your garter belt' giggled Clar.

The other two looked at her intrigued at this unusual comment from her. Clar had always been the quiet one, the peacemaker of the trio. She wasn't too ambitious or spectacularly sharp. She was, by and large quietly content with her lot. Pippa suddenly remembered.

'How did Leo get on with his Bar exam?'

Leo was Clar's long term boyfriend. He worked as a solicitor in the same chambers as she did. He was solid and dependable; a good man. He was no Adonis, being paunchy and ruddy cheeked with thinning ginger hair but he lover Clar dearly and would do anything for her.

'Well she replied barely able to contain herself, he got his results last week and...'

'Yes?' the other two were on tenterhooks now.

'He passed! And he's been offered a junior partnership in chambers from January next year when Sir Robert retires. Needless to say he is on cloud nine and...' looking like the cat who had just got the biggest bowl of cream, she slowly turned the silvery band in her left ring finger and revealed a beautiful platinum ring band with three good sized princess cut white diamonds.

Pippa and Chessie were stunned for a moment but they started squealing with delight and excitement. They hugged Clar with no envy or resentment and admired her ring with no jealousy. She had well and truly thumped them in this final round but they were extremely pleased for her.

With their traditional competition amicably settled in an unexpected three way draw they got onto the serious business of wedding plans and gossip. Half way through, Chessie's mobile started pinging, signalling a text message. She picked it up and checked the sender. She started swearing softly but profusely.

'What's wrong?' they asked.

'Oh it's bloody Yevgeni, the Chinese middleman. He keeps pestering me with requests for updates as well as sending me disgusting innuendo-filled text messages. What *was* I thinking when I agreed to give him my personal mobile phone number. Disgusting, sweaty, hairy bugger!'

Pippa was non-plussed. 'Yevgeni Rudkin?'

'How do *you* know him?'

'I've just sold him 2 large flats near Sloane square for £ 6 million.'

'Well it's not his bloody money, the Chinese are bankrolling him. Their credit is good though, so the sale won't fall through.'

Pippa's heart had missed a beat initially at the thought of losing a commission she had already half spent. Chessie's comment had reassured her but she would still double check tomorrow.

The rest of the evening passed pleasantly enough. The three women left well before the late rush for cabs.

Pippa got home and undressed herself. She slipped under the covers naked and snuggled up to Barry but he was too exhausted to notice. She kissed him gently and turned over to sleep. Maybe if she hadn't had a champagne too many she might have spent some time reflecting on her current status quo.

INHALE

Chapter 4

Barry cut a very different figure when he returned to work the following morning. He was well turned out in a lightweight navy blazer and cream cotton trousers, pale blue shirt and a dark tie. His shoes were polished to a high shine. He arrived 10 minutes before schedule. He toyed with the idea of changing into the palace uniform but, as his career prospect still hung in the balance, he decided against it; Conns might consider he was assuming he would pass his assessment. He was drinking a cup of coffee when Conns walked in, three minutes before schedule.

'Good morning Sir Ian.' Barry had almost stood to attention.

'Good morning Barry.' Sir Ian took in the improved figure. He nodded briefly in approval and picked and signed for the silver room key.

Barry and Sir Ian traced the now familiar route into the silver room. The inspection proceeded swiftly and smoothly. Even the dreaded silver tureen passed muster. They returned into the servant's dining area. A few people were drifting in, yawning and looking for the tea urn. Sir Ian's presence soon woke them up better than the strongest cup of tea!

'Very well Barry. As you know, because it is in your contract, your three month assessment was due yesterday. Unforeseen circumstances,' he said this without changing his expression, 'delayed it. If you have no objection I think we should not postpone it any further.'

Barry had been expecting this so he merely nodded in agreement.

They walked up the back stairs and into Sir Ian's office. It reflected the spiritual characteristics of the occupant. Sparsely furnished, but with exquisite furniture, there were a couple of old hunting prints on the walls and a beautiful Afghan carpet in the Bukhara style on the floor. The large desk was tidy, the in tray empty, the out tray had a few folders which were stacked in perfect alignment. Sir Ian opened a drawer and picked a manila coloured folder. Barry couldn't help noticing how thick it was despite his short tenure. Sir Ian opened it and slowly unscrewed the top of his Montblanc fountain pen. He put it to one side and gave the standard opening question: 'so, Barry, how do you think you are doing?' He leant backwards slightly in his chair with both hands on the desk.

Barry had been expected this question and had carefully rehearsed the answer in his mind while he travelled to work today. He had examined himself, and his performance uncritically and realised he was clearly lacking. Yesterday's events had thrown him a slender thread of hope; maybe he could keep both jobs.

'If I am honest, I don't think I have been performing well against the expected standards. My time-keeping and diligence have been substandard.'

Sir Ian nodded, his face was expressionless.

'I do feel, though, that yesterday I had an epiphany. Polishing all that silver made me realise how important teamwork is and how high the standards are at the palace.' This spiel didn't sound as good now as it had in his head. These were no more than platitudes and Barry was unsure whether Conns would buy it but he hoped he had managed to convey the right tone of sincerity and earnestness.

There was a long silence, punctuated by Sir Ian's tapping the desk with his right index finger. The taps gradually came further apart and then they stopped. Sir Ian leant forward, fixing his gaze on Barry who had started to perspire slightly.

'I am inclined to agree with you' he said eventually. 'Two days ago, signing your P45 would have constituted the highlight of my day but yesterday you showed a level of resourcefulness and diligence that stayed my hand. You accepted your punishment without complaining and worked hard.'

Brian swallowed hard. The tread was getting thicker.

'Unfortunately I feel I cannot offer you at present, a substantive position at the palace. I feel you should have your probationary period extended for a further three months with a first written warning on your file. Should there be any further infractions during this period I would have no option but to terminate your contract with two weeks notice. I feel this is an acceptable offer.'

And the thread started unravelling again.

'I can see your point of view Sir Ian, and I accept your terms.' He had no other option.

'Please resume your duties.' Sir Ian bent down and started writing in Barry's folder in his neat calligraphy.

Barry rose and started walking towards the door.

'Barry?'

He turned round. Conns' head was still bowed as he carried on writing.

'Yes sir.'

'I have noticed you have developed a good rapport with Melanie Hatton. She is an extremely capable person whose behaviour and work attitude are to be admired and followed. You should learn from her.' He had not stopped writing.

'Very well sir.' He let himself out, closing the door carefully as he did so.

As Barry walked into the kitchen, all the staffed stopped their chores and looked at Barry.

'I'm still gracing you with my presence' he said lightly.

This elicited a few smiles, mostly from the QARS club members. Barry got changed and went about his duties. The day went smoothly. He felt he had gained a higher level of acceptance from his colleagues. The atmosphere felt more relaxed and he kept receiving useful tips that made his job easier.

During his lunch break he updated Melanie on his appraisal and the unveiled threat attached. He chose not to pass on Conns parting comment. He acknowledged its wisdom but did not want to alert Mel to this, it would make his observing her a lot easier. He excused himself and went out to the courtyard for a postprandial cigarette and some discreet phone calls. He rang Pippa first. She had been fast asleep when he left and hadn't even stirred when he gently kissed her goodbye early that morning.

'Hi honey, can you talk?'

'Sure. You left early today.' There was an indistinct hubbub on Pippa's side of the line. She must be ordering her usual salad at her favourite deli.

'Yes, I had to be here before six. How did you get on with the rest of the coven?'

'Ha, Ha very funny. We had a great time. Some very exciting news: Clar is getting married! Leo passed his bar exams and has been offered a partnership in his chambers for next year. He is clearly going places' she added meaningfully

'That's great news!' Barry had met Clarissa a few times and Leo too. He liked them both; they had all the necessary ingredients to be a happy couple. He chose to ignore the innuendo about Leo's career taking definitely off compared to his. 'How about "ball breaker"' as he had christened Francesca. They didn't get on and it showed.

'Barry..' there was a warning tone in her voice.

'Sorry. What's happening with her?'

'She's just gained promotion and actually knows Yevgeni.'

'The gross Russian billionaire?'

'Actually no, I mean yes: it's him but it turns out he's not a billionaire. He is simply an agent for a large Chinese consortium.'

' What, Oil and gas?'

'No actually, he seems to dabble mostly in shares. Aeroplanes I think' Chessie said. 'Anyhow, where are you taking me out tonight? I'm looking forward to it.'

Bugger, bugger, bugger! He'd completely forgotten he'd promise to take Pippa out for dinner tonight. 'It's a surprise.' He tried to make it sound more mysterious than it really was.

'You haven't booked yet.'

'You'll see.'

'OK, ciao.'

'Love you.'

'Me too.' She hung up.

Barry looked at his phone deep in thought. A fake billionaire, working for a big Chinese corporation. He wasn't sure if it was mainland or Taiwan and didn't want to pry. Pippa wouldn't have known anyway. He knew he should ring his paper to pass this information on. He didn't want to speak to, or rather be barked at, by Jock. He thought he'd speak with the chief editor: Norman Sewell. He had only met him once briefly at the Christmas party but he had heard, and read, many good things about him. He was beginning to think more and more about a career in serious journalism. If the information passed were good, Norman, he suspected, would be keener to help than Jock who tended to treat hacks like disposable tissues.

Norman Sewell had been at his desk for a couple of hours. This was the time he normally started work unless there were any major developments. He was working on a draft for tomorrow's editorial. He always toyed with two or three ideas, depending on what major news was breaking. Unfortunately, the last two days had been rather lacking in these. He resorted to some old stalwarts for any editor: the decline of industrial output in Britain or the gradual deterioration in the NHS. His mobile phone rang; on the screen was a number he didn't recognise.

'Hello, Norman Sewell, Daily Herald.'

'Mr Sewell, it's Barry Smith here.'

Norman racked his brains. The name was familiar. 'Is that Barry at Buckingham palace?'

'That's correct sir.' Barry was amazed he remembered him or what was he doing but Norman had the vital journalistic skill of never forgetting a name, a face or their surrounding circumstances. This was one of the reasons he was so good. He continued. 'I have just had some unusual information about one Yevgeni Rudkin which I thought might be of interest to you.'

'Isn't he one of these tasteless and shady Russian oligarchs who seem hell-bent on purchasing half of Chelsea and sizeable chunks of the Home Counties?'

'It would appear so on first impressions.'

'What would the second impression be then?' Norman was mildly amused. This young whippersnapper had got hold of his phone number somehow and was now trying to impress him with some "breathtaking" news he had probably heard about three weeks ago.

'He had just spent £6 million in two large tatty houses near Sloane square as well being on the lookout for a small cheap house in South Derby. The really interesting thing is that the money isn't his, he appears to be a middleman for a large Chinese corporation who are also buying heavily into airplane shares.'

Norman, as usual, was jotting down a few notes with his mind working on other things. Two words closely together exploded in his mind: Chinese and airplanes. He sat bolt upright in his chair. This he had *definitely* not heard about!

'Wait a second. Airplane shares? What kind of airplane shares?'

'I'm afraid my source wasn't more specific.'

'How good and reliable is this source?'

Barry thought about this. He didn't want Pippa or Chessie to get into trouble. It could also lead to his cover being blown. 'They're a moderately senior executive working for a big investment corporation. I'm afraid I can't be more specific.'

Norman nodded approvingly; you should never reveal your sources. He also whistled softly. His day had just become *much* more interesting. 'Anything else?'

'I'm afraid that's all there is. The info about Rudkin came from two different sources but if I pump for too much detail it could blow my cover.' He was exaggerating slightly but Pippa could become suspicious and she could nag like the best. 'If anything else comes by I will let you know of course.'

'Fine, how's work at the palace?' Norman didn't possess Jock's pathological hatred for the royal family; he could take them or leave them. The only exception was the queen. He greatly admired her dedication and hard work. His mother was roughly the same age too and he knew how exhausted old ladies could get.

'It's not going too well, I'm still under probation. I feel people are beginning to trust me more so hopefully I'll start getting more substantial information. It will take time though.'

Norman caught the hint. 'I'll try to keep you out of Jock's radar screen then' he laughed.

'Thank you Mr Sewell.'

'Call me Norman, everybody here does.'

'Thank you Norman' he hesitated briefly.'I wonder if I could ask you something?'

'Let's hear it.'

'I would like to move more into mainstream journalism, national or international news. I know there aren't any vacancies at present but if any arose, could my name be considered?'

Norman thought about this. The lad had spotted useful information and relayed it appropriately. Yes, he might have the right instincts.'I'll certainly look into it with interest.' He couldn't promise more: Jock kept a tight rein on the budget.

'Thank you and good bye.' His phone clicked.

Norman looked at his mobile. He added Barry's number to his phone's memory card. He certainly appeared to be a bright chap. Something had not tallied in his mental abacus and he'd shared the disparity with him without revealing too many sources. He dialled an internal number.

'Yes boss?'

'Boris, can you come into my office please?'

A few moments later, Boris Kropotkin, one of sports subeditors, walked in tapping into his Blackberry.

'Boris, you're good at Russian, aren't you?'

'I should think so boss. My dad defected from Russia years ago but he insisted all his kids spoke good Russian.'

'Can you read it too?'This was important for his next step.

'Quite well just don't ask me to translate Mikhail Bulgakov!'

'I need a favour. I would like you to get onto the Russian Google and find out as much as you can about a chap called Rudkin.'

'Yevgeni Rudkin? The Russian tycoon?'

'Do you know him?'

'I know of him, made quite a big splash some months ago. Throws good parties. He has a bit of a reputation of being a moron and a brute. Nobody knows where his money comes from.'

Better and better thought Norman. 'I think we should try and find out a bit more about this gentleman don't you think?' He paused briefly. 'You don't sound too Russian to me if you don't mind my saying so.'

Boris laughed. 'I should very well hope so. I was born in England, spent most of my life in Derby.'

'Really?' Norman's eyes narrowed. 'So, what bought you to London? Apart from the cheap housing and the princely salaries of course.'

Boris sniggered, 'yeah, right. No, the fact is there isn't much going on in Derby and it's hard to earn a crust there. Also the local newspaper was too stolid and unadventurous for me.'

But I thought there was still a lot of mining and industry.' Norman feigned the typical Londoner's ignorance of anything beyond the M25.

'God that went ages ago! No, now all you have is small engineering firms which pay a pittance, Crown Derby china and Rolls Royce of course.'

'Hadn't they moved to Germany? Or is there still a factory there?

'No boss, this is the aero engine division. It's still British.' He frowned for a moment. 'At least I think it is.'

'Fine. Please look into it and let me know what you find out ASAP.'

'Sure thing boss.' He left the room closing the door behind him. Unlike Barry, he hadn't shown the slightest interest about the task assigned. Not serious journalist material.

As soon as the door closed Norman punched the air in triumph. His instincts had been right again. This was not out of vanity. He just loved the chase for a story and this one had all the hallmarks of a veritable humdinger! He pondered his next move. He would have to start talking with government officials and politicians. He hated doing it. Nowadays they were all slippery buggers, experts of the bland noncommittal statement. Oh to have Maggie back again! His eyes rested on the two drafts. He smiled slowly. He picked one of the drafts, crumpled it and threw it in the bin. Super bugs could very well fester for a few more days (that was their job after all!). It had been a long time since he had met or interviewed Helen Steele. A re-acquaintance was long overdue and *she* would ring first this time.

Before he needled Helen though, Norman needed a few more checks. He fast dialled a well-known number in Southern France.

'Allo?, ici Jean Pierre Calment.' The owner of the voice had a rich Rousillon lilt.

'Jean Pierre, mon vieux ami, comment ca va?'

' Tu m'apelles six mois depuis ma derriere defaite, sans chance de revanche espece de con!' Jean Pierre was not known to tolerate a defeat in his favourite game of boules, go unanswered for long periods.

'Tu auras ta revanche bien trop mon vieux. J'en ai besoin de ton aide' Norman's French was quite acceptable even if it was heavily accented.

'Professionelle?'

'Oui.'

'We will speek in Eenglish then, yes?' Jean Pierre and Norman had known each other for many years. They had initially met professionally when he had purchased a derelict farm near Toulouse. Jean Pierre had been the local notary who had dealt with all the legal aspects. Norman had always tried to speak in French, however atrociously, this had endeared him to Jean Pierre. From the initial professional relationship, a friendship had slowly evolved. As Norman slowly rebuilt the farm Jean Pierre was always ready to help with legal and bureaucratic advice. He had introduced Norman to the game of boules and they always played whenever Norman visited.

'I need to find out about any real estate purchases by a Russian chap called Yevgeni Rudkin.'

'Is it something criminal?' Jean Pierre knew what Norman's job was. Friendship or not, he was loath to expose his impeccably shaved neck into harm's way.

'No, it isn't.'

'Where is he buying?'

'Somewhere near the Airbus factory near Toulouse'

'Ang on! You said nozzing criminal. This looks like industrial espionage non?' When he got excited, Jean Pierre's accent and grammar tended to slip.

'No, no. I assure you this has got nothing to do with industrial espionage or any criminal activities. It is as clean as your boules before the southern Toulouse championship final' he joked.

'Bon. For you I do this, but only if you promise to come soon. I hear your British summer is very wet non? You need to give me a chance of revenge!'

'Sure, I will come very soon. Has Elodie ran out of tea?'

'Almost. Some of your excellent Earl Grey from Fortnum's would be greatly appreciated by her. Moi, I do not like it'

Norman picked the hint. 'Very well, I will arrange for a delivery for you. This leaves us quits non?' Norman slipped into Jean Pierre's vernacular

'Well maybe. Depends on how well you play next time. I will e-mail you the information by tonight.'

'Merci beaucoup.'

'A bien tot mon ami'

That had been a useful 5 minutes. He rang Fortnum's. he had a long-standing account there which was his only personal extravagance. He arranged for the delivery of three tins of Fortnum and Mason's finest Earl Grey tea as well as half a pound of Chinese extra strong crystallized ginger which Jean Pierre loved with the passion only reserved for his many epicurean weaknesses.

Norman now rang an old acquaintance in banking. Peter Walker was a broker who worked for a small finance firm. In the past he had provided Norman with some useful snippets of information. Norman had always tried to repay in kind.

'Hallo Peter, it's Norman. I wonder if you could let me know something.'

'That depends on what it is.' Like most people in finance, Peter never agreed to anything until he knew what he was committing for.

'Nothing harmful and indeed it could be beneficial for you.' Norman tried to put a positive spin on the request.

'I'm listening.'

'I need to know who owns large share packages in major aeronautical companies: Airbus, McDonnell Douglas, Boeing, BAe, as well as jet engine manufacturers like Rolls Royce and any others you can think of.'

'Well you should think of General electric, Embraer, CASA and SAAB too. How big a share package are we talking about?' Peter asked.

Norman thought about this. The Chinese had started small but he suspected they would now accelerate in their acquisitions and, now that the cat was out of the bag, they would be a bit less discreet. 'At least 1%. I would also need to know if anyone is buying or selling.

'Why do you need to know?' Peter hadn't committed himself yet and in fact was starting to sound a bit cagey.

'This is in complete confidence, yes?'

'Of course.'

'I think a major Chinese consortium, maybe even the Chinese government are buying major aero share packages, fast' Norman thought he heard a brief intake of breath at the end of the phone but he was slightly distracted, busily jotting down the other names Peter had given him.

'I'm not sure I can help you. Some of this information is extremely delicate. I could land myself in big trouble for revealing excessive data.'

'Peter, I'm not asking you to breach any confidential data. I could get hold of the shareholders names myself but it would take a long time. I need a short cut.'

'OK, OK. I'll see what I can find out for you. No promises though.' Peter was desperately trying to procrastinate. Norman had been dead right on the money. His firm, as well as many others, had been working for a far eastern consortium trying to buy as many shares as possible. They had also started to hoard shares of companies they hadn't been instructed to buy as advised by their analysts, in the hope that they would then be approached to sell them at a good profit. It was speculative capitalism at its worst. The last thing they needed was journalists poking their noses, even if they were as discreet as Norman Sewell. It could cause panic buying followed by a crash. Financial institutions didn't like crashes. They messed balance sheets!

Norman looked at his phone once Peter had hung up. He had sounded extremely wary, even more than usual. He took a sip of his now cold coffee. All in all it had been a productive hour. He had started spinning a big web and he hoped a few fat flies would land on it. He always used the personal touch when it came to investigative journalism. He would ask gently for a few favours, nothing major at the time, a small piece for his jigsaw. He would wait patiently. Time was usually on his side, as more elements surfaced of their own accord. Although he now was a chief editor, with many strings to his bow, he still liked to indulge in slow methodical research and once it was complete, he would deliver a comprehensive report. He was less in his element in press conferences, he preferred the discreet face to face interviews as he could read these extremely well. He checked his watch. It was well gone noon. He'd better go and catch a bite to eat before the early editors meeting.

Helen Stokes was sitting at her desk in the afternoon. She had been working flat out on the report Edward had requested. It was well ahead of schedule. Due to the highly sensitive contents in it, she had not used any assistance. At home she had accessed some rarely used websites (she did not want her internet trail checked at the DTI) and they had yielded a veritable cornucopia of information. The resulting report, expertly condensed in two sheets of A4, was now lying in front of her. She looked at it warily. The picture portrayed in it was very discomforting. The British economy, in fact the whole of the EU economy was in a far bigger mess than she had anticipated. She felt she would need an expert opinion to endorse it when she met with Edward. She rang Wilfred Wilkes on her mobile. She would had preferred to contact Sir Norman but knew that some worthless egos needed massaging for future favours.

'Hello, Wilfred here.'

'Hello, it's Helen. Can you talk?'

'Yes, let me close the door.' There was a brief pause. 'Where are you ?'

'I'm at the DTI, why?'

'You do remember it's Prime Ministers Questions in half an hour?' There was a note of reproach in his voice.

'Bother! I'd completely forgotten' Helen rarely swore, she felt it was common and it lost its impact if used constantly. 'Is there anything major going on today?'

'We suspect Gordon and his motley crew are going to try and roast Edward over the South China Sea incident.'

'Is it a three line whip?'

'Only if you don't have a good excuse not to be there.'

'That's my diary sorted then. I've just finished my report. Any news on John's?'

'He dropped it only five minutes ago.'

'I'm on my way. I'll drop it at Edward's office in parliament.'

'Why don't you just e-mail it?'

'I would rather not. I'm afraid I don't trust the internet when it comes to really confidential material. Hacking is a lot more widespread than we realise.'

'Aren't you being a teensy bit paranoid Helen? These *are* high security links. Not the kind of place some spotty youth can crack into in the afternoon.'

The condescending tone irritated Helen, her temper flared, how dare this pup question her? Normally she would have just let it pass but she was very tired; she had hardly slept for two days, slaving at the report and worrying about its findings. She knew only too well just how bad e-espionage was these days. She didn't even have her confidential laptop connected to the internet.

'Listen Wilfred, I have just spent a very hard two days slaving over a very confidential report which, if leaked, would cause major political and economic fallout. I am not prepared to risk it for you convenience so give it to him and arrange a meeting!... please' she added as an afterthought.

Wilfred's tone stiffened. 'Very well Miss Steele. I will deliver it personally as you request.'

By the time Helen got into the chamber, PMQs had just started. She slid onto the front bench almost unnoticed thanks to a heated exchange between Edward and Gordon Brown. The Conservatives, governing through the very precarious support of other parties, had been desperate to avoid any major political fallout for at least half a year until people got used to the idea of their being in power again. Labour, like a toddler who's had his favourite toy snatched unexpectedly, were in no mood to let them bed into people's consciousness. Since Edward had kissed the queen's hands they had submitted him to an incessant barrage of criticism, sniping and innuendo both in the House of Commons and from the national press which they still controlled through better contacts than the conservatives.

Edward was in excellent form. His rise to leadership of the conservative party and thence to Prime Minister had been quite swift but low profile. He had not had much chance to indulge in verbal sparring with the opposition front benchers so he was a relatively unknown quantity as a public speaker as far as they knew. Edward had kept his skills as a secret. He was in fact a phenomenal orator, Gordon Brown and his acolytes were beginning to find just how good he was and they didn't like it one bit. He was making them look like mumbling teenagers. Today, ably flanked by Rufus and John, he gave an excellent account of himself and made the opposition look like fools. The Lib-Dems were interested spectators who quietly congratulated themselves for choosing to support him.

He arrived home late. He was tired but elated. Sylvia was waiting for him in the sitting room. On the table there was a large mug of red bush tea and a plate with some biscuits. He smiled. His driver always informed Sylvia when he was about to arrive and she always tried to be around ready to talk and offer support if needed. She stood up and, checking no-one was with him, gave him a hug. He held on tightly, savouring the moment. She moved away slightly and they both sat down.

'How did PMQ go?'

'Not too bad. Brown tried to nail us down over the dead fishermen issue but between John, Rufus and myself we turned the tables on him. He looked even more disgruntled than usual!'

'It's those poor fishermen and their families I feel sorry for.'

'It was tragic but we will ensure they have financial support to soften the blow.'

She sensed he was beginning to eye his red box. She gave him a quick kiss and left but not before saying 'make sure Lhasa goes out!'

Edward opened the box. On top of the pile were two brown A4 envelopes kept together with a clip and a post-it attached to the top one. It was Wilfred's handwriting: "5pm tom post-HMQ".

Oh God! He had forgotten his weekly dispatch with the queen. That was probably the most irksome aspect of his job. She was an extremely well informed woman but she was so distant, so formal! Since he had started meeting with her she had never voiced an opinion, however inane, on anything. He fully understood her constitutional constraints but even when he'd enquired about Royal Ascot she'd been non committal. He hoped she wouldn't give him aggro over the short notice state visit! He opened the envelope with Helen's dossier and started reading. He became very worried.

Chapter 5

10000 miles away, MaTsien-Zu the Chinese premier was discussing the recent events with his foreign minister. Despite the early hour the atmosphere in the room was heavy due to their constant smoking. A cloud of cigarette smoke hung above their heads, its particles creating an unusual but pleasing swirling pattern; both men were too engrossed though to notice it.

'Very well comrade', Ma said 'how did the last meeting with the British ambassador go?'

'I feel it was quite satisfactory premier Ma.' The foreign minister didn't use the official title of Chairman Ma. It sounded too much like Chairman Mao; it would have been considered the epitome of hubris. Moreover, it was a known fact in some restricted circles that Ma Tsien-Zu held no fond memories of Mao Ze-Dong's regime. 'The British government have expressed their condolences for the unfortunate chain of events and have offered a respectable financial compensation package. They have also invited us to form a joint investigation commission to ensure this unfortunate event never happens again.'

Ma sneered. 'They do enjoy their "investigation commissions" don't they? It makes them look like they're taking things seriously and actions will occur. Nothing ever comes out of them. I do despise their hypocrisy. What about the sailor who insulted the memories of the dead fishermen as well as China? Will there be another "joint investigation commission"?' The irony was undisguised.

'No. This they seem to be taking more seriously. The Royal Navy have informed me that the sailor is off sick with stress. Officially...'

Ma noted the lingering pause. He took a long drag of his cigarette and exhaled. He then took a sip of green tea from the exquisite porcelain bowl at the table. His eyes had been fixed all the time on his foreign minister who wasn't squirming. He and Ma were allies and as friendly with each other as one could be in the rarefied political atmosphere of the upper echelons of Chinese government.

'And what has happened, "unofficially" comrade?' The question was heavily laced with irony.

'The Royal Navy have put him under house arrest. There will not be court martial but he will be dishonourably discharged with immediate loss of pension if he so much as breathes a word to the press. They lose no face and we receive satisfaction.'

'They certainly won't lose face. Westerners forget things quickly don't they? "Yesterday's news wraps tomorrow's fish" is they expression they use. It's a different way to control the press. More subtle'.

'This is very true premier Ma.'

'I also understand that the British prime minister has extended a formal invitation for a state visit.'

'He has indeed. The official reason is to commemorate the tenth anniversary of the British handover of Hong-Kong' he paused to check his notes and continued 'and "herald a new dawn of political and economical cooperation between our two great nations" they said.'

Ma raised his eyebrows in mock surprise. He lit a new cigarette with the end of the old one. He had a fit of coughing which lasted a few moments. Once it had settled he shifted his position in his chair, grunting as he did so. 'And when is this new "dawn" supposed to start?'

'On June the 28th, next week.'

'Next week? It sounds…precipitated. Is there any "unofficial" reason for this sudden rush of hospitality?

'I am inclined to agree it seems rather hasty, especially when they have appeared to try and lower the recent naval incident's profile. I do not know or heard of any ulterior motive though. In fairness there had been an invitation issued by the Labour government early in the year. Then their election came up and it was felt prudent to await developments. I have taken the liberty of checking your schedule. There is a five day window between your visit to the US and the brief summit with president Putin. There is the politburo meeting on July the 2nd of course but it could be postponed.'

Ma thought about this. Could they be already suspecting things? It would mean being away from the country for over two weeks. This was an extremely long time, especially when the balance of power and doctrine still hung so precariously. 'I will have to weigh the various arguments comrade. I will let you know by noon.'

Both men bowed, Ma noticeably less so. It sent a spasm of pain. The foreign minister left.

As soon as the door closed Ma tried to get up from his chair. He became extremely pale as he did so. His hands gripped the wooden armrests so tight, his knuckles became white. A small bead of sweat started trickling down his left temple, it wasn't caused by the room temperature, as it wasn't that warm. He only managed to hold back a yelp of pain as he became upright. He took off some of his weight by resting his left hand on the table while his right hand fumbled with the catch of an antique lacquer cigarette holder. It opened eventually. He grabbed an un-tipped cigarette with a small red dot at the end. He lit up and sucked in greedily. A few moments later the special morphine crystals mixed with the tobacco had started working their soothing effect on the pain nerve endings of his back. He lifted his body up slowly and gently eased the weight of his right hand, the fast rasping breaths settled into a normal breathing pattern. His pupils became narrow which blurred his vision slightly but this was a very short lived side effect and one he was happy to put up with in exchange for the fast relief the morphine gave. He walked up slowly towards the window overlooking Tian-an-Men square and looked down. His back pain was a direct consequence of Mao Ze-Dong's megalomania and paranoia. He had been a victim of the Cultural Revolution in 1966-67. He had been seized by a group of young red guards at the steel factory where he worked. They had beaten him senseless after extracting from him the most ludicrous confessions of being a rightist revisionist on Moscow's payroll. He had been kept in the "airplane position": body bent forwards with his hands tied at the back, jerked upwards, for hours on end. When they got tired he was thrown out of the window in the second floor and left for dead. His crime? Being the son of the governor of Manchuria; one of the few brave men who had dared challenge Mao during his "great leap forward" plan which had resulted in the greatest famine ever, during the late 50s. His father had been one of the first victims of the Cultural Revolution with Mao exacting the revenge for a previous challenge personally. Lin-Biao, Mao's sinister henchman, had also been present at his father's torture and execution. He too would have been yet another rotting corpse had a fellow worker not rescued him and hidden him for nearly a year. By then the worst excesses of that savage aberration that had been the Cultural Revolution were over. The red guards gone, the local commissar had put him under his discreet personal protection. He recovered from most of his wounds except for two crushed thoracic vertebrae. It was nothing short of a miracle he hadn't become paralysed. He had, however, been left with a severe chronic pain that only his personal physician could alleviate. It required almost daily sessions of massage and acupuncture. The morphine cigarettes were reserved for crises. He never smoked more than three a day as he was aware of the addiction risks. That had been the first one. On balance it may not be a good idea to have a very hectic two weeks.

His telephone rang and he moved slowly towards it. His secretary informed him that the deputy industry minister was waiting for him. He smiled and asked her to send him in.

Ma Jing-Tao walked into the room and bowed with a smile. 'Good morning premier Ma.'

'Come, come Jing-Tao we're alone, there's no need to stand on ceremony. I have told you this many times.'

Jing-Tao's smile became broader. 'Very good father, as you wish'. Ma-Jing-Tao's father was dead but his uncle Ma Tsien-Zu had filled the role for as long as he could remember. He sniffed the unmistakeable aroma of morphine and examined his uncle's pale features. 'Is the pain very bad today? Perhaps we can meet later.'

Ma Tsien-Zu had another coughing fit. He shook his head and gestured Jing-Tao to sit, which he did but not before helping his uncle sit down first. This was done with a tender solicitousness, which revealed the deep affection Jing-Tao felt for his uncle. His father was

Tsien-Zu's older brother. He had never met him. He had died in a "re-education camp" in Inner Mongolia when he was two years old. He had been seized by the political commissars when his mother was pregnant with him at the time. His uncle, already crippled by injury, and his mother, raised him. They had eventually married, hence his calling his uncle father. She had died 15 years later, shortly after Jing-Tao had started university. They both missed her dreadfully. He was one of the few people who knew the constant severe pain his uncle lived in. Ma Tsien-Zu didn't believe in advertising his weaknesses to his rivals!

'So, Jing, how are things going?'

'Very well. By the end of next week we will own 5-10% of all major airplane and aero engine manufacturers in Europe. The loan business is progressing well too.' He added cryptically.

'That is good news. What about America?'

'I'm afraid the news is nowhere as good.'

'Why?'

'They are extremely guarded about releasing shares of what they consider to be strategic industries to companies outside USA or the EU. Their stock is very fragmented in small share holders.' He hesitated, he was about to give some bad news. 'We also have a problem.'

Tsien-Zu lit up a filter tipped cigarette; he suddenly had become a lot less genial. 'What might this problem be?'

'When we decided to merge with the consortia of medium-sized shareholders we required consent from the Bank of England. In total they owned just over 5% percent. Any company who purchases shares over a certain percentage must obtain permission from the national bank. This is standard procedure. It used to be 10% but the rules were changed recently. By the time we found out, the alert had been triggered and it was too late to pull back. We felt it would have only given rise to more speculation.'

'Do you think they know?'

'I don't think they do. They would have created a huge fuss.'

Realisation suddenly struck Ma Tsien-Zu. 'They know, Jing-Tao, they already know.'

'How can you be so sure?'

Tsien-Zu relied to his nephew the unexpected invitation from the British government. He emphasised the phrase "political and economic dawn".

Jing Tao paled visibly. The game had suddenly become a lot more serious. 'Premier Ma, I have in my duties to you and the government of the PRC. You shall have my resignation letter on your desk by tonight.'

Tsien-Zu looked at his nephew with a mixture of surprise and affection. He reassured him poetically. 'My dear nephew, the surface of the road has just become rougher. Now, more than ever, the cart needs three horses to pull it.'

Jing-Tao breathed with relief. His uncle had included him in his nickname "two horse" Tsien-Zu. This came about because Ma means horse in Mandarin and he was born in 1942, the year of the horse. Although communists discouraged belief in astrology or portents, many Chinese, even high ranking officials, set great importance to such signs, especially when they are considered to be particularly auspicious.

'Very well, I will ensure the horses are well fed and shod.'

'You do that.'

'What should our next move be?'

Tsien-Zu closed his eyes and went into deep thought. Jing-Tao waited patiently. What should we do now? Obviously the British know. Have they warned the rest of the Europeans as well as the Americans? Will they still have the arrogance to try and resist us alone or will they be realistic about their situation? This technology will act as a foundation stone. On it we will learn how to do proper research and development. We have lagged badly behind for too many centuries, living on past glories. I hope the British don't start panicking. Scared people make rash decisions, mistakes. These would be costly for them and make us look aggressive. I do not want world domination; I just want China to take its rightful place in the world order.

His eyes opened again. He had decided on a course of action. He smiled benignly. 'First we will practice talking in English.' Jing-Tao spoke perfect English after spending 10 years training in Canada, USA and Britain. They practiced together in private. It irked him that this was the "lingua franca" of the world but that was the situation. He never revealed his level of proficiency in public. It was a useful delaying tactic when speaking with English-speaking dignitaries; while the interpreter translated it allowed him extra time to plan his answer.

'Very well, what then?'

'You will stay here while I go to USA, I'll take with me the Industry minister as well as the foreign minister. You need to find out as much as possible about the new British ministers. We also need to know about what their "free press" are saying. You will arrive on the 26th in England and prepare a dossier. We continue with our investments as scheduled with a special reinforcement of the loan aspect. I will need an updated dossier by the time I arrive on the 28th; it will include the latest shares update with special interest in airbus-linked companies and high quality steel producers.'

'What of the USA investments?'

'Forget about them. It's a no-go zone. My trip has almost become redundant but we still need to show we can observe formalities. We will concentrate on poaching their best IT consultants. Capitalism has its advantages and the fact that many are Chinese is just a bonus. By the way, no telephone or e-mail contact. Use couriers if there are any major developments and let our "cultural attaches" earn their keep.' He popped a cherry in his mouth and ate it with great satisfaction. This year's crop was excellent he thought as he spat out the stone.

They conversed in English for a while. Tsien-Zu's English was quite correct grammatically but it took him a long time to translate in his mind and speak out with a heavily accented Chinese. It was also very taxing mentally. Eventually he signalled he was tired. He had been up since dawn. Jing-Tao bowed respectfully as he left, but stopped when Tsien-Zu mentioned almost casually:

'Isn't it our dear Chung Hing-Lai's birthday tomorrow?'

Jing-Tao frowned in puzzlement. His uncle positively loathed his immediate superior, the industry minister. He had needed to accommodate him in the cabinet as a compromise with the most reactionary current of the CPC. They were still a powerful voice in the party and had demanded, and obtained, two important ministries. Fortunately Chung was a torpid, venal brute who thought himself far more cunning than he really was. He was, of course, aware of the relationship between his deputy and his boss but, having obtained plum postings for his two sons (who were hardly an improvement on the master copy), he had no option but let it be. Why was his uncle being so solicitous about him?

'Yes uncle, I believe it is.'

'I thought it would be a nice gesture if we arranged a surprise dinner party for him. We should invite some close friends such as the other ministers and their deputies. No spouses. Maybe some dancers. Hopefully no-one will be inconvenienced.'

Jing-Tao smiled inwardly. This was a direct order of the Chairman. Of course no-one would be inconvenienced! They would jump through the hoops as instructed, or else. He felt China was long overdue a political overhaul but in the meantime, why not take advantage of the current status quo? He also realised that with the ministers' and their deputies' bellies full they would be in a far less alert mood to resist any impromptu changes. Birthdays are not a common celebration in China and most people would see through this; he hoped their interest would overcome their wariness. 'Very well uncle. Perhaps the invitation should emanate from your office?'

Tsien-Zu looked at his nephew. What a clever lad! If he summoned senior party members, however diplomatic the invitation, they might take offence, think he was getting ideas above his station and incite them to bring Jing-Tao down a peg or two. This he couldn't afford to do. He had long term plans for this lad. Very long term plans which shouldn't be upset by a silly slip. 'Of course it will come from my office!' he barked. He still wouldn't allow himself to be corrected, however gently, by this pup. 'Your job is to arrange the food and the dancers!'

'Yes Premier Ma.' Jing-Tao responded meekly. He understood his slip and his true position.

'Make sure the rice wine is of the best quality, plentiful and well warmed. I understand our good friend Chung appreciates the good things in life.'

Jing-Tao bowed again only lower this time, trying hard to stifle the wave of laughter building up inside him. His uncle was using the oldest trick in the book. Getting Chung drunk so he wouldn't create a fuss!

Ma Tsien-Zu nodded curtly at the retreating figure of his nephew. He then rubbed his hands with unconcealed glee. Maybe this could be used to his advantage. At the end of the meal he would mention he had accepted the invitation for a state visit next week. He would ask his ally, Hsien Fang-La, the interior minister to express his concern at the length of time he would be away especially with the politburo meeting scheduled for a long time. He would then suggest in all innocence an impromptu cabinet meeting there and then. Most of them would agree. Chung would probably try to object. The trick was to have him drunk enough that he wouldn't object. but not so drunk he would become aggressive. It was fortuitous that the second, more formidable reactionary element of opposition was away on manoeuvres in Manchuria. Marshal Wang was a far more dangerous opponent. He was teetotal, a survivor of the long march and blinded in his veneration for Mao. Yes, he felt he could turn this apparent setback to his advantage.

He asked his assistant to inform the British embassy of his acceptance unofficially with a formal acceptance to follow the following day. He also arranged for the guests to attend tomorrow's meal. Finally he had a very long conversation with the interior minister.

Chapter 6

Barry was back at work. He was, once again, on time. He wasn't in a good mood. Having managed to secure a table at Pippa's favourite restaurant, a promising evening had turned into an unmitigated disaster. Clarissa's forthcoming engagement had aroused Pippa's own yearning to settle down. She also wanted to at least beat Chessie to the altar, something Barry suspected even if she would never admit to it. The whole meal had been a third degree on Barry's "career prospects" and "where do you think our relationship is going". Although Barry was fond of her, he wasn't sure she was the ideal partner for him. Her looks and ambition massaged his ego, but there were character traits in her which resonated with past memories.

Barry's parents had eventually divorced when he was twelve, a very vulnerable age for a young person. His sister Lily had been two years younger and suffered even more. Their parents considered them mere pawns in their hatred battle had used them accordingly. Simple tools of blackmail, one minute the apple of either parent's eye, the next sent packing to the other faction's home depending on their mood. Mercifully the paternal grandparents had stepped into this maelstrom of conflicting emotions and had rescued them. They obtained a restraining court order and fostered them. It was with them that he and Lily had eventually found a safe haven, which offered stability, love and affection. Gramps and Nana were the flipside of the marital coin. Even now, after 55 years of marriage, they were still devoted, caring and respectful of each other. His bitterness about his parents had eventually abated but he was still wary around them and their respective new partners. Lily still refused to see them. He was more flexible but ould leave either house the moment there were any sniping comments about their exes, regardless of time or weather. He rarely finished a meal with them. He and Lily would go regularly to visit their grandparents and it was a given that they would spend Boxing Day with them. All four would eat cold cut sandwiches with homemade chips, which Nana still fried better that any 3 Michelin star restaurants, play scrabble and fall asleep in front of the telly. Pippa's nagging and attempts at manipulation indicated that their marriage would end in a bitter and acrimonious split however "civilised" their intentions might be. His faint reassurances, laced with a distinct lack of commitment, had not pleased Pippa.

'Are you OK?'

Melanie's question had raised him from his reverie.

'What? Oh yes, I'm fine. Spot of daydreaming.'

'Well you'd better stop that. The Prime Minister's due to meet with the queen and you are on car door duty so you need to go and practice.'

'Practice? Car door duty? I think I can work that one out. Car arrives, car stops, I open door, man gets out, I bow, close car door, back inside.' He tried to sound sarcastic but his heart wasn't in it.

Melanie was sitting askance, her right check resting on her right hand, her expression a mixture of bemusement, pity and exasperation. 'You still don't get it do you? Three months here and you still don't get it.'

Barry remembered Conn's parting comment. He decided against any irony and asked politely: 'I'm sorry if I sound a bit obtuse. I have seen it a few times on the television. It appears quite straightforward.

'Did you ever laugh when you saw it?'

'Laugh?' Had quota lost her marbles? He thought about it though. 'No, I never did. I would have if the footman had tripped or had to run behind the car…' his voiced faded, he had just realised what she had been trying to tell him.

'Exactly!' Melanie had straightened up suddenly; her face was inches away from Barry's face with her eyes wide open as she slapped her right hand on the table. 'You don't laugh at a footman's mishaps because they never happen. They all practice like mad so the performance is always flawless!'

'Always?'

Melanie blushed slightly, as if caught telling a big lie. 'Well as a matter of fact Jeremy was on duty once and he mistimed it. He had two walk a further two steps. It is believed the driver did it on purpose. That's how he joined QARS.'

Barry's face was a mixture of horror and incredulity. 'Just one big fat second here. Are *you* telling me Jezza had to polish 150 pieces of silverware because he mistimed the arrival of a sodding car?' He was almost shouting.

Melanie had leant back again. Her expression was less intent. 'Barry, Buckingham palace is one of the most photographed places in the world. It is part of the magic that everything appears to run faultlessly. Like a ballet by the Kirov. No one ever realises the amount of elbow grease, of sweat, tears and tantrums involved to achieve this. Why do you think this place has a list of candidates longer than your arm?' She had leant forward again.

Barry shook his head silently. He had never seen Mel looking this intense, almost possessed!

'Training and discipline! We have people from all walks of life applying for a position here. Some of the best families in Britain send their children to work here. Not for the money, not for loyalty to the crown – though that helps – but because this place teaches you that only perfection will do. A lot of people do a 2-3 year stint and their next job is in junior management on the fast track to the keys to the executive loo!'

'Why did you join then?' Barry was very confused, he had never thought of people taking a position at the palace as part of a long term career plan.

'Partly because I'm a monarchist, a dying breed, partly because I was fed up with living in a two horse village where everyone knew your business, but more importantly because I'm doing a degree in tourism and catering. I have been working at my degree for two years. In twelve months it will be finished, I'll start applying for top hotels in London or in the countryside with a stint working in a cruise ship as an alternative.'

'Wow! You do want to get on with life.'

'Too right I do. Anyway you'd better get to the west wing where your training awaits. Incidentally, this job is considered a small promotion, Sir Ian seems to have taken a shine to you!' She couldn't help smirking as she said it.

'And who is going to initiate me in the sacred mysteries of door opening?'

Melanie took a sip of tea while she cross referenced the rota with Barry's name.

'Ooooh!' She said with exactly the same tone as an elderly aunt spotting the last strawberry cream in a tin of roses. 'You training will have unexpected lustre. You have been bestowed the great honour of having Mr Patrick O'Malley MC as your personal trainer!'

'Whaaat? "Psycho" Pat?'

'The very one and only, the sublimely inimitable Mr O'Malley.' Melanie gave Barry a look in which beatitude and schadenfreude were mixed in just the exact proportions. She wouldn't miss this training exercise for all the gin in the world! 'You'd better get there in time. Mr O'Malley makes Conn's hatred of lack of punctuality look like a teddy bear's picnic and he can be soooo imaginative when it comes to discipline! You're due to start in five minutes.'

'Pah! As a veteran of QARS nothing frightens me any more.' Barry added boastfully.

Mel fluttered her eyelashes and added brightly 'do you know how many windows this place has? It's four minutes now by the way.'

Barry was out of the kitchen by the time the chair he'd been sitting on had hit the floor.

Mel stood up, picked the chair up and put it under the table. She sat down again, sighed contentedly and nibbled at the ginger nut she had been dunking in her tea.

Barry was sprinting down the corridors slowing down slightly to avoid any oncoming people. Fortunately there were few staff at the time and no royals. 'Oh shit, oh shit, oh shit! I'd better get there on time or I'll be dead as a bloody Dodo by the time "Psycho's" finished with me.' He had just reached the beginning of the corridor leading onto the West wing hallway when the clocks started chiming the quarters before eight o'clock. A cheetah off its face on cocaine and steroids wouldn't have moved quicker than Barry those last thirty yards. His feet were a mere blur over the carpet-less floor. He screeched to a halt in front of the door, composed himself and walked into the west wing as the last chime struck.

A veritable mountain of a man eclipsed the light at the entrance of the West wing. He stood six foot five barefoot. He was so wide that he couldn't walk straight through a normal doorway. His bulbous nose zigzagged across his face, having been broken more times than he cared to remember. His right eye was covered by a patch with a black elastic band, (a memento from the Falklands) over his shaved head keeping it in place. He limped ostensibly as he progressed towards Barry who watched him as he moved as inexorably as a glacier. He had lost his left leg in the first Gulf war where he had been awarded a bar to the MC he won in Goose Green. His C.O., whose life he had saved at the expense of his leg, was an old comrade of Sir Ian's. He had recommended him for a position at Buckingham Palace. Sir Ian, a military man to the core, instantly recognised the special qualities of RSM Patrick O'Malley MC (Bar): he could train anyone, even the worst slack jawed yokel, to perform any task by instilling the fear of God and "Psycho" in them! By the time he was finished with any of his charges they would follow him blindly to the ends of the world.

'And a top of the morning to you my lad! It warms the cockles of my heart to see you so keen and punctual, so it does.' His remaining blue eye twinkled mischievously with anticipation at the thought of yet another charge whom to mould to his exacting standards. He affected an Irish accent to appear friendly and slightly dopey but he was in fact an east Londoner born and bred. His family were originally from Wexford whence his great-great-grandfather had emigrated as a child when the potato famine blighted Ireland. His ancestors had helped build the embankment and most of the original London underground. His physique would have made him the ideal henchman for one of the many east London gangs; his mother had different ideas however and had packed him into the Royal marines as soon as had been old enough to enlist; that's were he had earned him the nickname.

'G-good morning Mr O'Malley. I have been put on car duty and I believe you are to instruct me on the correct procedures.' Barry made sure there wasn't a scintilla of cheekiness in his voice. The stories regarding punishment meted out to anyone moronic enough to think they could outwit Pat were terrifying even if only 10% of it were true.

'So I am, so I am.' He still sounded pleasantly genial. 'Let's get started.'

Outside, at the far end of the courtyard, a regulation governmental Jaguar XJ8 was in readiness, the engine running already. Pat stood at the top of the steps and signalled it to move. This it did at a sedate pace. When the car was twenty yards away Pat walked down the stairs, his limp now almost imperceptible. He reached the bottom exactly at the same time as the car stopped in front of him. With one fluid movement he opened the car door and stood to attention behind it. A footman stepped out nodded at Pat, waited till a second footman had joined them and walked up the stairs. As soon as they were halfway up Pat closed the car door without slamming it and walked up the stairs to stand at the left side of the open doorway. Barry couldn't help feeling impressed at the coordinated choreography and the apparent effortlessness of the whole procedure. He began to understand what Melanie had been on about.

'So lad, can you tell me what happened there?'

Barry was fortunate enough to have a near photographic memory. He had certainly been watching carefully and gave a detailed account of the preceding events.

'Good, good. At least you have been paying attention. I'll do it a couple of times more and then we'll see how you fare.'

And so the procedure was repeated twice. Barry still watched carefully, assessing landmarks to establish when to start going down the stairs. He worked out that two of "Psycho's" steps would equate to three of his and recalculated the timing accordingly. He felt reasonably sure he would not make a complete fool of himself.

'Right lad. Your go.'

The Jaguar approached, he timed it correctly and managed to be at the right position on time. He bent over to pull the door open in the same fluid movement… Christ! The damn thing weighed a ton!

He almost pulled his shoulder out. He staggered slightly as the door eventually opened. The footman inside sniggered.

"Psycho" spoke: 'didn't I tell you? How very remiss of me. The car is bullet proof so the doors can be just a tad heavier than usual.'

Barry kept quiet. He practiced opening the door a couple of times so as to find the correct leverage.

Training went on for several hours. Every conceivable possibility was explored. Faster, slower, closer of further apart from the steps, holding an umbrella, assisting the passenger with their walking sticks etc. etc. Fortunately Barry was a quick learner and he avoided any major scathing remarks from "Psycho" who, when all was said and done, was a fair person if he felt his trainees were giving their very best. They were now in a small waiting room opening into the hallway, waiting for the Prime Minister to arrive.

'You did well Barry.' His mock Irish accent was gone.

'Thanks Mr O'Malley.' Barry carried on devouring a sandwich while massaging his throbbing right shoulder. He had lost count of how many times he had opened that wretched door. At his side was a mug of strong, sweet, black tea fortified with a generous measure of Pat's Irish whiskey ('purely for medicinal purposes').

The phone rang. Pat leant over to pick it up. He listened in for a few seconds.

'Righty-ho lad, actions stations, the Prime Minister will be here in three minutes.'

Barry knew by now that three minutes meant exactly one hundred and eighty seconds. Almost simultaneously, the smiling head of Sir Hugh Argyle, the queen's private secretary popped into the room.

'Good morning Mr O'Malley!' he said with a smile. 'I trust you are well? Rheumatics not troubling you too much?' He nodded towards the two empty mugs.

Pat stood up. 'Doing fine Sir Hugh. Medicine does help.' He winked. 'I've just been showing this young lad some of the finer points of car door opening.'

Sir Hugh turned to assess Barry. 'So, Mr...'

'Smith, Sir Hugh, Barry Smith.'

'Barry Smith' he repeated, 'good. Enjoyed the rehearsal?'

'Yes Sir Hugh.'

'Excellent!' He sounded like he meant it. 'Let's get on with the matinee.' He reversed swiftly, and then allowed Barry and Pat to move ahead of him to the top of the steps.

On cue, the Prime Minister's car drove in. Barry opened the car without mishap like all the previous rehearsals except, instead of a footman, Edward Faulkner emerged.

Sir Hugh greeted him. 'Good afternoon Prime Minister, her majesty is expecting you.'

They walked down the corridor. Barry had remembered to close the door on time before the car left. He returned to the servant's quarters.

'Everything all right Mr Faulkner?' Sir Hugh was a stickler for protocol, not unlike Sir Norman. Eventually he might call Edward by his first name but not now, not yet.

'What? Oh yes, fine, fine.' Edward was distracted. He had received a call from the Chinese ambassador advising of Ma-Tsien-Zu's unofficial acceptance to a short state visit. An official response would arrive within two days. The wheels had already been set in motion; Sir Norman had contacted Sir Hugh earlier on to warn him of the recent developments. Sir Hugh had informed the queen. She wasn't too fond of unexpected changes in schedule unless there was a very good reason!

Edward and Sir Hugh reached Queen Elizabeth's office. Entry was not immediate; there was always a ceremony attached. Sir Hugh would walk in first, he would advise the queen of his arrival and then he would open the door to let him in.

'The Prime Minister your majesty.' He announced.

Edward walked towards the sofa and armchairs where the queen was waiting. Queen Elizabeth was standing up, waiting for him. When he was close enough he bowed and outstretched his hand.

'Good afternoon Ma'am.'

'Good afternoon Prime Minister.' Her handshake was firm and brief. 'Shall we take a seat?'

They both sat down with the queen sitting in an armchair facing the sofa where Edward had accommodated himself. He back was completely straight. Edward was also sitting bolt upright. The whole formality and ceremonial of the occasion irritated him. It was inefficient.

On the coffee table there was a tea set. Both cups were already full. His was white with one sugar and hers was black, no sugar and a slice of lemon. (Incidentally it was Earl Grey, not PG tips!)

The queen made the opening move. 'I saw you yesterday at PMQs. It would appear the tragic incident in the South China Sea is being resolved to everyone's satisfaction.'

'Indeed Ma'am. The Chinese government have fully accepted this was an unforeseen tragedy and have graciously accepted our offer to support the families of the deceased.'

'I am very glad to hear it. So often the dependants can be left in a very vulnerable position. If my government approves I would like to send a personal message of condolence.'

'I am sure it will be well received Ma'am.'

The queen took sip of her tea. She put the cup down noiselessly. Her hands rested on her lap again while she looked unblinkingly at Edward for a few seconds.

'I believe my government have extended an invitation to Premier Ma Tsien-Zu.' Her piercing blue eyes continued fixed on Edward. He felt uncomfortable under her scrutiny.

'This is correct Ma'am.'

'In some circles this might be perceived as overreacting, hasty almost.'

She was not being critical or obstructive. Queen Elizabeth had met many Prime Ministers in her fifty-five years of reign. Some she had admired deeply, like Sir Winston Churchill, the war-time stalwart and solicitous mentor in the early days of her reign. Others she had found harder to connect with. Edward was the eleventh Prime Minister to kiss her hands. He was the first to govern in a loose coalition but not the first to be embattled and harassed from the day he had started. She remained unsure as to how well would they interact but watching him yesterday at PMQs she had been pleasantly surprised by the fire in his belly as well as appreciative of his oratorical skills.

Edward studied her expression. She had leant forwards slightly, as if offering support, the eyes weren't hard and her head was slightly tilted. He interpreted correctly she wasn't being critical. She was offering, discreetly, her wealth of experience at gauging the reaction of the public and the press. Edward felt a surge of gratitude at her unspoken kindness. Instinctively he decided to show his hand.

'Most observant Ma'am. Your point would be very valid were it not for certain developments in the financial markets which make it imperative we establish contacts of the highest level urgently. Regardless of the fallout.'

The queen digested this information. She liked what she had just heard. This Prime Minister was ready to take a beating to protect his country and not his party's interests. He was behaving like a statesman rather than like a politician. She decided to reveal a bit more about herself.

'Would this have anything to do with recent developments in the aeronautical industry?' she asked almost innocently.

Edward was dumbstruck. He had some of the best brains in the country working for him full time and here was this old biddy, almost twice his age, whose main concern should be her pension and her family, showing a mastery of her file that would have made most ministers proud!

He took a deep breath. 'Indeed Ma'am that is the case. Unfortunately there is more to it.'

He had not planned on discussing Helen's dossier but now he felt it was the right thing to do. He knew a large portion of the queen's personal fortune was concentrated in a very discreet financial portfolio; he didn't insult her intelligence by "dumbing down" the explanation. He realised now that when she met with her financial advisors she made a lot more decisions about it than he would have thought five minutes ago.

For the first time since they had ever met the queen's expression became incredibly serious. 'This is a very important matter Prime Minister. Who else has seen this document?'

'Only a very few senior government ministers. I actually photocopied it myself. I am meeting with the FOS, the DTI secretary, the chancellor, the governor of the bank of England and Sir Norman.'

'I see.'

'I can update you with the conclusions later on if you would like me to?' He wouldn't have volunteered to do this last week but his respect for the queen's political acumen had just gone up several notches.

'I would be most grateful if you could inform me of your conclusions. As long as no-one objects.' She always avoided putting people in awkward positions. She had also made it clear she wasn't going to interfere or offer advice unless it was requested.

They went through the rest of the government's business swiftly, the queen making a few pertinent observations. They had finished well ahead of schedule. The queen looked at her watch and then out of the window. It was a clear afternoon, the sun was shining. She pressed a buzzer.

'Do you have a few minutes to spare Prime Minister?'

Edward checked his watch, more for show than anything else. The queen was revealing previously unknown facets and he was keen to learn more about her. 'Certainly Ma'am.'

'Perhaps we could go for a short walk in the grounds. This summer has been so wet; I have hardly seen any sunshine. It does one good to go out and feel the sun and the fresh air; it blows away the cobwebs I think.'

'I couldn't agree more Ma'am.'

They both stood up. The queen's corgis had been silent witnesses throughout the meeting. They stood up and started yapping around. Their internal clocks reminding them this was the time their mistress took them out for a walk. Edward was rather taken aback by this noisy eruption. He liked dogs, he had one himself, but he had heard some ugly rumours about how the queen's corgis could be vicious little brutes, with a proven predilection for other people's ankles!

'Hep!' It sounded like the crack of a whip. The queen had just reminded the pack who was in charge with one short, sharp syllable. The dogs stopped their racket and trooped obediently out of the door, which had just been opened by Sir Hugh.

'Thank you Sir Hugh. The Prime Minister and I are going to take some fresh air in the grounds. I wonder if you could be so kind as to join me in my office in half an hour.'

'As you wish Ma'am.' He bowed and left.

They walked silently down the corridor at a good pace. The corgis were scouting ahead, occasionally running back. Edward had never been invited for a walk before and was uncertain of the objective or the best course of action. He wisely chose to let the queen lead on this one. The reached the doors opening onto the gardens. The queen paused briefly. She closed her eyes and let the sun warm her face and took a deep breath. The garden was in full bloom and the recent rain followed by sunshine was the perfect time for all the scents to be at their peak. She opened her eyes and breathed out contentedly. She loved being outdoors. Ever since she was a girl, something her parents had nurtured. It didn't matter if it was a trek on horseback or tramping the moors with Prince Phillip or even alone with the dogs. She firmly believed it kept her sane.

'You have a dog I believe?' She had started walking.

'Yes Ma'am, a champagne Chow-Chow bitch by the name of Lhasa.'

'I've always found them an intriguing breed with those blue tongues, as if they had stuffed themselves with brambles!'

The chatted amicably about dog for a few minutes. The corgis kept running up and down the garden paths, returning to their mistress at regular intervals. They sniffed Edward and wagged their tails; they even allowed themselves to be petted. It was as if they could sense the queen's growing approval of Edward and they were reacting accordingly.

They were both returning slowly to the palace when the queen stopped and turned round to face Edward.

'Have you ever met Premier Ma?'

'I'm afraid I haven't Ma'am. In view of recent events I wish I had.'

They started walking again. 'I actually met him once. It was in Peking' -she couldn't be bothered to use the correct name- 'back in, oh 1986 during the state visit. He had just been appointed governor of the Peking district.'

Edward looked at her. He had heard about her amazing memory for names and faces likes and dislikes of people.

'He was a very pleasant man. He joked about his nickname: two

90

horses. He was also very keen on ornithology; he wanted to set up a bird sanctuary in the capital but was not sure if the air would be good enough. I wonder if he ever did?'

They had reached the doorway into the palace. A footman was waiting for them.

'Your car is ready Prime Minister.'

The queen turned round and stretched her hand out. 'Good afternoon Mr Faulkner. I hope the fresh air did you good. I would be glad to be updated on this evening's events if at all possible.'

Edward shook her hand and bowed, this time with a lot more respect. He had also clocked she had called him by his surname rather than by his title. He stood still and watched as she walked down the corridor. Her carriage erect, her steps firm. She was flanked by her dogs who only had eyes for her.

'This way Prime Minister' the footman smiled as he gestured towards the opposite corridor.

He got into the car in a daze and almost forgot to thank Barry, who gave yet another faultless performance, much to "Psycho's" satisfaction.

Chapter 7

Helen's afternoon hadn't been as pleasant or rewarding. She was struggling with the latest draft from the Health and Safety Executive regulations regarding mining. She was fully aware there was hardly any mining left in the country but felt this would be the death knell of what precious little was left. She knew there should be a reservoir of people with the skills and knowledge to know how to run a mine but the HSE was hell bent on making mining a thing of the past. There was a discreet knock at the door.

'Come in.'

It was Patsy, her private secretary. She had followed her faithfully from posting to posting. That was a non-negotiable issue for Helen whenever she changed posts. Patsy knew and understood her better than anyone. Helen personally supplemented her meagre civil service income with an additional allowance. It was money well spent as far as she was concerned. Patsy was carrying a copy of the Daily Herald. Helen frowned. This could only mean bad news. She normally read FT and Wall Street Journal cover to cover. She would rotate which broadsheet she took but avoided the tabloids. She particularly disliked the Daily Herald's rabid anti monarchic stance.

'Yes Patsy, what is the problem?'

She handed her the newspaper carefully, as if it could go off at any moment. 'I think you should read today's editorial.'

Helen laid the newspaper on her desk and started reading. It wasn't particularly controversial: the usual maudlin moan about the parlous state of what was left of British industry. The last paragraph started picking up pace; it concentrated on the threat posed by cheap imports from China. It was the last sentence which caused the explosion in Helen's mind: "What the Daily Herald readers would really like to know is how is this new Conservative government –in particular, the very business savvy but politically naive DTI Secretary Helen Stokes– going to cope with the new challenges, in particular the ever more competitive aeronautical industry." Helen read this several times. It didn't matter: the words were still the same, as was the meaning. The editorial was unsigned of course. She took her reading glasses off and looked enquiringly at Patsy. She was toying with a pencil.

'Who is the editor in chief at the Daily Herald?' She tried to sound as insouciant as possible.

Patsy winced as she gave the answer; Helen was NOT going to like this: 'It's Norman Sewell, Helen.'

There was a brief pause. The pencil in Helen's hands snapped in two with a loud crack.

'Very well. Thank you for bringing it to my attention Patsy.'

'May I remind you there is a meeting at number ten in one hour?'

'Please make sure the car is ready in half an hour.'

Patsy walked out. As she was closing the door she thought she heard her boss swearing softly. She shook her head. Helen needed a new dose of Norman Sewell like she needed a hole in the head!

Indeed Helen *was* swearing. 'Fucking bloody hell.' Of all the damned hacks in the sodding press it had to be bloody Norman Sewell who picked up the scent. He had obviously read the BAe and RR shares story and already made some enquiries. That editorial wasn't a senseless rant! He *knew* he was onto something and he had just challenged Helen to run the Gauntlet. He expected her to ring. She knew there was no option but to do it before things got a lot worse. As she was about to pick up the phone something caught her attention. She had a TV switched on but on mute and BBC news 24 was on. The continuous strip at the bottom of the screen read: suspected outbreak of foot and mouth in Surrey. She put the volume up. Huw Edwards was commenting on the last news on the outbreak which apparently was just confirmed. Behind Huw, a small screen showed a gaggle of reporters outside the farm. She had suddenly remembered a comment by a junior minister at DEFRA. She picked the phone and dialled a number which wasn't the Daily Herald. Her smile indicated she had just had thought of a much, *much* better idea.

Edward walked into his office just before five. Everybody was waiting for him seated in front of his desk. He sat down and thanked everybody for coming. He updated Harold the Chancellor and George Wilson the Governor of the Bank of England. Wilfred was taking notes. Everyone had a copy of both dossiers. Edward allowed John to start.

John cleared his throat. 'I must warn everyone that some of the conclusions are pure conjecture. Information gathering in China is notoriously difficult especially when it comes to the highest ranking officials. The little that we know seldom matches Wikipedia.' He smiled at his little joke. As far as we know, Ma Tsien-Zu is a dedicated lifelong communist. His father was with Mao at the time of the long march. They weren't particularly close but Ma senior was always loyal to Mao and the party until 1958. That is when the severe famines, a consequence of Mao's "Great Leap Forward" plan started decimating people. He was the governor of Manchuria, where the hunger wreaked most havoc. He and the Chinese president, Liu Shao-Chi were the frontrunners of the politburo rebellion which forced Mao to back down and countermand the plan which caused the worst non-war death toll in the 20th century. Mao never forgot the people who "betrayed" him and he exacted terrible revenge in the very early stages of the Cultural Revolution. Both Ma senior and Liu were killed in '66. Ma Junior also suffered through his family association. He was expelled from Beijing University, where he was studying engineering in the early 60s, and sent to work in a factory. In '67 he disappeared for nearly 2 years. He continued working in the factory but his luck changed from '74 onwards when Den Xiao-Ping started to offer discreet patronage. He finished his degree in engineering in '78 and Deng, who was a very close friend of his father's, rehabilitated him then. He was fast-tracked into the CC of the CPC and quickly progressed up the party ranks. He was appointed governor of the Beijing district in '85 where he is believed to have first suggested Beijing's candidacy to host the Olympic games around '88 or '89. He became deputy foreign minister, his first major cabinet post, in 1990.

He advanced steadily through the ranks until he became premier two years ago. So far the hard facts. Here is where it becomes interesting but slightly more speculative.'

'Ever since becoming governor of Beijing he has been sponsoring the brightest university graduates to go abroad. Usually they went to the US or here, but also to Canada and Australia. He ensured their credentials were impeccable and concentrated mostly on science and technology graduates. Interestingly enough, a few politics and economics students were allowed to go abroad too.'

'Since he joined the cabinet he has been slowly but steadily promoting these "bright sparks" into positions of responsibility in industry and research centres but also within the party. This trend accelerated when he became premier. His protégés are now doing exactly what he did and are promoting the best below them. Ma Jing-Tao, who is his nephew, is particularly active in this area without being brazen.'

'Within the cabinet, his strongest senior allies are the interior minister, the finance minister and the justice minister. All appointed by him. His most obdurate opponents are Marshal Wang, the armed forces minister and Chung-Hing-Lai the industry minister. Incidentally Ma Jing-Tao is his deputy. They represent the party hardliners, resistant to change in any way, shape or form. Marshall Wang is due to retire very soon, the three most likely successors are either pro Tsien-Zu or neutral. Marshall Yu, Wang's current deputy is cautiously pro reform but it remains to be seen whether the CC will allow his elevation. Maybe he will wait until the Olympics to implement further reforms then, when his popularity is at his highest.'

'What about the central committee?' asked Edward

'The overall impression is that he has the support of 40-50% of people who either owe their elevation to him or are by temperament, favourably disposed towards him.'

'What about the hardliners?'

'A dying breed, literally. Most of them are quite old. There are some young hotheads but they are being kept in check by having power denied to them. Ma is doing to the CPC now what Stalin did to the CPSU in the 20s and 30s. Very slowly. In a couple of years he will probably control over 60% of the CC.'

'What do your experts think are his long term plans?' asked Helen.

John took a deep breath. 'Here we go into the realms of conjecture and crystal ball gazing really. As far as I can understand, he still appears to want the party in full control. The recent deal with Google shows he doesn't want "dangerous" ideas permeating too easily into the system. The man was partly responsible for the Tian an Men slaughters for heaven's sake. And yet…'

'And yet, what!' exclaimed Edward, he felt John was beginning to behave like a story teller in Jackanory.

John refused to be rushed. He was enjoying himself and he felt people were enthralled by the story he was relating. 'Those politics and economics students. They all are the fastest rising stars. They were all top of their class at university and all, without exception, saw a parent, sometimes both, die as a consequence of Mao and the CPC's repressive methods. They all know what a force for evil the party can be. None of their parents was particularly high ranking by the way. Most of them have stuck their neck out and expressed cautious wishes of society reform and modernisation. The most glaring example is Ma's nephew.'

'Is that Ma Jing-Tao?' asked George. He was enjoying the story!

'The very one. He is the trailblazer, the brightest new kid on the block by a country mile. He graduated in Politics in Beijing but he also got an engineering degree from MIT. He very often acts as an interpreter for his uncle. This raises his profile internationally without raising people's hackles too much. He is the only protégé to have cabinet rank. We believe Ma-Tsien Zu uses him as a foil for Chung. He is already allowing loose workers associations in small industries and has introduced suggestion boxes in the large mining and steel complexes. His mother married Ma Tsien-Zu who is the only father figure he has ever known.' He raised his hand to stop the inevitable question. 'Before you ask, no, he will not be the next Chinese premier. He will be kicked sideways so he develops his own powerbase in as many ministries as possible. Another reason is he is too young and it could raise questions as to Tsien-Zu planning to start his own dynasty. That would be the epitome of hubris; that is something Ma hates. He insists on being known as Premier Ma rather than Chairman Ma as the latter sounds too much like Mao's official title.

'What happened to Jing-Tao's father?' asked Wilfred.

He was Ma Tsien-Zu's elder brother. He was arrested before the cultural revolution and sent to a re-education camp in inner Mongolia. He died there after two years of starvation and repeated beatings. His wife was pregnant when he was arrested so he never knew his son. Rumour has it he was never told if the child born was a boy or a girl.' This drew a few horrified looks. John continued. Ma and his brother were extremely close, so much so that Ma married his sister-in-law after a decorous period. She died fifteen years later, the cause is unclear but ovarian cancer was suspected.'

'I'm sure all this is very interesting John' said Edward rather testily, 'but I would like to know what are his long term plans, what do we expect from him.'

John Looked around the room. 'I'm sorry if this has been a rather long preamble, but I felt it was needed so you could all understand my final conclusion.'

'I think that Ma-Tsien-Zu is slowly laying strong foundations of a structure that will eventually release the grip of the CPC from power and turn China into a democracy. I suspect he also wants his nephew to be the first democratically elected president of China in 20 years or so; this would add lustre to his own memory. That's what his final objective is and he will pulverise anyone or anything that gets in his way and that includes us!'

There was a stunned silence in the room. Wilfred had paused to look up. Harold broke the impasse.

'Are you sure John? Don't get me wrong, China as a democracy seems like an impossible dream.'

'As I explained before Harold, there is a lot of speculation and conjecture going on. You must remember how Yuri Andropov, Ex-head of KGB and the epitome of a CPSU apparatchik, promoted Mikhail Gorbachov to the Politburo. While Yeltsin's rightly credited with the final push towards democracy, with Gorbachov's glasnost and perestroika as the foundations that allowed this to happen, it was Andropov who made the crucial appointments.'

'Very well John' said Edward, 'we will go with your hunch and try to foster friendship and support as long as it doesn't screw us. As you all know, the Chinese have already accepted our invitation for a short State visit between June the 28th and July the 2nd. The official confirmation will be tomorrow when he informs his cabinet. The queen has been informed and we should be able to give the full works between those dates albeit with everyone working double time and twice as smart.'

'What shall we tell the press?' Helen had an ulterior motive to ask this.

'In the finest British tradition: we do not lie but we do not tell the whole truth. As luck would have it, July 1st is the actual 10th anniversary of the handover of Hong Kong. We will use that. We will also mention the pre-existing invitation and how it all fitted nicely into the schedule. We will gloss over the South China Sea incident but if asked we will admit, reluctantly, that it was good diplomacy to try and pour oil over troubled waters. Let's move on. Helen, have they got us by the short and curlies then?' He was trying to soften the impact of the incoming report with some schoolboy humour.

Helen peered over her glasses. She didn't feel that jokes were appropriate. 'Gentlemen, the situation is extremely serious. At the risk of sounding overwrought and dramatic I would say it is critical. I took the liberty of presenting my figures and findings with George Wilson,' she nodded at the portly figure of the governor of the Bank of England, 'and Harold who, as Chancellor of the Exchequer should be aware of the seriousness of the situation. They both checked my findings and reached similar, if not worse, conclusions. I will try to explain the situation succinctly in three main areas: shares, raw materials and bank loans.'

Helen helped herself to a glass of water. This was going to take some time.

'In terms of shares, the PRC have, or are about to have between 7.5 and 15% of: Rolls Royce, BAe, SNECMA, MBB, Fokker and CASA. All of them are major aerospace industries with indirect control of Airbus. They also bought 25% of Embraer, a brazilian company which produces excellent short haul planes. They have also purchased sizeable share packages of Krupp and Corus who produce specialized steel for the above companies. They have also got 3-5% of Natwest, Abbey, BNP, Deustche Bank and Argentaria. All these are banks who happen to be important shareholders in the aerospace industry. They also attempted to penetrate major aerospace and banks in the US with very poor results. They do have 1% of Boeing and McDonnel Douglas but the Americans have been extremely cagey. New York Stock Exchange tightened their rules after 9/11 and also many Americans enjoy having shares in these companies usually handed down for generations. They have been buying steadily for the last five years and as their packages have become bigger they have become a lot more aggressive. 60% of their acquisitions happened in the last 18 months.'

'How did they manage to avoid scrutiny by the Bank of England?' Harold asked.

George intervened. 'Allow me Helen. By being very clever. You are right in that any major purchase of shares above 5-10% requires approval by ourselves. The Chinese have been buying below the threshold of approval most of the time. Six months ago we changed the minimum threshold which requires Bank of England approval. This applied especially to the aeronautical industries and Banks. We reduced it to 4% and we didn't advertise it too much. We had been noticing some funny goings on for some time and we decided to change the rules. It worked. Only once, which was all we needed. We do not only count money at Threadneedle street.' He chuckled.

'Thank you George.' Helen continued. 'In terms of raw materials, the PRC have, over the last three years, struck major deals with oil and strategic mineral producing African countries. Unlike the Europeans or the Americans, they ask no questions: no demands on human rights, no requests for democracy or curbing of corruption. Hard cash, on delivery, every time.'

'Surely we could cut funding to African countries if they did this?'

'No John, we can't. The world press would crucify us.' Helen continued. 'The most worrisome aspect are the loans. Since the collapse of the sub-prime mortgages in the US, money has become a very expensive commodity. Most national banks, including ours have raised interest rates. The average interest is about 5%, the Chinese have been offering loans at 4%. They are short term rolling loans with a three-month recall. This means that anyone who has been lent money has to return the entire amount by the end of September 2007 if the Chinese demand it back today. It is a non-negotiable clause. They have been lending heavily and they have concentrated on the aforementioned banks who are desperate for funds. If they decide to pull the plug, they could make the '29 Wall Street crash look like a walk in the park. In reply to your previous question Edward, no, they do not have us by the short and curlies. If only. They have strapped half a ton of Semtex on us, tied us to a post at low tide and have a Heckler and Koch laser guided gun pointing to our head!'

The only noise in the room was the frantic scribbling of Wilfred. Most people in the room had a higher than average grounding in economics. They understood very well the implications of Helen's presentation.

Harold broke the silence. 'How much do you reckon they have spent in the last five years, including their planned share purchases.?'

Helen checked her notes. 'About £150 billion give or take 5 billion.'

'Where the blazes did all that money come from?'

'All the bloody happy meal toys, lead paint tainted Barbie dolls, every single bit of cheap tat you can get on the markets. They haven't been spending it on improving the quality of life of their people that's for sure. They literally have more money than God.'

'How much have they invested in loans?'

'That's the scary bit: about £100 billion. Between the share dividends and interest they are making about half a billion minimum *every* year. Not only are they trying to take over, they are making us foot the bill!'

Edward looked at the Governor of the Bank of England. 'George, is there anything you want to add?'

'Yes Edward, I'm afraid there is some really bad news round the corner. There is a major mortgage lender who is teetering on the edge of bankruptcy. Mercifully it isn't one of the banks Helen mentioned. In view of the new developments we will definitely need to rescue them. The bill could come to £10 to £20 billion, maybe more.'

Edward barely managed to control his shaking hands. Unless they managed to cut a deal, his would be the shortest premiership in one hundred and fifty years. It was a record he did not wish to achieve. He asked wearily. 'Is there any more bad news?'

Helen hesitated but finally raised her hand. She felt sorry for Edward. He didn't deserve being hammered on all sides.

Edward gave a wry smile. 'Dear Helen: you definitely aren't my blue bird of happiness today. You're more like a storm crow!'

This raised some smiles. At least he hadn't exploded in a rage. He was taking all the news with remarkable equanimity.
'I'm afraid Norman Sewell is in the know.' She passed photocopies of the Daily Herald editorial. The relevant fragment had been highlighted.

Everybody knew Norman. He was well respected, even liked. Today he was feared. A slip of the keyboard, his keyboard, and they would all be toast.

'Have you spoken with him yet?'

'No Edward, I haven't. I was going to but the news of the outbreak of foot and mouth made me stop.'

'Why?'

'The news has just broken out. He will be concentrating hard on it. I have just dropped temporarily off his radar screen. In his editorial he threw me a challenge. He wants to speak with me, face to face. His favourite way. He loves a good sparring partner and if a deal is offered he will stick to it. He is that most rare creature in journalism: a man of his word.'

Harold asked Helen: 'how can you be so sure?'

'I have known Norman for nearly twenty years. We aren't friends but as close as. I think there is a certain amount of mutual respect. He will enjoy analysing the intellectual challenges posed by the current situation. He will also understand this is not the time for a scoop! I will need your help though.'

'In what way?'

Helen explained. This drew a storm of protest.

'This is a suicidal plan! We should try to steer clear from him. Only speak when spoken to and then we are economical with the actualite!'

Helen shook her head. 'No Edward, It's the only option. Keeping quiet or avoiding him is suicide. Lying or bullshitting him is even worse. If he found out we had been doing either he would be ruthless and implacable; the worst enemy ever.'

'Do you realise what will happen if you miscalculate, the consequences of failure?'

Helen got out a sheet of typed paper. It was headed by her details on the House of Commons. She stood up, walked round the table and handed it to Edward. 'This is my letter of resignation; signed but undated. If I screw up all you have to do is add the date. That's how serious I am.'

Edward read the letter carefully. He handed it over to Sir Norman who, too, studied it carefully. He nodded. He folded the letter carefully and put it in an envelope.

Edward sighed. 'Very well Helen. We'll play it your way. Desperate times require desperate measures. If everything goes according to plan, which I sincerely hope, I want you and John to get cracking with the package of measures for the Chinese. Once again I cannot emphasise enough the importance for discretion. Avoid the press like the plague. We will issue an official communiqué in two days time. On a lighter note. Do we have any twitchers in the cabinet?'

Everyone looked puzzled. Edward explained what the queen had explained to him about Ma's hobbies.

Sir Norman raised a hand. 'I understand Dr Christopher Ward, the Northern Ireland secretary is quite a keen ornithologist.'

'Excellent. Let's make sure he is on the guest list. Oh! and Bill Oddie too. Just make sure we get him out of those mucky clothes!'

The meeting broke up. In the room there were only Edward and Sir Norman.

'I have to give it to Helen; she has certainly shown "cojones" in the current circumstances.'

'Indeed Prime Minister.'

'The queen mentioned something else about premier Ma. She said he joked about his nickname: "two horses". Is he fond of Citroen's?'

Sir Norman did all he could to not smile. 'No, Prime Minister. In

Mandarin, Ma means horse. The premier was born in 1942: the year of the horse. In Chinese astrology it is considered an extremely auspicious combination when your surname coincides with the birth animal. Especially if it's the horse.'

'How do you know this?'

'Sir Hugh kindly rang me. The queen noticed you slightly puzzled expression when she said "two horses". She knew the reason for the nickname but didn't want to patronize you. I was already aware about the astrological implication. A little knowledge I picked up while stationed in Beijing.'

'I see. I have to say my meeting with her today was a true eye opener. I had never realised how sharp and up to date she is. It must be quite frustrating for her to see the whole picture and not being able to intervene.'

'Indeed. Her main concern is for her country and her subjects.' Sir Norman hesitated. What he was about to say could be considered a dangerous insubordination. He weighed the situation and took the plunge. 'I understand the queen mentioned something about a bird sanctuary.'

'Yes, that fits with his interest in birds.'

'Actually, I think, although I am not 100% sure, that the queen was hinting that premier Ma is more concerned with environmental matters than he can actually show. China is one of the world's worst polluters. There is a big environmental meeting in Bali at the end of the year, the follow up of Kyoto. The Chinese are going to be asked a lot of questions they don't appear to have answers for at the moment.'

Edward looked at his cabinet secretary. His body stiffened momentarily as the bile rose. Had he understood correctly? Was Sir Norman trying to dictate policy? He realised they were alone. He certainly hadn't mentioned it at the meeting so maybe he was just trying to send him a lifeline. Edward had noticed the original hesitation when he had started to mention the issue. He knew he could be accused of overstepping the mark but had done it to try and help him. He took the advice in the spirit it was offered.

'Very well. Please make sure John and Helen are aware of this information.'

'I will make sure they receive you message Prime Minister.' Sir Norman had understood Edward's thoughts.

Later on Edward spoke with the queen and updated her on events. He didn't mention Helen's high risk strategy plan to deal with the press. The Windsors had never been overtly fond of the fourth estate.

'Thank you Mr Faulkner. Sir Hugh has identified two possible dates for the state banquet. Friday the 29th or Saturday the 30th. Perhaps Saturday would be more appropriate as it would be exactly ten years since the Hong Kong handover. The return banquet can only be on the 2nd as I have some unavoidable long standing commitments on Monday evening.'

Edward thought about this. Yes Saturday would be perfect. 'Very well Ma'am, we shall pencil Saturday in then. I will inform Sir Norman. Perhaps he and Sir Hugh can liaise between us and the Chinese embassy.'

'Yes, that would be acceptable. Good evening Mr Faulkner.'

'Good evening Ma'am.' The line went dead. The queen didn't waste time on the phone.

It was eleven o'clock in the evening. Norman was at his desk looking at all the recent information regarding the new foot and mouth outbreak. It would be interesting to see how the new government reacted to their first crisis. So far they had created a five mile exclusion zone. His mind wasn't entirely focused on the breaking news; China loomed too. Several pieces had fallen into place. E-mail from Jean-Pierre confirmed the purchase of two flats in Toulouse. Boris had told him that no-one in Russia really knew anything about Yevgeni Rudkin and commented this was strange. Peter sent an unhelpful e-mail full of ifs and buts with nothing definitive except for news of a new player who was buying heavily, above the odds, to get hold of as many shares as quickly as possible in the open market. Norman correctly surmised Peter's firm were on the game. He wondered who this new buyer was. It jarred with the rest of the procedure. His mobile phone rang; it was Jock, China went into the back burner.

'What was that crap editorial you published today about?'

'And a good evening to you Jock(!)'

'I'm not paying you £200.000 a year to spout platitudes on the paper!' Jock was away at some foreign press freebie in Greece. By Norman's reckoning it would be one in the morning and he had clearly been partaking of the local tinctures! Norman fervently wished him the hangover from hell the following morning. He was becoming increasingly frustrated with his boorish boss. Jock spent more time trying to be in the news, raising his profile, than actually working to save the Daily Herald. Being rung at this time of the night while trying to think of a catchy front page headline and being accused by his drunken boss of lack of competence was the straw that broke the camel's back. With careful tact and politeness he explained there hadn't been much in the news. He also explained the recent outbreak and reassured him that tomorrows editorial would be better. He decided against sharing his suspicions with Jock. Chances were he would only blab drunkenly and torpedo the whole story!

His mobile rang again. This time it was the PMs Press officer. He began a long winded and whining tirade against the paper's attitude in the early stages of government. Norman could see the large clock handles ticking inexorably towards midnight, the witching hour. The paper had to be completed by then or its distribution schedule would be jeopardised. He could see his secretary through the glass window mouthing environment ministry as she waved the phone. He fobbed the press secretary off and walked into the main newsroom.

'What is it Jane?' His voice revealed how exasperated he had become.

'It's some press secretary at the environment ministry wanting to discuss press arrangements for the Bali conference in November. Also there is another call on wait but I don't know who it is.'

Norman hid his face in his hands and took a deep breath. Had everyone gone mad? He had a paper to put to bed for heaven's sake! He took a deep breath and uncovered his face. 'Tell them, as politely as possible, to piss off! I have the final editorial meeting and I want no interruptions whatsoever.'

'No one?' She sounded dubitative.

'Absolutely no one!' He stormed off into the conference room where all the other editors were waiting.

Jane switched the caller on. 'I'm terribly sorry but Mr Sewell has just gone into a very important meeting and cannot be disturbed.' May I take a number so he can ring you back?'

'There's no need' replied John Stokes, not the environment ministry's press officer. 'I'll ring again tomorrow at a more convenient time.'

'Very well sir.' She flicked another button on the switchboard. 'Hello? Norman Sewell's office.'

'Good evening. This is Helen Steele. The DTI secretary. I would like to speak with Mr Sewell.' She tried to sound as if she didn't know him.

'I'm terribly sorry Miss Steele but Mr Sewell is at a very important meeting and has left clear instructions he should not be disturbed.'

'Are you sure?' Helen tried to sound pompous and disappointed. 'It will only take two minutes.'

Jane toyed with the idea of giving in. She had only worked for Norman for six months. She perceived him as a nice enough man. Tonight's outburst showed he could get very angry. She wasn't in the mood to have her head chewed off! Also Helen's tone irritated her. These politicians! They just thought they could click their fingers and everyone would come scurrying to do their bidding! Her tone became firmer. 'I'm terribly sorry Miss Steele but he was quite definite about no interruptions.'

Helen switched her tone to deflated. 'Very well, I'm sure he has a busy schedule at the moment. Could you please let him know I rang tonight as soon as possible? I would be grateful if he could ring me on my mobile between 10 and 1030 tomorrow.'

'I will make sure he receives the message tonight. May I have your phone number please?'

Helen gave it to her. She made sure Jane checked it twice. Once she went off the phone she switched her mobile phone off. She had just planted the ball firmly in Norman's court.

Helen remembered the first time she and Norman had met. She was the youngest executive VP in her bank. She was cocksure and a bit arrogant. She had granted a young Norman an interview. (In fact Norman was 30, slightly older but his untidy hair and boyish looks made him look like a young and gullible reporter, this trapped people into saying more than they would normally have!). He came to enquire about rumours of her bank's hostile takeover bid. She had tried to fob him off and fed him a different story that would hopefully send him barking up the wrong tree. Fortunately she had not told any lies. She felt it was morally wrong and they always caught up with you. After he left she had felt stupidly smug about her own cleverness. The following morning, a devastating article on the FT tore strips out of her. Norman was aware of all the facts already. Her attempts at giving him a cock and bull story and feeble half truths were exposed. The takeover still took place but at a higher cost and she spent a very uncomfortable half hour in the chairman's office explaining herself.

They met again a few days later at a press conference in one of London's swanky hotels. She approached him and shook his hand.

'Well done Mr Sewell. I deserved that.'

Norman didn't know what to say. He shook the proffered hand gingerly. 'I'm sorry I don't think I understand.'

'I haven't had much experience with the press. I underestimated you; I thought I could fob you off. You have taught me a lesson I won't forget in a hurry.'

Norman was quite taken aback. He had never expected this reaction. He was bracing himself for a slap in the face, not for a grudging thanks! 'I hope I didn't land you in too much bother.'

Helen had shrugged. 'A bit, but I'll survive.'

Since that second meeting, Helen and Norman had crossed swords many more times. They had developed a grudging mutual respect that had grown steadily over the years. Sometimes Helen won; sometimes Norman got the upper hand. They never stabbed each other in the back, Sometimes Helen gave more information than was required or offered him new leads, in exchange, Norman had withheld a couple of important reports. The tally was heavily balanced on Helen's side which was just as well as she was about to ask him the mother of all favours.

It was well past midnight. Norman was in his office reading the latest edition of the Daily Herald. He could have looked it up on the internet but there was something inherently satisfactory about holding a freshly printed newspaper, even if his fingers got stained! He loved the smell of fresh ink in the morning! His office door was open. Jane tapped discreetly at the door. He looked up and smiled. 'What can I do for you Jane?' His previous belligerence was gone.

'There are a couple of messages for you.'

'Oh yes, I forgot. Sorry about earlier on. I always become a bit twitchy at this time of the evening!'

'Don't mention it. The environment ministry's Press secretary rang. He said he'd ring tomorrow.'

'Fine. And the other message?'

'Helen Steele rang.'

'Personally?'

'Yes, I recognised her voice. She was most insistent she needed to speak to you. She eventually gave up and gave me her mobile number. She asked if you could ring her today between 10 and 1030 in the morning.' She put a post-it on the table.

Norman could barely contain his anger. He picked the note up. 'Thank you Jane. Please close the door after you.'

As soon as the door closed Norman banged his fist on the table. He stood up and started pacing up and down his Spartan office. Bugger! He thought. The one person he had really wanted to speak to last night. All he had had was Jock and the two sodding press secretaries from number 10 and the environment… He stopped in his tracks. It suddenly hit him and he laughed out loud. Clever, clever Helen! He had thrown a Yorker and she had flicked it to the boundary. He had to give it to her: the girl still had class and a sense of humour. He didn't bother to try ringing. It was too late and there was no doubt Helen would have switched her mobile off but the missed call would be logged. No, he would ring tomorrow at 1015. Not too early, not too late. Niceties *had* to be observed!

Chapter 8

In Beijing, at the Industry minister's birthday dinner, things were going swimmingly. Especially in Chung Hing-La's head. He had been drinking rice wine all night. He had a prodigious capacity for drinking but he was now reaching the edge of incoherence. The remaining guests were more restrained. Some, Ma's allies understood the reason for the impromptu party, others were unsure. Most were intrigued at Ma's solicitousness with the guest of honour. Always choosing the choicest morsels, ensuring his cup was always full. The oldest in the room felt there were echoes of Mao and Lin-Biao's last meal together. Ma's attentiveness was due to his ensuring Chung drunk enough that he did not challenge him too hard, but not so drunk that he became incapacitated, or worse, aggressive. Ma had collected him at his office and driven together to the banqueting hall. He had presented him with an exquisite T'ang horse. He explained the western tradition. Chung's eyes lit up when he saw the gift: it was worth a king's ransom! It showed respect towards him. Thus mollified he allowed Ma to pamper him, feed his ego and wet his whistle!

Ma looked around. All in all, the evening was going well. The hardest part was about to begin. He stood up with some difficulty. His back was extremely painful but he had drunk some wine himself and feared the combination of alcohol and morphine would muddle his brains. Of one thing he was sure: he needed his wits about him tonight. The general hubbub of conversation gradually died down.

'My dear comrades, as you all know we are here to celebrate our esteemed colleague Chung's 68th birthday. You are all aware, too, than I am due to leave tomorrow for a Sino-American summit with President GW Bush. I am also scheduled to meet President Putin briefly shortly after that. In between I had a few days to prepare and attend the Politburo meeting. Following the sad deaths of fishermen in our territorial waters, the British government has re-issued a previous invitation for a state visit. I feel that I should accept.'

This last statement was received with a lot of murmuring. Ma had expected this.

The interior minister rose. 'Is this wise comrade? They not only killed three fishermen; they also insulted us. Are we to do their bidding? One click of their fingers and off we scurry?'

Some heads nodded at this point. This could be interpreted as loss of face to the now toothless British lion. It was unacceptable.

'*One* person insulted us. Just one. That part of the incident was never published. He was severely punished, by their soft pathetic standards. It is *they* who are grovelling.'

'What do we need from these people anyway?' asked Chung.

'Technology, comrade, high technology'

'Pah, technology. We have technology. Do we not possess the atomic bomb? Do we not produce jet airplanes and computers?'

'This is very true. However, our standards are nowhere near to theirs. Our technology is antiquated, we are learning to develop it but we need to start from a higher level. They aren't keen to share it but now we can grab it!' He closed both hands simulating the gesture.

The mood in the room was uncertain. It was time to remind them of past humiliations, of previous shortcomings. It was time to go for the kill! 'For too long have we lagged behind the western world. We turned our backs to it and fell behind. We became weaker and they humiliated us time and time again. If we tried to fight back they brushed us aside; like a minor irritation. In the last fifty years, as comrade Chung has pointed out, we have advanced enormously. Yes we have the atomic bomb, yes we have the world largest army but it is not enough. The west fear us, yes but they also despise us. What are we good for? Manufacturing toys and cheap trinkets they give away as an enticement to buy their horrible food.' (Ma had tasted a hamburger; it was the worst experience of his life!) 'They use us, they say they want to be our partners but they still sneer behind our backs. We have become accustomed to the breadcrumbs that fall from their table. We daren't ask to sit with them. Us! The country that has given the most things to the world. We used to be a great country. Now we are just a big lumbering country. I want China to become great again! We will sit at their table! At the head of it!'

This unexpected piece of oratory had certainly roused their spirits. Quite a few ministers and their deputies were banging their fists on the table to signal their approval. Some still looked dubious.

Chung rose. He was feeling slightly sick, he felt unsteady but he knew he had to create obstacles. His words were slightly slurred, this reduced their impact; just as Ma had anticipated. 'Premier Ma, this is a worthwhile plan. But what about the costs? These foreign devils will expect us to pay.'

'My good friend Chung. How very observant of you. It will cost money but not that much. I will ask my esteemed colleague the finance minister to explain the finer points of what we have been doing.'

Sun Tze-Yang rose. He had collaborated with Ma for many years. He explained what had been going on. The shares and, especially, the loans. These were a recent neat touch. He did not give the exact figure involved.

Chung sprang to his feet. He managed to avoid falling over, only just. '$25 billion!' He shouted. 'We could have bought entire factories and built the planes here for a fraction of the cost!'

Jing-Tao was about to rise to explain some facts to this oaf. Ma caught his eye and shook his head imperceptibly. He didn't want to expose him to Chung's fury at this stage.

He replied himself. 'My dear Chung, what would that achieve? Nothing more than a short term gains. The west would boycott all our products. We would have nowhere to sell our products. The west would pass legislation that would prevent us from trying that tactic again. We would also debase ourselves as nothing more than cheap tricksters. Incapable of original thought. The plan I present shows them we can beat them at their own capitalist game; it forces them to make us partners, real partners. No more cheap rhetoric from them. We also get them to foot part of the bill.' He added with a smile.

Ma could sense the approving mood. He decided to request an endorsement to this policy.

'So, comrades, do I have your approval to negotiate the forcing of the western powers to share their technological secrets with us, while getting them to foot the bill?'

Chung was up again. His drunkenness has almost evaporated. 'Comrade Ma,' he almost spat out the name of his hated rival. 'Do you realise you are proposing far reaching economic and ideological changes at the end of a party? Is that how we do things now? We ignore the rest of the Politburo, the CC?'

Ma had been expecting this. He realised he was no longer drunk, even tipsy. 'This is very true. In normal circumstances I would have followed the normal procedure. Unfortunately there was no time to convene a formal meeting. The most senior members of the party are here and we must seize the opportunities when they arise. I completely agree with you that once the treaty is presented, it will need, indeed it must, be approved by the politburo, in a formal meeting. However the next scheduled meeting is on July the 2nd so it will be difficult to approve a visit while it is already happening and to approve a treaty while it is being discussed. I am requesting from you comrades, the core, the elite of the politburo, to offer informal assent to this visit. I would like to have a show of hands.' Almost everyone agreed. Only Chung kept his hand down. Just as well he is scheduled to come with me thought Ma. That is one loose cannon I need to keep a very close eye on.

The party broke up soon after that. The two Mas and Hsieng Fang-La hung on. They were all standing quietly.

Fang-la broke the silence. 'You could have a lot of problems with Chung. He still commands a lot of following in the CC and the politburo. He could cause trouble at the meeting.'

'That's why I'm taking him with me. It certainly isn't for his good looks or charming personality!'

'He could still insist on coming after the US visit; claim this was too important a meeting to miss.'

'I will keep Chung firmly by my side whether he likes it or not!' Ma said sharply. He continued in a softer tone. 'I will need your help and that of our supporters to ensure the visit and any agreements derived aren't rejected before we have a deal. If we have to stall them, we will.'

Jing-Tao coughed discreetly. 'What about Marshall Wang?'

The other two men turned round to look at him.

'He wasn't here today; he was supervising the army manoeuvres but these are scheduled to finish in ten days, just before the politburo meeting. Chung is sure to speak with him. Together they will be a formidable threat to your plans.'

Ma Tsien-Zu swore softly. Wang! Jing-Tao was right. He and that son of a turtle Chung would make life very difficult. Of that there was no doubt. 'Marshall Wu was here today. If I remember correctly he voted in favour. Fang-La: I need you to speak with Wu tonight. Wang will not make my life difficult. You and Wu may need to activate some dormant resources too' he added cryptically. Fang-La nodded silently. 'Wu needs to ensure there are no unauthorised troop movements within a 300 kilometre radius from Beijing. Fortunately he is liked by his men; unlike Wang. We also need to tap all of Chung's phone lines. I want it done tonight.'

'What if they become dangerous?' asked Fang-La.

'Then you will have to ensure they lack the resources for it. I will not have a bloodbath or warlords on the rampage. China has had its fair share of both. We cannot afford to have any mishaps.'

'What would you like me to do?' asked Jing-Tao.

'Nothing more than you have already been instructed.'

'But I can do more!'

Both men smiled. Ma spoke: 'Jing-Tao, I know you want to do more. I am glad you are so enthusiastic. Some things will happen in the next few days that could haunt you in the future if you were involved. As a matter of fact you are already in danger. Chung and Wang might try to hurt me through you. And they would succeed. Fang-La: I suddenly realised. We will need protection for my nephew. I want all round police escort. No lesser rank than an inspector.'

Fang-La nodded. 'I will also speak with Wu, we will also need military police protection. Again high ranking. Captain at least.'

'Good idea.'

'This looks a bit extreme. I am not some poor clerk or peasant who can be pushed around.'

Ma put his arm around his nephew's shoulder. 'My dear boy. You have not experienced the things my good friend Fang-La and I have.

We have both known Wang and Chung for a very long time. We know they are extremely dangerous. Not just for you: also for us. They learned some very questionable tactics before you were born. They have used them successfully and they will try them again.'

Hsien Fang-La merely nodded. They all left the room and started to get their various plans rolling.

Helen's phone rang midmorning. She checked her watch. 1015. Norman had seen through the plan but accepted defeat graciously. She was relieved to note he hadn't lost his sense of humour.

'Hello, Helen Steele speaking.' She tried to sound very business like.

'Helen, it's Norman Sewell here.'

'Norman!' she gushed. 'How kind of you to return my call. It was such a shame you were busy last night. It's my fault of course. I should have remembered what a busy time late evening is for you!'

'Helen.'

'Yes Norman?' she replied sweetly.

'Cut the crap please.'

'Very well, I shall. I read your editorial yesterday. I may be mistaken but I feel you were challenging me to contact you.'

'This is correct.'

'We need to talk.'

'Very well. Where and when?'

'Today, at three. Not at the DTI though. I would rather it was my place. Flat 3, 6 Cadogan place. No promises though.'

'We shall have to see.'

'Indeed. See you at three.' She hung up.

Norman felt elated. Once again his instincts had proven him right. He had rattled Helen's cage. This could end up being a hell of a story!

Helen wasn't feeling as positive. So far so good though. She had read the Daily Herald and all the other dailies from top to bottom. No one seemed to have followed on Norman. Everyone's attention was focused on the foot and mouth crisis. She had been lucky but she knew better than to rely on that fickle tart! She confirmed a few details about foot and mouth with nervous DEFRA officials. Sir Norman had done the background work very well indeed!

Norman was visiting his elderly mother at her nursing home. It was one of the best, with fees to match. Norman didn't care. He adored his mother. That's why he had joined the Daily Herald. His salary allowed him to pay the fees. Irene Sewell had worked hard all her life. She had made untold sacrifices for her adored only son. She became a widow very young. Her husband died in a car crash when Norman was a baby. Now, crippled with rheumatoid arthritis and diabetes she could no longer cope alone. Norman's hours were too erratic for him to provide adequate care. She had reluctantly agreed to go into a home. She was still bright as a button and would do the Times and Daily Herald crosswords and sudoku in record time.

'How are you today mother?'

'Not too bad. These new morphine patches help with the pain but I think they are slowing me down. I couldn't complete the super fiendish sudoku today. It's either that or I'm definitely losing my marbles!'

Norman laughed. 'That'll never happen mother.' His mobile rang.

'Where the hell are you?' The voice and tone were unmistakeable

'I'm visiting my mother as I do every Friday and Sunday. It *was* included in my contract if you remember.' Norman had made this a non-negotiable clause. After working with Jock for one month he was even gladder he had insisted on it.

'Paper was better today. Try and see if you can throw some mud in the government's handling of this foot and mouth crisis.'

'I'll see what I can do.' Norman was incensed. Jock's constant interference with the editorial content of the paper was beginning to rankle seriously. 'Good-bye Jock.' The other phone had already clicked off.

'Was that Jock?'

'Yup.'

'Arrogant little tosser. Made my knuckles itch when he was a lad.'

Norman was surprised. 'You know Jock?'

'Oh yes. Had I never told you?'

Norman shook his head.

'Hmph. I'm sure I had. I'm definitely losing it. Now let me see. It was shortly after your father died. I worked at Balmoral for some time.

Your aunt Ruth took care of you for a while. It broke my heart to have to leave you but it was in the middle of the Suez crisis and times were hard.'

'How did you get that position?'

'I had worked as a maid in Buckingham palace before I married your father. I reapplied but they couldn't fit me in. There was a temporary vacancy at Balmoral Castle so I accepted. Pay wasn't great but I was able to save most of it. The duties weren't onerous either so I managed to complete a typing correspondence course while I was there.'

Norman was amazed. He had never realised this facet of his mother's. 'How did you meet Jock?'

'Jock was an orphan. His parents had died during the war. His aunt cared for him. She worked as a maid as well as being a crofter in the estate. She had a bad drinking problem. She also had a very short fuse, especially if she'd been at the tinctures. While I was there she got quite drunk one day. She was walking down a corridor and young prince Charles was running in the opposite direction. They bumped into each other. Charles apologised and tried to help her get up. He's a kind lad by the way, always was. She smacked him across the face. She was sacked instantly and kicked out of her croft. The queen was said to be furious but she never showed it in public.'

'Wow! What happened to Jock?'

'From what I gather, he got taken into care. He was an unpleasant child. Very bright I'll give you that but he had a chip on his shoulder. He always had his nose in the air. He felt he was destined for greater things. He was rude too. I clipped him once behind the ear for cheeking me!'

Norman knew what a swift backhand his mother had. She had seldom used it though. Jock must have provoked her badly.

'Anyway' she continued 'maybe it was the best thing that could have happened to Jock. He was in an orphanage but the queen's factor received specific instructions to look out for him, make sure he was well taken care of. I know they ended up pulling some strings so he could go to a grammar school. I don't think he knows that either.'

'How did you find out all this?'

'I bumped into one of the Balmoral senior maids in London years ago. She let me know what had happened after I left. They're not a bad lot you know. The royal family I mean. If you're hard-working and loyal they look after you. I still get a Christmas card every year.'

'So you stayed for six months.'

'Nine in fact. I had my contract extended when she was sacked. They even offered me a permanent position but I missed London and my boy.' She stroked Norman's face. 'They waited until I got a position as a secretary. I think they might have pulled some strings there. In many ways we did well thanks to them.'

Norman could hardly believe his ears. It certainly explained Jock's pathological hatred for the royal family. 'Surely someone should tell Jock.'

Irene turned round and glared at her son. 'You will bloody well keep your mouth shut!' she hissed. 'They probably know who he is and what he is doing. *They* chose not to tell. It is *their* privilege. One good turn may deserve another but it doesn't demand it! Promise me you will never tell anyone about Jock.' She grabbed his hand.

'I promise mother.'

Irene relaxed her grip. They chatted pleasantly for a few more minutes until Norman realised he had to leave or he would be late for his meeting with Helen. He kissed his mother farewell, left the nursing home and got into a taxi.

He arrived at his destination just before three. Number 6 Cadogan place was an old townhouse which had been converted into luxury flats. He pressed at number three button. The door buzzed. He let himself in. There was a plain clothes policeman at the bottom of the staircase. He smiled and pointed upstairs. Norman walked up. Helen was waiting at the door and she let him in.

Helen's flat was a masterpiece of understated elegance and good taste. The sitting room had two two-seater dark brown leather sofas facing each other. In between there was a glass-topped coffee table with a notepad on it. On the mantelpiece there was a superb Laszlo watercolour of a handsome woman wearing an evening gown. She had a more than passing resemblance with the current flat owner.

Helen noticed he was looking at it. 'My grandmother' she said. 'She insisted I inherit it when she died.' And if this goes tits up I might have to sell it she thought. She offered Norman a seat in one of the sofas. 'Do you still drink diet coke?'

'Yes please.'

She poured one into a cut glass tumbler. She had a glass of water already. She sat opposite Norman.

'How's life working for Jock Robertson?'

'Helen, I'm not hear to have a social chit chat. I'm here to talk about the Chinese plans to take over the western aeronautical industries.'

Helen raised her hand. 'Norman, this is not the time, nor the place to speak in headline terms. It's not your style. It's definitely not mine. Now please tell me what you know.'

Norman told her all the facts as he knew them. Helen frowned when she heard the name Rudkin.

'What do you know about this Rudkin fellow Norman?'

'Not a lot. He has been throwing his weight about, pretending he is a big businessman but he doesn't possess that many assets. I believe the Chinese are using him as a front. London's full of Russians flush with money; another one wouldn't raise many suspicions.'

Helen nodded while she jotted the name down. 'I'm inclined to agree. Please continue.'

He explained about the purchase of flats in Toulouse and the intended purchase in Derby. He also mentioned the recent mystery buyer who was paying above the odds.

'What do you think of Ma Tsien-Zu Norman?'

'I think he is an odd one. He definitely wants to catch up with the west from the high-tech industry point of view. I am unsure about his politics. He has promoted quite a few bright young things. Maybe he wants to open society slowly, very slowly.'

Helen looked at him admiringly. He was still the best nose in the business, still as straight as an arrow.

'Have you purchased any shares in RR or BAe?' she asked innocently.

'No. I do not have enough money to fritter it away on a hunch. What about you?'

Helen shook her head. 'No. It's not allowed. As a matter of fact I had to offload most of my investments quickly as soon as they appointed me secretary of state for the DTI. Cost me a lot of money.' In fact it had cost her a fortune especially in capital gains tax. The sale had come at the wrong time especially as she was still paying for the flat and was supporting her parents so she wasn't joking about the Laszlo. She went in for the kill. If she got it wrong she would be yet another flash in the pan of politics. She looked at Norman intently. 'Do you know that Jock Robertson has been purchasing shares of RR and BAe?'

Norman nearly spilled his drink. 'Whaaaat?'

Bingo thought Helen. Venality and greed are such useful tools sometimes. She plunged the knife even deeper. 'He has been buying heavily in the open market. That's your mysterious buyer. Jock is in deep slurry too. He has spent £10 million buying shares and he has been borrowing heavily against the Daily Herald's pension fund. Echoes of Rob Maxwell eh?'

Norman was horrified. He remembered the Daily Mirror's fiasco. Fortunately he hadn't worked there but some friends and mentors were now living in precarious circumstances because of it. He wiped his mouth with his handkerchief. 'How do you know this?'

'My dear friend. I *am* the head of the DTI. This kind of stuff gets brought to my attention. More so now. If he gets it wrong, a lot of people could suffer.'

'How can he get it wrong? From your invitation, I take it I am right. Once the story is in the open the shares will go through the roof. We will all benefit in the long term. Don't get me wrong. He is sailing close to the wind but he didn't have insider dealing. I told him what was going on but anyone could have worked it out.'

Helen decided to break the news gently. 'Norman, Jock is using the pension fund as *personal* collateral. He will skim the profits but he will not increase the fund.'

'Are you sure?'

'I have never lied to you and I'm not going to start now. As a matter of fact the investment is extremely risky and there might be doubts about the legality of his financing the deal. Moreover we are facing what is possibly our worst economic, not financial, crisis ever.'

'Come on now Helen. Who's talking in headlines now?'

Helen opened her briefcase, which lied at her feet and handed over her secret dossier. 'If you choose to read this, you are implicitly signing the official secrets act.'

Norman opened the file. He studied it carefully for several minutes. He was horrified. He handed it back to Helen.

'You have checked all this.' It was not a question.

She nodded sombrely. 'Thrice. Harold Butler and George Wilson have gone over the facts too. They are even more pessimistic than I am. I will be extremely blunt. We think the Chinese have purchased these shares because they want to cooperate with the west, especially the EU. They will negotiate from a position of strength of course but if this gets out into the open they won't pull their punches. If you release the information you have, you could push the Chinese into a corner. They might lash out and cause unprecedented harm. They can effect a series of hostile takeovers in no time. It would cause the worst ever financial, political and economic crisis ever. The government would have to resign. Accused of something we had nothing to do with.'

'Trying to save your job?' he joked.

Helen handed him an unsigned copy of her resignation letter. 'The PM has a signed, undated copy.'

Norman read the letter. He looked at Helen. She was sitting up straight. Her face was expressionless. She wasn't begging for mercy or calling in favours. She had presented him with the facts and put the decision in his hands. What impressed Norman most was her willingness to put her head above the parapet.

'OK Helen. You win. What do you want me to do?'

'Are you sure about this Norman? This could be your biggest story ever.'

'Helen' he sighed, 'I have spent a very unhappy six months working for the most venal incompetent prick in Christendom. He is trying to profit from information I gave him. In doing so he has chosen to put the pensions of loyal workers at risk. I have always respected your honesty and integrity. Today you have reaffirmed it beyond doubt.'

'Despite our first interview?' she smiled.

'Despite that. Even then you didn't lie. How did you manage to convince the PM?'

'I explained our long standing working relationship. I also told him you would not react kindly to bullshitting or lies. I also offered myself as a sacrificial lamb.'

Norman smiled. 'You are incredible. A first. A politician I can respect.' His face suddenly hardened. 'I do want something in exchange.'

She had anticipated this. 'Jock will get a very unpleasant visit from IR and the Serious Fraud Office. He will swing. As a matter of fact nothing would give me more pleasure. I will make sure the Daily Herald survives too.'

'Then the slate is clean.'

They both shook on it.

'Good. I'm about to do you a favour.'

'You have the cheek of the devil Miss Steele!'

'No, I have just started a new tally!'

'What is it?'

'Ma-Tsien-Zu is coming on a state visit very soon. On the 28th to be precise.'

'After George Bush?'

'Yes. We are using the 10th anniversary of the handover of Hong Kong as the official motive.'

'Is that when you will try to cut a deal?'

'That's what I do best; even if I am developing some skills at muzzling the press!'

They both laughed.

Helen dived again into her briefcase. 'I nearly forgot. This is a gift, not to be added on the tally.' She gave him some printed e-mails. 'There is a research laboratory next to the farm. They share drains. This lab actually deals with foot and moth specimens. There have been complaints about the state of the drains and the risk of cross contamination.'

Norman read the papers greedily. This was a veritable scoop; not as good as the Chinese share dealing though. He looked up. If I hadn't agreed to keep shtum would you have given me this?'

Helen examined her fingernails. 'Eventually. About twenty-four hours after the rest of the newspapers! We would have buried your scoop with a news item closer to the peoples hearts.'

'God, you politicians are a devious bunch sometimes.'

'We try our best.'

Norman stood up and gallantly kissed Helen's hand. 'Always a pleasure doing business with you Miss Steele.'

Helen remained sitting and said nothing. She smiled as she watched him walk out. She looked at the fireplace. Her vision became blurred as she felt tears coursing down her cheeks. She cried for a couple of minutes allowing the tension to ebb away. She then wiped her eyes and blew her nose. She stood up and gave herself a little pep admonition. 'No time to laze around Helen; there's work to be done.' She looked up at her grandmother's serene gaze in the portrait. Her fingertips brushed the gilded frame. 'Still with me gan-gan, still with me.'

Edward was on the phone to John. He was in a buoyant mood. 'She did it John! I don't exactly know how, but she pulled it off. She refuses to give me the full details but that's her privilege. You two had better get cracking. Tomorrow if possible. Speak to you soon.'

Sir Norman walked in the office. He was smiling too. So far it had been a good day. 'Prime Minister, I have just spoken with Sir Hugh, the Chinese embassy and the rest of the cabinet. The queen's original suggestion of June the 30th is the best possible one. Dinner will have to start a bit later than usual though. Around half nine in the evening.

Very good. We will try and create an available, "unexpected" slot for tomorrow afternoon Let's say BBC 24 h. It's a good thing it will all break out during the weekend. With that and the foot and mouth outbreak it will give us some breathing space.

Helen was back at work in her office. Her mobile rang, it was John.

'Hello Helen, I understand congratulations are in order.'

'I'd rather wait until tomorrow.'

'He shook on it.'

'He did and I trust him but I will feel happier when I don't see it in the newspaper.'

'I suppose you're right. When shall we two meet again?'

'Hold on Shakespeare, let me check my diary.'

Her schedule was pretty full already. So was John's. Eventually they agreed that tomorrow was the only time they could both have a few uninterrupted hours.

'Where do you want to meet?'

Helen thought about it. She disliked her office at the DTI. It was OK for routine work but there was something in the place that irked her and seemed to block her mind. 'At the risk of sounding forward. Do you mind if we meet in my apartment? Less opportunities for distractions and less people nosing around.'

'That makes sense. I'm OK if you're OK. What time do you want to meet?'

'Shall we say 10 in the morning?'

'Sounds good. Where do you live?'

She gave him her address. He jotted it down. 'See you tomorrow Helen.'

'See you tomorrow.'

At the same time as Helen was pulling her amazing coup, there was an emergency meeting of the Lord Chancellor's committee. It normally comprised the seven most senior members of the queen's household but the Director of the Royal Collection was away. Fortunately his presence wasn't essential.

Lord Carruthers was the current Lord Chamberlain. He coordinated the six other departments and chaired the weekly meetings. To his right was Sir Hugh Argyle. It was he who had requested the meeting after liaising with Sir Norman. He was the closest non-royal confidant. He normally advised the queen on political and constitutional matters and was the closest man to meet the standards of the legendary Sir Alan Lascelles. To Sir Hugh's right sat Sir Ian Connaught, Master of the Household Department. He was in charge of of staff and domestic arrangements at the palace as well as dealing with protection issues in the Royal Households. Michael Fagan wouldn't have had a cat's chance in hell if Sir Ian had been in charge!

To Lord Carruther's left sat Sir Henry Gosting, Keeper of the Privy Purse. This was a far more complex role than the title suggested as he dealt with all the financial matters of the queen's estate. To Sir Henry's left sat Brigadier General Sir Alan Reynolds Crown Equerry in charge of carriage processions as well as chauffer driven cars.

Finally, sitting opposite the Lord Chancellor was Sir Fergus Macleod, the Comptroller in charge of the Lord Chancellor's office as well as all ceremonial matters appertaining to State visits and State ceremonies.

These men were the ultimate great and good of the queen's household. They knew their roles backwards and were equipped to deal with the most inconceivable situations. A short notice state visit was mere grist to their mill. They had been there, done it perfectly with panache and savoir-faire and they had got the gong to hang from their T-shirts. (Not that any of them would ever contemplate wearing such a common piece of clothing!)

Lord Carruthers opened the proceedings. 'I am very grateful for everyone's prompt reply to this emergency meeting. If nobody minds I will go through the schedule and check for any problems as we allocate duties. Please feel free to interrupt if you foresee any problems. I spoke today with Her Majesty. She has informed me that there are vital state interests at stake and we should ensure, more than ever, that no stone is left unturned to guarantee the success of this visit.'

'I understand premier Ma travels with a very limited entourage; no more than twenty or thirty people. This should ease transport problems. They are scheduled to arrive in London Heathrow around 1600 hours on Thursday the 28th. The State banquet will happen on Saturday the 30th. Sir Fergus, if you could kindly liaise with the Chinese embassy, find out any likes or dislikes or allergies our guest may have and please advise likewise about her majesty. Could you remind me which regiment which regiment is scheduled for the guard of honour?'

Sir Fergus checked his notes. 'The Welsh Guards my Lord.

'Very good. Make sure their C.O. is aware today. We will have the usual 21 gun salute. There may also be a military parade but we will need to check with the Chinese if they feel it will be to premier Ma's liking. Sir Alan.'

'Yes my Lord.'

'We will need extremely accurate weather reports. Her majesty would prefer it if we could use open carriages but we cannot have everybody drenched. It is Wimbledon fortnight after all!'

This elicited a few smiles.

'I can get the most accurate report four hours in advance. Will that suffice?'

Lord Carruthers thought about it. He nodded in agreement. 'Yes that should suffice. We will have car backup as usual should the need arise.'

'Yes my Lord.'

'Sir Ian?'

'Yes my Lord.'

'Are there any staffing issues?'

'We have identified a problem due to the annual leave schedule. Quite a large number of staff have gone or are about to go on leave. We have already started ringing and asking if they could postpone. If Sir Fergus agrees I feel we should offer an additional two days leave to those who acquiesce. We do have a full complement of staff butt hey are the most junior and inexperienced. If worse come to worse Mr O'Malley and I have devised a training regime which should leave them well prepared to cope with any eventuality.'

'Is that Patrick O'Malley MC?' asked Sir Alan.

'Yes general.'

'Good god man! Are you sure about this? The man is positively corybantic!'

Sir Ian became quite defensive. 'I have known Mr O'Malley for a few years. I admit his looks and some of his idiosyncrasies go slightly against him but he is a superb trainer of men and women. We have inexperienced staff, we have a very important state banquet. We can avoid problems.'

Sir Hugh intervened. 'I am inclined to agree with Sir Ian. Mr O'Malley is an excellent trainer and motivator, even if the motivation is to learn quickly to avoid the punishment!'

'That settles it' said Lord Carruthers.

The rest of the meeting proceeded smoothly. Every small detail was analysed, all possible case scenarios were studied and suitable contingency plans outlined. Nothing was left to chance. Nothing would go wrong; their reputations depended on it.

Chapter 9

On Saturday morning Edward had been reading the papers. He was pleased to note that the Daily Herald carried no news about any Chinese takeover. Sir Norman walked in and handed him an unsealed envelope. Edward looked at the document contained therein and processed it. He added a short note in his own hand and put it in the envelope with the original document. He sealed the envelope and handed it to Sir Norman.

'This letter needs to be delivered personally Sir Norman.'

'I know where it has to go' he replied.

John arrived at Helen's flat on time. He dismissed his police escort. He knew there would be someone on duty in Helen's quarters. He pressed the button for flat number three. The door buzzed and he let himself in. Helen's protection officer was at the bottom of the stairs. He stood up as John walked in.

'Miss Steele is waiting for you Mr Stokes.' He gestured at the staircase.

He went up and knocked at the door. It swung inwards.

'Door's open!' shouted Helen.

He let himself into her apartment. Helen was sitting at the dining table in the large space which doubled as sitting room and dining room. She was tapping into her laptop and didn't look up as he walked in. She was wearing blue jeans, a vest, covered by a light blue blouse and some Salvatore Ferragamo red loafers which matched her belt. Her long hair was tied in a bun held in place by two pencils. She looked effortlessly chic except for the reading glasses that were perched at the end of her nose. John couldn't help but stare.

Helen was still typing; she pointed vaguely into the flat. 'There's coffee and croissants in the kitchen. If you want tea there are some teabags.' She noticed the silence and looked up. 'Are you OK?'

'Sorry Helen, I am so used to seeing you in your work clothes that I didn't recognise you. For one second I thought I had walked into a complete stranger's home!'

Helen shrugged good-naturedly. 'Yes, I know. I do give this image of a suit but as soon as I get home I go as scruffy and as unreconstructed as possible. It drives my mother nuts. Go and get yourself a drink and some grub.'

He walked into the kitchen and poured himself a cup of black coffee from the filter machine. He resisted the temptation to snoop in her cupboards. She was showing him trust and he didn't want to abuse this. He walked back and used a copy of the Daily Herald as a mat.

'I see Norman came good.' He had read it too.

'Yes. I expected him to do so. I'll give him that. Once he strikes a deal he never pulls back unless the other party has lied, in which case all bets are off.'

'Were you worried he wouldn't agree to withhold?'

'Extremely. The thing that swung it for us was the fact that his boss was buying shares for himself; using the pension fund as a guarantee. That and the fact that breaking out the story could cause a financial meltdown. He is an intelligent man. He understands the consequences of his actions.'

'Does it bother you that you're beholden to him? Especially if Jock threatens him with the sack?'

'No, he owed me a few favours and we wiped the slate clean. Also I gave him the information about the vaccine lab. As for Jock Robertson, he won't in a position to threaten anybody by the time I'm finished with him.' Her green eyes flashed with anger as she said this.

'OK, let's gets started. Any ideas?'

'I have a few. I think we should group the work streams in three major areas: what leverage can we get with the help of our European partners, what do we think the Chinese want and what are we prepared to give and finally additional technologies we could offer to lower their demands and sweeten the deal. What do you think?'

'I was thinking along the same lines. Shall we concentrate first on what the Chinese want?'

'I think it's the best starting point. From what we have gleaned, we know that the Chinese are after the latest technology in air travel. Airbus have finished developing the super jumbo. I don't think they would go after that one. I think they're more interested in the mid-range aircraft and that's where the major bargaining will occur. Also they are looking into specialised steel so they're not dependent on the west or even the US to produce it. They are going to want to produce the whole airplane themselves and that, we cannot give.'

'Why not?'

'Airbus has spent billions researching and developing their planes. Most of the fleet is less than ten years old, that's negligible time. They will not be prepared to give away that level of investment.'

'What do we do to convince them?'

'Explain to them how we build the planes. Each country produces a certain number of parts. They fly them all to Toulouse where the planes are assembled. I think we could offer the Chinese some parts and they produce them in limited numbers. We send them other parts and exchange them. If we could convince them to take the most labour intensive but least profitable parts it would be great.'

'Which parts are you thinking of, the wings?'

'No, never the wings. That's the crucial aspect of a plane. I was thinking more along the lines of fuselage. It gives them bulk but little substance.'

'Will they buy it?'

'Let's hope so.'

'I think we should concentrate now on the political aspect of things. The Chinese may have made a crucial tactical mistake here.'

'You mean by trying to take on the whole of the EU John?'

'Precisely. If they had concentrated on a single country they would have exerted more leverage.'

Helen doubted this. 'I think this may have been their strategy all the way. Negotiate with the whole of the EU.'

'But they aren't. They are only negotiating with us. We picked up the scent first. We are the ones who are most at risk currently'

'It may be so but I think we altered their timetable.'

'And now we alter the number of players involved.'

'What do you mean?'

'Helen, are you aware there is a Franco German summit in Strasbourg on Tuesday?'

'Of course! they meet once a year don't they?'

'Once every six months as a matter of fact.' John couldn't help feeling a bit smug that he knew more about this that Helen.

'If we could get Wolfgang and Mario there it would make things much easier.'

'Who are they?'

'Chairman and deputy chairman of the European Central Bank. They are the real power brokers in Europe. They determine ultimate economic policy in the EU.'

'I take it you know them.'

Helen waved and old fashioned address book.' This is worth its weight in diamonds. As a matter of fact I spoke with them earlier on the week, as well as the chairmen of all the affected banks. They are a very unhappy lot I can tell you. They realise they are vulnerable like never before and are, for once very keen to cooperate.'

'I will have to clear it with Edward but I could sneak you into the summit so you could speak with Merckel and Sarkozy as well as the ECB top brass. '

'To what end John?' She knew what he was after but wanted him to say it. She was realising what a political animal John was; very adept at seeing the whole picture.

'As I see it, the main problem are these short term loans, the PRC have the banks over a barrel. They will have no option but to be at their beck and call. They would definitely control, direct or indirectly, a majority or as close to a majority of shares in the major industries. If the ECB can offer to underwrite these debts, with less generous terms of course, they would be less inclined to bend over. They would also owe us a huge favour.'

'That's the main objective. If you can arrange a meeting, secret of course, I will fly on Monday to Strasbourg and speak to the Angela and Nicolas as well as the ECB. I need clearance by tonight though. Do you think Edward will buy it?'

There was a knock at the door. Helen opened it. Her plain clothes protection officer was standing next to a dispatch rider.

'I am sorry to interrupt Miss Steele but he said it was urgent, from the top.'

'That's all right Brian.' She looked at the dispatch driver 'do you have something for me?'

'Yes Miss Steele, personal delivery.' He handed a bulging plain white envelope.

Helen thanked him and went back indoors. She looked questioningly at John who just shrugged. She opened the envelope. A load of confetti fell from it. A folded note also fell.

'What the...?' Helen recognised part of her signature in a fragment of paper. The note simply read "Thanks, but no thanks: Edward." It had today's date. She showed the note to John who smiled.

'There's your answer. Your resignation letter has been returned. You can do no wrong at the moment in Edward's eyes so take advantage!'

'Believe me, I will. I do note he didn't send it until today though.' She walked to a cupboard and opened it. Inside was a another computer but already connected to the internet. She quickly fired off an e-mail to Edward's office requesting permission to go to Strasbourg late on Monday explaining the reasons for the request. She got a reply within two minutes: "OK" is all it said. Helen deleted it and walked back to the dining table.

'Right, Edward has agreed.'

John pointed at Helen's laptop on the table. Why don't you send it from here?'

'This laptop has a special encryption device with three variable passwords, it is disabled for the internet. I only use it for strictly confidential stuff. That computer is permanently linked to the net' she jerked a thumb at the computer in the cupboard, 'but there aren't any confidential files in it. I don't trust the Internet. Too many big organisations spend an unhealthy amount of their IT budgets in finding about hacking.'

'Surely to fight it?'

Helen gave him a withering look. 'No John. To do e-espionage. A lot of the most powerful financial firms do not keep their important files on Internet linked computers. They know how easy they are to penetrate. If you have any important files in such a computer, chances are other people already know about them.'

'I will bear it in mind.'

'Please do. Right, the Spanish are our next objective. They are also major shareholders in airbus.'

'I actually know their economy minister, Pedro Solbes.'

'Good, I know the Botin family. They run Banco de Santander, the biggest bank in Spain and they own Abbey so it affects them. They also have valuable worldwide contacts. I will try to arrange a meeting on Tuesday. Can you make it then?'

'I'm sure I can.'

'We'll have to clear it with the cabinet on Monday.'

'That won't be a problem. What do we need from them?'

'The same as from ECB, the Germans and the French: money, a shed load of it. If you meet the Spanish on Tuesday, chances are Wolfgang will have already spoken with Emilio Botin so you should have no problems.'

'What do you know about this Solbes chap? I have only met him at an EU summit. A bit strange but pleasant enough.'

'He's sound, there is a weird economic think thank in the Spanish government that makes a lot of policy decisions, he doesn't see eye to eye with them but the Spanish president will have to listen to him this time. Why do they have a president if they have a king by the way?'

'Something to do with Franco. He was head of the government but in the mid to late 60s he appointed a president of the government in case something happened to him. He didn't use the term prime minister in case people accused him of behaving even more like a king. The term remained.'

'Oh well, that explains it.'

'I have to admit I hate how we have to crawl to these people!'

'I'm not sure I follow you.'

'They have all the trump cards and a spare deck to boot. All we can do is beg them not to destroy us by causing a huge financial meltdown, which they can, almost on a whim, if the mood takes them!'

'John, you are too emotional about this. The have set themselves an objective. We have some bargaining chips, they have their bargaining chips. If it was just us and them we'd be stuffed. They chose to engage with the whole of the EU, on purpose or not. This changes the playing field. We are on a level pegging. All they're after is a take over, perhaps the biggest ever, but a takeover nevertheless. It can be challenged, it *will* be challenged.'

'You are relishing this.'

Helen thought about this. 'Yes, I suppose I am. It is quite a simple situation.'

'Simple? We are talking jobs, livelihoods political repercussions. If we balls this up we would be out of office in no time!'

'John, calm down, if we only concentrate on the worst case scenarios, we will lose. I prefer to have a very detached look at it. It is nothing more than a commercial exercise. They have assets, we have assets. We analyse these. We then study, sometimes speculate, what they want and what they need. Sometimes they aren't the same thing. We create internal markets for them. They are 1.3 billion people for heavens sake! All we have to do is convince them to direct their energy into their internal markets. Exactly the same as the USA, only a small percentage of their GDP goes outside. They like it like that. Why can't we convince the Chinese to think likewise? If we achieve it the threat of major competition disappears. Our exports will probably suffer in the long term but we adapt. It happened in the 80s when major industry and mining went down the tube. We adapted and we emerged stronger. I'm sure it will happen again.'

'I had never looked at it in this way.'

'In my view, it is the only way to look at it.'

John reappraised his impression of Helen. Not only was she very attractive (more than Helen realised) she also was a complete pragmatist with an amazing intellect. 'You weren't that optimistic two days ago. In fact you were so despairing. Now all you can think of is what an incredible opportunity this is.'

'Very true. I was exhausted having just been working flat out for two days and I had Norman to contend with. It is amazing what a good night's sleep and the disappearance of one major problem will do to your outlook.'

'I know what you mean. Shall we get on with the third part of the negotiation?

'The additional bargaining chips?'

'Precisely. What do you think we can entice them with?'

'This is the tough part. We don't know how interested they are going to be in different technologies.'

'Let's start with the ecology issue.'

The next few hours were spent pooling knowledge on alternative energy, better use of industry and increasing recycling. The internet was used extensively with the printer working full time. Around mid-late afternoon a clap of thunder distracted them. The day had been mostly overcast but it had suddenly become very dark. It started raining heavily. Helen looked at her watch.

'Good heavens, look at the time. We have been at work for six hours. Are you hungry?'

John was used to erratic eating patterns but with only a bowl of cereal since breakfast he realised he needed some sustenance. He nodded.

Helen walked into the kitchen. Her fridge was a virtually empty shell. Her freezer revealed a couple of pizzas. She walked back to where John was. 'I'm terribly sorry but I only have a couple of pizzas left. They are thin crust too. '

'I prefer thin crust.'

'Good! I could never abide the thick stodgy stuff. It bloats me, so I end up looking like a Michelin man!'

'I find that hard to believe' John said gallantly.

'Thank you!' She felt quite pleased at the subtle compliment. I'll go down and check on Brian.'

'Sorry?'

'The protection officer. They spend hours on end looking after us and fitting into our timetables. The least I can do is make sure he is not going hungry.' I'll be back in a tick.' She rushed out of the door.

John paced around the room. He walked towards the mantelpiece and admired the painting. He stretched himself, groaning as he did. Helen walked in as he was doing this. She admired his figure. He was a trim man with brown hair which was beginning to grey at the temples. There were unexpected sides to John. He was an undoubted political animal but he didn't appear to be cynical with it. John sensed he was being watched and turned round.

'Hi, I was admiring the portrait. Laszlo isn't it?'

She nodded; she was quite impressed, few people could identify him. 'It was my grandmother, I adored her and so did she. When she died she specifically bequeathed it to me. She knew how I loved seeing her in the painting.'

'I can see where you get your good looks!' He coughed in embarrassment. Maybe he had been too forward. 'He sometimes reminds me of Joaquin Sorolla, a Spanish painter, in the use of light.'

She looked at him slightly puzzled. Was he flirting with her? It didn't displease her. The only problem was that there was a time and a place for this sort of things and today wasn't one of them. 'I'll get the pizzas started. Are you OK with some white wine?'

'Yes please. '

She went back into the kitchen and returned presently with an open bottle of Chablis and two glasses. 'Would you mind if I switched on the news?'

'Not at all, please do.'

She flicked on the television, BBC news 24 was on. Edward was being interviewed by Fiona Bruce. They were already halfway through.

'Prime minister, can you please explain the reason for this unexpected visit from the Chinese premier?'

'Certainly. I agree it looks somewhat unexpected but not as much as you think. The previous government had already extended an invitation back in February, when they decided to anticipate the elections it was deemed prudent by all parts to have an expectant attitude. As you doubtless know, Premier Ma is on his way to Washington for a summit with President Bush. He is also due to visit President Putin a few days later. It was felt by all parties involved that the timing was good.'

'I'm sure some of our viewers wonder if this surprise visit has anything to do with the tragic events a few days ago when three fishermen died.'

Edward was suddenly a bit sharper. 'As I have already stated, this isn't a surprise visit. I agree it was a tragic incident, the consequence of an unfortunate chain of events. The British government have offered their condolences as well as support for the families of the victims. The PRC's government have accepted our proposals and the matter has been closed.'

'What will you be discussing with Premier Ma?'

'Mostly trade agreements with the EU and Britain. We will also assess how Hong Kong has fared after 10 years as a special administrative region within China.'

'What about contamination? The PRC is considered to be one of the world's greatest pollutants.'

'I am sure that we will touch on environmental issues. The Kyoto protocol is due to be reviewed in Bali in November. We will probably analyse the impact this could have on China's industrial development.'

'Will you discuss human rights? There are still serious concerns, according to amnesty international, on China's track record on this matter.'

'It could possibly be discussed but we feel that China is slowly adapting to the world expectations and is addressing these matters. We feel interference could be counterproductive.'

The producer warned Fiona that she should start wrapping up. She chose to ignore this and throw Edward a curved ball. 'Finally PM, how come, news of the impending visit first came to be known through a leak rather than an official announcement?'

Edward had been expecting this. 'We received unofficial confirmation of acceptance recently. The PRC wanted to wait until today to give an official announcement. Preparations were already under way to give Premier Ma a reception fitting to his status. In these circumstances it is possible that minor leaks will occur, especially if a lot of people become involved.'

'Thank you Prime Minister.' Fiona looked slightly deflated at the slick response to her question.

'Thank you Fiona.' Edward tried not to look to smug after handling well a tricky question.

Helen turned to John. 'I think he handled that reasonably well don't you?'

John nodded. 'It was interesting how they gave the worst question at the end. He knew it was bound to come up. He had the answer well rehearsed.'

They watched the rest of the news including a disgruntled looking Francine; she could see this visit was stealing her thunder. There was a ping coming from the kitchen, the pizzas were ready.

They both ate with good appetite. They also drank a glass of excellent Chablis. By common unspoken agreement they avoided talking about work so they chose to talk about art which they both enjoyed.

'How do you know so much about art?' Helen asked.

'I took history of modern art as one of my A levels. I chose it initially as an easy subject but my tutor was extremely knowledgeable and enthusiastic. I became hooked on it. Larissa also loved going to exhibitions and we would drag the children to the National Gallery every six months whether they liked it or not. As a "revenge" now they drag me to Tate modern!'

Helen paused before she spoke. 'I was sorry to hear about Larissa's death. I met her once at a party conference three years ago. She had just had a course of chemotherapy but she bore the whole thing with remarkable fortitude. I thought she was very brave and very sweet.'

John looked surprised.

'I'm sorry' she blurted. I was away at an international conference when she died and I never passed on my condolences. Sorry.'

He smiled sadly. 'Thank you Helen. Yes she was wonderful. She coped very well throughout; we had an excellent support from our GP. The children were old enough by then and they were a great comfort during her illness and after she passed away. Edward too was a tower of strength.'

'I'm glad to hear that.'

John looked at the table with the empty plates. 'Come on' he said briskly, 'let's clear this mess up and finalise the plan!'

They both went to the kitchen; John helped tidy up. They sat at the table again.

Helen started. 'Let's wrap this up. From the Chinese demands we know they will want major components from mid-range airbus planes. They may also want to produce jet engines. We hang on to those for the time being.'

John continued seamlessly. 'With regards to external support, you are going to Strasbourg Monday evening and sneak into the Franco-German summit and explain things to the money men; trying to get as much financial back up from our European partners as possible. I will go to Madrid and do likewise with the Spanish. All this subject to Edward's approval of course.'

Helen nodded. 'We'll need at least £ 100 billion of committed backup. Now comes the tricky part. The additional bargaining chips. I have recently heard we have developed a new, more efficient and less polluting coal fired power station. I think we could offer them that.'

John agreed. 'We could also advise them on wind farms and solar panels. We can't convince the local NIMBYs to install them but they should be able to do so. "People's Democracies" do have their advantages!'

Helen was looking pensive. 'I keep thinking it's not going to be enough.'

John chewed his thumb. Edward would have quickly identified he was about to drop a bombshell. 'There's always Hong Kong.'

'I'm not sure I follow.'

'When we handed over Hong Kong, Britain and China agreed it would have a different set of rules. It controls its own police, banking system, press and local elections. It is known as a Special Administrative Region or SAR. The Chinese describe it as "one country two systems". They can't get any revenue from them until 2052. They cannot meddle in their internal affairs until then either. Britain guarantees this. We could offer to reduce the length of time we guarantee the SAR status by twenty years, until 2032.'

Helen was aghast. She stood up and started pacing the room. 'We cannot do it. We signed a treaty and offered them guarantees. If we did what you suggest we would be nothing more than strumpets at China's beck and call. We would become the world's laughing stock!'

'Who's thinking like a politician now' joked John.

Helen's voice became slightly shrill. 'This isn't about politics. A deal is a deal is a deal. It could set a very dangerous precedent.'

John gestured to her, inviting her to sit down. 'I'm not offering this at a whim. This is our nuclear option, a last ditch resort.'

She sat down. 'Very well. I would rather this wasn't discussed at cabinet level on Monday. Or with Edward at any point' she added as an afterthought.

'I can't promise you that. But I won't float it immediately. Right, I think I should get home and start putting my parts in a presentable form. I'll have a word with the Spanish, the French and the Germans. I'll let you speak with the money men. We should try and meet with Edward half an hour before the cabinet meeting.'

'OK, I'll make my phone calls and update you on Monday.'

They both stood up and walked to the door. There was an awkward pause as Helen opened the door.

John thought: sod it! and plunged in. 'Listen, when all this mess is over, regardless of either of us still having a job, I wonder…' he started blushing and cursed himself for doing so.

Helen face was a mixture of puzzlement and amusement.

'I wonder if we could go out for a meal or catch an exhibition.' There! He'd said it!

Helen blinked in surprise. She paused to collect her thoughts and gave an encouraging smile. 'Yes, I think I would like that.'

'Good!' John felt like a huge weight had been lifted from his shoulders. He shook hands with her. 'Good bye.'

'Good bye.' She closed the door and leant her back against it. She chewed her lower lip. Had John just asked her out on a date? Was she imagining things? She laughed out loud. There they were, in the middle of what was possibly the worst crisis they would ever face and there he was, blushing like a teenager and asking her out while their world collapsed! She liked John and would like to go out with him but it amused her to think how two middle-aged people sometimes chose weird timings. She shook her head and started working on her computer. Two minutes later John Stokes's gentlemanly invitation had disappeared from her consciousness as she struggled to find the exact level of pitch for the Chinese proposal.

Edward was watching his interview at number 10. It was taped on video. He rewound it several times assessing how he had responded to the various questions. He pronounced himself satisfied. He had a brief chat with John about the planning meeting and joined Sylvia in the sitting room.

Francine Weekes had taped her interview too. She had looked too sulky and, in her opinion, with good reason. How dare Edward steal her thunder? She knew she was never going to be Prime Minister but she had worked hard all her life for a small space under the sun. This was supposed to be her best opportunity and now it was disappearing before her eyes.

Norman had been watching the news too. He was pleased about the coverage with regards to the Daily Herald on two counts. It added to his reputation. Jock had given him some aggro over the moderate tone of the headlines but he reassured him that everyone was buying their paper because they were the only ones with the inside story.

Barry had been watching the news too. Pippa was out at the gym so he could, for once, commandeer the remote. He had also read the relevant articles very carefully. There was no significant mention of shares. He rang Norman.

'Hi Norman, it's Barry.'

'Hi Barry, what can I do for you.'

'Congratulations on the Chinese visit scoop.'

'Thank you.' Norman self preservation instincts moved to Defcon 3.

'Does this have anything to do with the information I gave you about those share purchases?'

Bugger! thought Norman. The last thing I need is this young whippersnapper upsetting the apple cart. 'There might be some bearing but the visit had been partially scheduled for some time. I suggest we wait and see.'

'Oh, very well. Any more thoughts on my transfer request?'

'As I explained to you, I will try and look favourably into it. Unfortunately Jock has a very tight control on the editorial purse strings'. I would like to ask you a favour though.'

'Go ahead.'

'Keep these thoughts under your hat. I understand there are some delicate negotiations afoot after the South China Sea incident and the last thing we need is pointless speculation.'

'Sure. Thank you Norman.'

'You're welcome Barry.' He flicked his mobile off. Definitely he had a nose. Well worth watching, and helping. He made a small annotation in his diary.

Barry hung up. He felt slightly uneasy. He was positive Norman was keeping things from him. He didn't want to challenge him, not through Jock at any rate. The strings attached would eventually strangle him! He wisely decided to await developments.

In the meantime, and sensing possible photo opportunities, he decided to check his spy camera. It was fitted inside an old fashioned looking chunky ring with a blue stone at the centre. The stone was the lens. He never wore it at home; Pippa would have deemed it too naff. It didn't raise much comment at Buckingham Palace. He was quite amazed at this remarkable piece of equipment. He was impressed at the detail in the pictures it took. It could show faces clearly up to ten feet but worked at its best from three feet. The pictures were automatically relied into his mobile whence he could e-mail them anywhere in the world. He had already managed to catch a premiership footballer carousing with two blondes while his wife was at home!

He tried a several snaps always calculating position and distance. His innate triangulating skills were certainly an asset for the job! He checked the results. He was 100% accurate. He put the ring back in his briefcase.

Chapter 10

Barry arrived at work on Monday morning. The staff notice board had a new notice, which dwarfed the rest of the announcements. It summoned him and other members of staff to a meeting in the common room. He scanned all the names. As far as he could see none of them had been working at the palace for more than six months. He wondered if his job was at risk through redundancies. He was definitely at risk on "the last in first out principle". If it were decided on the basis of the last appraisal he would be the first on the queue! He enquired around, asking various maids and footmen if they had any ideas as to the reason for this meeting. He drew blank every time. Everybody was as clueless as he.

At the announced time, he joined a group of approximately twenty junior maids and footmen in the staff common room. He saw the chairs arranged in rows, like school assembly, he thought. Barry had arrived among the first. He positioned himself in the second row. The room filled up quickly. Nobody dared ignore a summons from Sir Ian who was already seated at the table at the top of the room. As soon as everyone was seated Sir Ian started proceedings. He spent little time in niceties.

'Ladies and gentlemen, thank you for coming today. You are no doubt aware of recent developments in the press. The Chinese premier, Mr Ma Tsien-Zu is due to come on a state visit this Thursday, invited by the government. On Saturday there will be a state banquet in his honour. This visit has not long been scheduled and we have lower than desirable levels of staffing. We have been informed that this is a crucial state visit and everything must be perfect. You are the most junior members of staff. To the best of my knowledge, none of you has taken part in a state visit. This will be your first. In order to cope with it, you will receive additional training on the special requirements a state visit demands. It will be hard work. Anybody who fails to give their utmost and fails to perform to the highest standard will incur in my displeasure as well as that of your trainer.'

At this point, the door at the back of the room opened, somebody let himself in and closed the door with a slight click. The footsteps of a heavy man could be felt rather than heard. Every other footstep had a squeak added to it.

'I apologise for my delay Sir Ian.' The familiar voice sent a shiver through most spines.

'That's quite all right Mr O'Malley.' Sir Ian's tone was pleasant. They had scheduled his late arrival on purpose. 'Please take a seat.' He gestured to the empty chair next to him.

Patrick O'Malley advanced to the top of the room. The squeak of his artificial limb appeared to be magnified progressively as he walked. He sat down. The chair groaned as it took his vast weight. He looked at his new charges and offered a wolfish smile. A few tried to sink into their seat. Barry was not one of them. This was about to get quite interesting and, if he played his cards right, it would give him a chance of getting right in the middle of things.

Sir Ian continued. 'Ladies and gentlemen, I believe most of you already know Mr O'Malley. As your instructor, he will ensure you achieve the desired standard which is nothing less than perfection. Failure to deliver will have …consequences. Mr O'Malley if you please.'

Psycho stood up. As he did his right leg squeaked again. 'As Sir Ian has already explained I am going to achieve the impossible. To turn you into the best damn staff in record time. Anyone not pulling their weight or perceived to be slacking will make the windows of this place shine like gold. Understood?' He almost shouted the last words.

There was a strangled chorus replied 'Yes Mr O'Malley.'

'Good, lets go into the banqueting hall. Sir Ian,' he nodded.

'Mr O'Malley.' He nodded back.

The staff were herded towards the banqueting hall. Sir Ian went to join the Lord Chamberlain's Committee.

That meeting ran smoothly. The various departments had already swung into action and the bulk of preparations were all but complete. Heathrow was in readiness and the Chinese embassy had already exchanged information with the palace. There had been an interesting development there. Sir Fergus Macleod raised the point.

'My Lord, we have received an unusual request.'

'Unusual in what way?'

'As you already know, Premier Ma had already met the queen when he was governor of the Beijing district back in '86. Apparently they established a good rapport at the time.'

'I am aware of this. What is the request?'

'He has asked for an informal meeting, no more than six to eight people after the state banquet, for a "friendly chat".'

Lord Carruthers turned to Sir Hugh. 'Is her majesty aware of this?'

Sir Hugh nodded. 'Yes she is. She was slightly surprised but, bearing in mind the importance of success, she has graciously acceded.'

'In that case we will arrange the blue room next to the banqueting hall.'

The rest of the agenda was dispatched swiftly.

Sir Hugh went to meet the queen. He knocked at the door of her office.

'Come in.'

Sir Hugh walked in and bowed. The queen was working through the inevitable red box at her desk. Prince Phillip was sitting in an armchair reading a newspaper. He acknowledged Sir Hugh with a nod. He looked enquiringly at his wife who shook her head briefly. He became engrossed in his newspaper again.

'How are the preparations going Sir Hugh?'

'Very well Ma'am. We have arranged the blue room for after dinner coffee. I understand none of our guests are too keen on spirits or liqueurs so I will not order any if you approve.'

The queen nodded. 'Who will be attending?

'From the Chinese delegation we understand it will be Premier Ma and his nephew, the deputy industry minister who will also act as an interpreter. From number 10 we will have the prime minister and his wife as well as a 3rd party. Your majesty and prince Phillip from the palace.'

'Maybe you should also join us too Sir Hugh.'

'As you wish Ma'am.' Sir Hugh bowed and left.

Phillip folded his paper back irritably. 'Dammit Lilibet! Do you realise it will be well past midnight? Why do we have to bow and scrape to these buggers anyway?'

The queen smiled indulgently at her husband's latest outburst. She understood perfectly well he was protecting her from exhaustion. They were, after all, both octogenarians. She spoke softly but with authority. 'We have to bow and scrape because we are in no position to do anything else. This visit is vital; I will explain everything in a few days. We endeavour to make their stay a memorable one, for the right reasons, not because someone makes some crack about "slitty eyes" Phillip.' Her smiling face had morphed into a warning glare.

Prince Phillip got the message. He shook the paper ostensibly and hid behind it. The queen carried on working unperturbed while the corgis dozed.

Ma Jing-Tao boarded the plane with a sigh of relief and thanked mentally his uncle and Hsien Fang-La for their foresight. Beijing had become quite a dangerous place. Minister Chung and Marshall Wang had clearly been in touch. There had been two arrest attempts in the last two days. The first time it had been a member of the Chinese secret police. He had tried to barge into his office. The second time a military policeman of sergeant rank had banged at his home door. The paperwork they had submitted had been shoddy; some vague accusations of corruption. In both occasions the protection offered by Minister Hsien and Marshall Wu had been more than enough as both times his would-be captors had been vastly outranked. He feared he would not be so lucky next time so he decided to leave for England one day earlier than planned. Even now as he sat in the comfortable first class seat there was a police inspector sitting next to him. The plane became airborne. His police escort grunted as he tried to get comfortable and muttered darkly about the smoking ban in long haul flights. Jing-Tao ignored him. He had pulled out his laptop and was busily updating his negotiation plans.

The cabinet meeting had started. The atmosphere today was nowhere as relaxed as last week's. The true significance of Saturday's "press leak" about Premier Ma's impending visit had set everyone on edge. Helen had been directed to the "hot seat" by Sir Norman. Unusually, John as a senior Cabinet minister was sitting next to her on Edward's instructions. Edward looked grim as he walked into the room.

'Ladies and gentlemen: I will not spend much time explaining the seriousness of the situation. You have all got copies of Helen and John's dossier. This document is, and I cannot emphasise this enough, top secret. The Chinese government have accepted our invitation. Their delegation arrives in four days. We need to cut a deal that preserves our high tech industries as well as our economic status quo for the foreseeable future. Unpleasant as it may be, given their track record on human rights and contamination, we will kowtow to them like our lives depend on it. Helen and John have developed a package of measures which we hope will help us negotiate from a better position than the one outlined in their dossier. John, if you could start.'

'Thanks Edward. We think there may be a possible weak spot in their whole strategy. They appear to have overstretched themselves by going for the whole airbus complex. In doing so they are confronting Europe's heavyweights. Tomorrow is the start of the bi-annual Franco-German summit. We have arranged for Helen to have a discreet conference with the German chancellor, the French President and the chairman and deputy chairman of the ECB. I too will be travelling tomorrow to Madrid to meet with the Spanish economy minister and the chairman of Banco de Santander; they are major stakeholders in this venture too. The rest of the member countries will be appraised in the next two weeks with the full picture emerging at the next EU summit in September. We will have to cooperate with them as never before. There cannot be any Euro scepticism. We are in desperate need of their aid. Alone we sink especially as they seem to have concentrated their highest stakes in our industrial and financial institutions. Helen, do you want to talk about the financial package?'

Helen stood up. She wasn't fazed by being in the spotlight. 'As you already know, the Chinese have long desired to advance technologically. Their main Achilles heel is pollution and efficiency. They are the world's worst CO_2 producers as well as other unpleasant pollutants. We have recently developed a new coal-fired power station.

It is 30% more efficient and is 40% less polluting. We are also going to offer advice on wind farms and solar powered homes. We will export this and start sharing technology in joint ventures. Long term everybody wins from the environment point of view. Short term it, could even be advantageous for us as we send technicians to set up these power sources, we learn from any mistakes they make as do they. On the efficiency front, the Chinese are way behind. They have a policy of virtually full employment. They will employ five people to perform a task which would be easily done by two people in the west. Any new industries we set up would have to comply with EU efficiency and health and safety regulations.'

'Surely this will eventually backfire on us' said Harold.

'If I can finish explaining the plan I will gladly address that very valid point. We will have to offer partial production of some airbus plane parts as a joint venture. The fuselage is bulky and would probably look good on their achievement sheet. We agree they produce a certain number for internal production and a certain number for export. These export numbers can then be bartered for other parts of the plane. We still export and they don't spend as much. Also we control the amount of planes they produce. Regarding Rolls Royce we should apply the same principle.'

Helen paused and took a sip of water. Nobody talked. She resumed her presentation. 'With regards to competition in the world markets, if John's predictions are accurate, they will develop their internal markets brutally. They have a population of 1.3 billion. Places like Shanghai are not dissimilar to us. They have skyscrapers, slums, traffic jams – caused by non-Chinese cars incidentally- and shopping malls which are making good business. This will eventually spread to the rest of the country. They are going to have to start manufacturing for this vast internal market. Their GDP growth is enormous at present but partly it is because of the expansion. Eventually this will stop because everybody will compete and undercut each other. The Americans for one will not allow this to progress unchecked.'

'Why don't we just let them build a certain number of fully built planes? No disrespect but your proposal sounds somewhat inefficient.'

'It is inefficient but if they produce the complete plane they could swamp the markets. We could control matters for a few years but eventually they would become very good. Remember that Jumbos started flying in 1971, they are still being used with production schedules already running into 2012. Air travel is quite deregulated. Easy Jet, Ryan air etc these companies would buy planes designed twenty years ago with newer engines at a fraction of the cost of newer planes. Buy keeping control of parts we control the production chain output.'

'Surely they will realise that?' asked Edward.

Helen shrugged, 'probably they will. They know how we work regarding airbus. They know that if they force our hand they will be challenging the whole of the EU. They will realise that USA won't stand on the sidelines either.'

Edward decided to cut the debate short. There wasn't any time. 'Right, if everyone is in agreement we will proceed according to Helen and John's plans including tomorrow's meetings. If any of you have any suggestions please pass them on to Helen and John in a brief A4 sheet preferably. I think we will adjourn for ten days until Wednesday the 4th when we will analyse the success of the visit. In the meantime we all devote our energies to bring this to good port. Hopefully we will meet socially at the state banquet which has been scheduled for this Saturday. Any questions or any disagreements?' There was a hint in his tone there had better be none.

Francine's cough aborted the initial scraping of chairs. 'If I may Edward, this would be an excellent opportunity to export our concept of a smoking ban to which as you all know it starts this Sunday after midnight. I think we should try to make maximum effort to raise the profile of this worthwhile cause for the benefit of our Chinese visitors.'

For your benefit you mean, you smug cow. Christopher Ward was careful not to voice these thoughts.

Edward blinked; his face expressionless. He was quite taken aback by Francine's chutzpah. He managed to curb the rising ball of fury building up with great difficulty. 'It's an interesting idea Mrs Weekes, I'm sure you can submit it in writing as I have just outlined.'

People's ears pricked when they heard him use Francine's surname. Her career had just taken a serious nosedive which would be reflected in the next cabinet reshuffle. The nearest ministers edged away from her instinctively. Francine appeared to be unaware. She ploughed on: 'What is there to submit? The plan is in place in the NHS website, she can download it and make a brief précis. She is so good at these,' she waved Helen's dossier as she gave a nauseatingly sweet smile.

Helen could not believe her ears. 'Sorry?'

'Yes, the plan is available in the website, have a quick read and make a few notes so you can present it to the Chinese.' She had carried on smiling but now there was an element of sneering and condescension attached.

Helen was barely managing to control her temper. Her first thought was that Francine had suddenly gone mad. She started speaking calmly and reasonably. She didn't want to appear arrogant or confrontational. 'Francine, as you have just heard, I have to got to Strasbourg tonight and spend most of tomorrow convincing the French, the Germans as well as the top brass at the ECB to support us. I have to prepare a complex dossier, summarise it and arrange a presentation which is pitched exactly at them. Then I will fly back and report here and gain further updates on developments and plan accordingly. As you have pointed out correctly, a small presentation regarding the smoking ban implementation shouldn't take long. At the moment I don't have the time, or the inclination, to write down a further report. Edward has just laid down the rules: if you have an idea, submit it in writing. We will try and fit them in. Everybody else is happy with this; we all agree this is the most efficient way. Chances are it will be my turn to do the same when asked to muck in. I will do it gladly.'

'Little "Miss perfect prefect" bossing around. Just like school eh Nells?' Francine sneered.

Helen's temper finally snapped. 'Oh shut up "Fanny Buns"! You've had a bloody chip on your shoulder since school. I did well at school and you didn't. Diddums! I put a lot more hard work in than you ever realised; I got on with it and never made a song and dance about it.'

'ENOUGH!' Edward had just slammed his hand on the table. Everyone around it jumped. They had been fascinated and horrified by this vitriolic exchange. In a lower voice he continued. 'I have just asked everyone to help the government and the country at a very difficult juncture. Not me, not Helen nor John. They happen to be the conducting rod at present. We all muck in and that includes you Francine. I will not have any bitching around when so much is at stake, including our jobs, if this goes tits up understood?' the last question was directed specifically at Francine who, at last, realised she had overstepped the mark.

'Very well Prime minister' she replied meekly even if inwardly she was seething. How dare he shout at her like that? When Edward looked away she shot him a look of pure venom. Only Christopher Ward saw it.

The cabinet walked out. Christopher whispered to the Scottish secretary: 'better than Mallory Towers this is!' She had read the famous Enid Blyton series and had to stuff a handkerchief in her mouth to avoid bursting with laughter.

Sir Norman detained Christopher as he was walking out. 'Mr Ward, the Prime Minister would like a word with you please.'

He walked into Edward's office completely mystified.

'Hello Chris thanks for staying back. Do take a seat.' He gestured towards an armchair. He appeared to have calmed down at any rate.

He sat down and waited for Edward to take the initiative. He had no idea as to why did Edward want to speak with him.

'I hope you can make it to the state banquet.'

'If I don't the missus will kill me. She complains we never go out. Why is my presence so important though?'

'It appears Premier Ma is quite a keen ornithologist. I have been told you are a bit of a twitcher yourself. Is that correct?'

Christopher merely nodded.

'At the end of the meal, Premier Ma wants to have a private chat with the queen and a few other guests. Sylvia is coming of course but I would be grateful if you could be there too. Just yourself though.'

'I can come if you want me to but I would have thought it would make more sense if Helen or John went to this late soiree.'

'I don't think he wants to talk shop. Apparently he knows the queen of old and wants to have a relaxed chat. Your hobby would be helpful as an ice breaker as well as the fact that you are very good at lightening the atmosphere if things get too heavy going.'

'The court jester then.' Christopher replied dryly.

'No Chris, not the court jester. Over the years I have noticed you have some very good interpersonal skills. Perhaps it was all those years working as a GP, perhaps it's a knack. You can read the mood in a room far more quickly than I do. You can always defuse tension quickly with "le mot juste", an ability I do not possess. I need your help to make this visit a success.' He was almost pleading now.

'No pressure then. Fine, I'll come. I'd better brush up on my James Bond though.'

'James Bond?'

'He was a very famous ornithologist of the 40s and 50s. Ian Fleming used his name for the action hero.'

'I didn't know that.'

'Few people do. On a far more serious note, what do you plan to do about "Fanny Buns"?'

'I'm not sure as follow.'

'Speaking strictly as a GP, I think Francine has some very serious narcissistic personality traits. I think she's about to crack.'

'You're joking!'

'No Edward, I'm not speaking as the court jester. I'm speaking as a GP with many years of experience under my belt. She sees herself as a dependable plodder who will be rewarded at the end. She has seized on the smoking ban implementation as her best opportunity to have her place in the sun. Ma's visit is screwing this up and she's not taking kindly to it. She has become desperate to draw attention on herself. Witness today's episode. When you put your foot down just now she gave you a look of pure venom. Matters are made worse by the fact that Helen, whom she loathes, has become the centre of attention.'

Edward massaged his temples. He really didn't need this. 'What would you do?'

'It's difficult to say. I know that we are running a very tight schedule but if you have the chance I would try and praise the good work she is doing towards the smoking ban.'

'Wouldn't that make me look weak in front of the rest of the cabinet?'

Christopher shrugged. 'You have just told me how important it is that this visit is a success. Keeping Francine happy may very well be a necessary part of it. It's your call.'

'Thanks for that. I'll bear it in mind.'

Christopher took the hint and left.

Edward turned round to Sir Norman. 'What do you think?'

He thought long and hard before answering. Once again he was moving beyond the confines of his responsibility and his portfolio. This time involuntarily. He was definitely unhappy about this. 'I do not possess Dr Ward's great powers of perception and diagnosis. My impression is that he has identified a potential problem area and he's trying to help you.' He tried to be as non-committal as possible.

'You don't think he's trying to help himself?' Edward regretted it as soon as he said it.

'I fear Prime Minister that you are now asking me things which are way beyond my agenda of responsibilities. I feel compelled to ignore this question.'

Edward felt quashed at the put down. He retained enough common sense to realise Sir Norman was right. 'I apologise Sir Norman. I had no right to ask you the last question.'

Sir Norman bowed his head in acknowledgement. 'Will that be all Prime Minister?'

'Yes thank you very much.' He tried to put as much warmth in the phrase as possible to emphasise his contriteness.

They both left his office. Edward walked upstairs to his private rooms. Sylvia was in the kitchen making some tea. He enjoyed the picture of domesticity. She looked up and smiled.

'Hello darling. I didn't hear you come. Everything go all right at the cabinet meeting?'

Edward sighed and shook his head.

'Are you all right?' She put the mug down and gave him a hug. He held her tight allowing the gentle caress and her fresh smell ease the tensions off. She broke off and looked at him with a worried expression. 'Do you want to talk?' She had never seen Edward look so forlorn.

'There was a bit of a to do at the cabinet meeting just now.' He explained the spat; he omitted nothing including how he had imposed order or his conversation with Christopher or Sir Norman.

'Oh dear. I did wonder if it would happen when you appointed them.'

'What do you mean?'

'Do you know Rebecca?'

'Your cousin?'

'Yes. She also went to Cheltenham Ladies College. Apparently their rivalry was legendary. Francine usually came a poor second.'

'Wait a minute. Do you mean this is a long-standing feud?'

She nodded as she bit her thumb. She didn't want to appear as interfering.

'Come on. Out with it!'

'You may not know this but Helen was always top of the class. She was also sports captain, prefect and, eventually head girl. Francine was nowhere in her league and she was insanely jealous, from what Rebecca told me. She was forever sniping and trying to create an anti-Helen clique. It never worked. Helen was too well liked. She ignored Francine most of the time but occasionally she would lash out. She is responsible for the "Fanny Buns" nickname. Apparently Francine was quite er.. rotund at the time. The nickname stuck. From what Rebecca told me, Helen was phenomenally patient and even tried to befriend her. Eventually she gave up and ignored her only hitting back under extreme provocation.'

'For fucks sake!' he swore.

'Edward! Language!' Sylvia was very prudish when it came to swearing.

'Sorry darling. I just find it hard to believe that two adult women, in a position of high responsibility, can carry on like this. Especially' he sniggered, ' "Fanny Buns".'

'Edward! Please don't. You will only antagonise her.'

'OK, OK. I won't.'

At that moment the phone rang. Edward picked it up.

'Excuse me Prime Minister but Charles Grigg the Home Office Secretary wants to speak with you. He says it's urgent.'

'Put him through please.' The phone clicked. 'Yes Charles?'

'Edward, this has just arrived. Ma-Jing-Tao, the deputy industry minister and also Premier Ma's nephew is flying in tomorrow.'

'Not officially?'

'No, in private. He was scheduled to arrive early on Wednesday but he has taken an early flight. I took the liberty of checking all incoming flights from Beijing and checking if any senior politburo or ministers were in them. His name pinged the system today. Do you want me to alert the DTI?'

Edward thought about it. The Chinese government had not warned them so they didn't want a fuss. He had to respect that. But it was Ma's nephew. Some courtesies had to be observed. 'No Charles, we make no fuss. Who are they travelling with?

'BA, they are scheduled to land in Heathrow at 0600. Business class.'

'Fine. Alert the captain of the flight. I want someone of the cabin crew to discreetly point him out. Get a plain clothes senior officer to zip him through customs. Have an official Jag ready with one unmarked escort in readiness. If the Chinese embassy is providing transport, let them. Otherwise we will offer him a lift. Also offer him contacts with DTI and FO. He can take them or leave them.'

'I know just the man for the job. Leave it with me.'

'Let me know if there are any problems. Well done Charles. Good thinking.'

'Only trying to help. 'Bye.'

'Everything OK?' asked Sylvia.

'Yes, it's fine. Ma's nephew is flying in tomorrow incognito. I suspect he is just preparing the ground for when his uncle arrives from the US. Right, where's that cup of tea? The service in this joint isn't what it used to be!'

Sylvia gave him a withering look. 'Do you want to sleep in you office sofa? That Chesterfield looks mighty uncomfortable!'

Chapter 11

Barry was exhausted by the time he arrived at Pippa's flat. Psycho, true to his word had put his new charges through their paces. Opening and closing doors, walking through miles of corridors carrying plates, serving and removing them. All this was done under Psycho's single eyed glare. He had acquitted himself well but an unfortunate footman had incurred in his wrath. He was last seen walking disconsolately down the corridor, not likely to be seen for many hours, carrying a bucket full of soapy water and a squeegee.

Pippa was sitting on the sofa; she was wearing a bathrobe and reading Tatler. She seemed distracted. He kissed her. He noticed how she wrinkled her nose.

'Is there any hot water left?' The immersion boiler in her flat was a rather decrepit and temperamental contraption; more prone to being on the blink than to delivering the goods!

'I think so. I've just had one.'

'Excellent. I'll go and have one.' He walked towards the bathroom.

'Barry?'

'Yes love?'

'We have been invited to Cissie and Leo's pre-engagement dinner party. Just a few friends.'

'That's nice. When is it?'

'This Saturday. You're free. I've checked your rota.'

Barry walked back into the sitting room wearing an apologetic expression Pippa knew only too well.

'Oh no! Don't tell me you've made plans!'

'Not plans as such. There has been a change in the rota.'

'Does that mean you're working?' Her voice was now raised to a screech.

'Almost certainly. The Chinese premier is coming on a state visit at very short notice. We are short staffed so it's all hands on deck.'

'I don't believe it! The one chance we have, to go out and spend a nice evening with some of my friends you suddenly have to go and kowtow to some bloody Chinese bigwigs!'

'Sweetheart.'

'Don't you sweetheart me Barry Smith!'

'As soon as I'm finished I'll come and join you.'

'When is it supposed to finish?'

'Around ten or eleven o'clock.'

'Wonderful! That means you won't be there until gone midnight. What am I supposed to do in the meantime? Put on some Marigolds and wash up all on my own?'

'Come on. It's the nature of the job.' He decided to go on the offensive. 'You have been late many a time because you were trying to complete a sale.'

'At least it was worth it.'

'You mean my job isn't?'

'If you ask me. No.' She flicked the television on and ignored him.

Barry knew there was no point in pursuing the argument. He went back to the bathroom. The bathtub was half full. His mobile was beeping. He checked his messages. There was another misspelled offer. He thought about ignoring the summons but he decided against it. The last thing he needed today was Jock in a fire-breathing mood. He rang.

'Yes?'

'Hi Jock. How did the conference in Greece go?'

'None of your business! Anything at the palace?'

'Nothing much. The Chinese premier is arriving on Thursday. There should be some chances of slip-ups at the state banquet.' Not if Psycho has anything to do with it he thought. 'Even if nothing untoward happens we can still spin a good yarn.'

'Of another boring state banquet?'

'This one is short notice. We could mention the extra training involved.'

'Wasn't that covered by the Mirror?'

'Nope. We could also link it to the fact that the Daily Herald was the first to break the news about the visit.'

'I'll see.'

'Jock, I need a favour.'

'Do you think you are in a position to ask for bloody favours given your recent crappy record?'

Barry let that pass. 'It's dependent on success. If I deliver a good story, my cover will be blown. I will have to go back to full time with you. If so, can I join the national or international desk please?'

'If you deliver a story that goes round the world, I'll consider it.' Jock never made promises if he could avoid it. He hung up.

Barry looked at his phone. He knew it was as good as it was going to get. Chances were he would be stuck in the gossip column until Jock decided to sack him. He undressed and sank gratefully into the warm water.

Jock was looking at his computer screen when Norman walked in.

'Hi Jock. How was Greece?'

'Vile. Hot and sticky and I didn't make any new contacts. You got two good scoops on Saturday he conceded grudgingly. Why didn't you mention the shares issue?' He was being entirely partisan. He had seen a rise of 5% in the value of his shares. A handsome return for a week's work! He was a greedy man though. He wanted more.

Norman was aware of what was in Jock's mind demurred. 'It isn't the right time for the story. We should see what developments does this visit bring.'

'I just spoke with Barry Smith. He hopes he will get a scoop. He has asked for a transfer to the national or international desk. What do you think?' He had suddenly become unusually friendly.

Norman eyed him warily. He decided to hedge his bets. The last thing he wanted was to be beholden to a greedy brute like Jock. As far as he knew Jock wasn't aware of Barry's role in the whole story and Norman had made no further revelations to Jock. 'He might be good' he said non-committaly. 'I'm inclined to wait and see what can he deliver.' He looked ostensibly at his watch. 'Good heavens! Look at the time. I'd better see to the newspaper.' He hurried away.

Jock sat at his desk tugging at his lower lip. Maybe it wasn't a bad thing Norman hadn't broken the story. It would give him a further chance to increase his profits. He used his personal mobile phone to ring his broker. He had never cared for other peoples timetables.

In the southern Cotswolds a digitally activated recorder started taping.

Ma-Jing-Tao landed in Heathrow on time. He was among the first to leave the plane. He and his police escort didn't notice the plane's chief steward's discreet signal. A man in his late 40's approached him not ten yards after he had left the plane. Despite his non-descript navy blue suit he still looked like a policeman.

He walked alongside Ma accommodating his stride to Ma's. 'Mr Ma Jing-Tao?'

Jing-Tao eyed him warily. 'Yes, it's me.' He had his diplomatic passport and a very fit, albeit tired back-up. He rapped a quick instruction in Mandarin and his police escort moved two steps back. It made it harder to immobilise them simultaneously. The policemen eyed the incident with polite interest and shook his head.

'That will not be necessary Mr Ma. I am Chief Inspector Richard Cowper from Immigration. I would like to welcome you to the United Kingdom on behalf of her majesty's government.' He showed his badge and additional credentials discreetly to Ma. Richard Cowper was a veteran of the immigration service. He was very good at sensing anxiety and disquiet. He normally used these to his advantage and exploited people's fears. Today he endeavoured to calm his charges. 'We noted a high ranking official from the PRC was flying in today. We want to ensure you go through immigration unimpeded. This way please.'

After some hesitation Ma and his bodyguard followed CI Cowper down the corridor. Not many travellers had noticed this exchange. The flight attendants, as instructed, had stopped any more passengers from leaving the plane. Ma noticed this. It convinced him that CI

Cowper was the real thing. They walked down the corridor until they reached a side door. CI Cowper swiped his access card and they all went in. The corridor was narrow and not as well illuminated. They went down some steps and through another door and found themselves in the baggage reclaim area. The baggage carrousel corresponding to their flight was deserted. Their luggage was already there though. The Chinese policeman retrieved it swiftly.

'What about our entry visas?' Ma asked

The English policeman extended his hand. 'Your passports please.' He checked them quickly, more for show than anything else, and stamped the pages with a three month visa.

Ma eyed the stamps critically. They appeared to be in order. 'Thank you Mr Cowper.'

'Not at all Mr Ma. As I explained earlier, we noticed you wished to enter the country discreetly but we felt it would be appropriate that we assisted you. Have you got any transport arranged?'

Ma shook his head. He had planned to jump into a cab and get to the embassy on his own steam.

'If it is acceptable, we have a car ready to take you to the address of your choice. Would that be the Chinese embassy?' Richard Cowper was enjoying his role play of the perfect English butler. He could see his two charges were bewildered by the display of speed and efficiency of their hosts.

Ma understood what mind tricks were being played. He regained his composure and tried to recapture some of the lost ground. 'That would be very helpful thank you.'

'This way please.'

They walked into the arrivals lounge. As they crossed the door they were swiftly flanked by two plainclothes police officers. The five man procession walked out into the muggy outdoors. On the sidewalk there were two cars waiting for them. A couple of traffic wardens watched warily. Richard Cowper had told them in no uncertain terms what a poor career move would it be to even think of slapping a ticket!

CI Cowper opened the door of the first car. 'There you are Sir. Oh! Forget my head next. I have a message from Mr Faulkner, the Prime Minister. He will be delighted to offer any assistance should you wish to meet with any officials from the DTI or the FO. Here is his telephone number.' He gave Ma a sealed envelope. 'Have a safe trip.'

'Thank you Chief Inspector. Your assistance has been invaluable.'

The door closed CI Cowper stood up and nodded. Both cars left simultaneously. He walked back to the airport and returned the immigration stamps. Even if it had been a standard procedure, the change of routine had been enjoyable. He decided to treat himself to a full English breakfast; Glenys needn't know!

In the car, as he was going into London, Ma Jing-Tao analysed the recent event. The English had been waiting for him. They had put on an understated display of efficiency. He had been given a subliminal red carpet treatment. Good, he thought. This meant they were treating the whole visit seriously. He ignored the views of warehouses and ugly blocks of flats and entered some more data in his computer.

Edward was having breakfast when his mobile rang. It was Charles Grigg. 'Hello Charles, everything go all right?'

'Smooth as a baby's bottom! They were out of the airport within ten minutes we must have set a world record! Our discreet guest appeared to be quite impressed. He got your message too.'

'Excellent Charles. Well done.'

'Let's hope it is a good omen.'

'Indeed. Good-bye.'

Edward resumed his breakfast in a mellower frame of mind. He didn't expect Jing-Tao to contact Helen or John but they had shown him they were beginning to anticipate his moves. The following morning Edward and his emergency work group were at his office. Wilfred was taking notes as usual.

'So John, how did it go in Madrid?'

'Not bad at all. I met with Solbes and Botin as well as a couple of number crunchers from the bank of Spain. It was all very hush hush. My plane was diverted to a military aerodrome and we stayed there all the time.

'John, you're not Smiley and this isn't a Le Carre novel.'

'Sorry. It is a bit cloak and dagger anyway! The long and short of it is that they are going to create a contingency fund of around £10 billion. If ECB don't come up with anything they will try and dig deeper. I understand Mr. Botin had already been in touch with the ECB. This comes with strings though.'

'What strings?' asked Harold.

'No more nuclear subs in Gibraltar. The issue of "Tireless" pissed them off no end. They want it public by the way.'

Edward thought about this. 'It seems reasonable. I'll have to check with Rufus though. If we agreed how do we present it to the public?'

'Usual guff of reorganisation and redeployment of the naval bases. Also we give some spin about the environmental impact of subs in the Med.'

'I wouldn't use the last bit Edward,' Harold intervened. 'We'd have the SNP all over our bases in Scotland. They do have an obsession about Gibraltar don't they?'

'See how would you like a permanent Spanish military base in Land's End Harold' said Helen.

Harold blushed. He was the MP for Cornwall South. 'Point taken.'

Edward cut in. He didn't want a long discussion on military bases in foreign countries and the political ramifications. 'Let's crack on. Helen; how did it go in Strasbourg?'

'Initially not very well. They are fully aware of the seriousness of the situation but the initial reaction was to let us get it in the neck and give themselves time to prepare for the next round.'

'You're joking!'

'Nope. Believe me, it was quite ugly. I explained to them how once they had hammered us they would then go for some of the smaller weaker EU countries and hold them to ransom thus being able to dictate policy in the back room. I hinted we might well be willing to negotiate such a deal. I also reminded them of their unenviable record of sluggishness when it came to implementing laws and the speed at which the Chinese moved. I finally threatened them with the worst EU constitution referendum result ever thus torpedoing any chance of progression in the EU especially with us blocking negotiations and budgets at every turn.'

'Was that wise?' asked George.

'Maybe not but it was the only way to show those idiots how desperate the situation was.'

'It smacks of bullying tactics' said John. He looked uneasy.

'I agree, but with Angela Merkel being particularly obstructive and Sarkozy dragging his heels I couldn't find any other way. Eventually Wolfgang knocked a few heads together explaining the worst financial case scenario. It soon made them change their tune. They knew they would be out of office, particularly Merkel, before the year was over.'

Edward asked what was on everybody's mind. 'What was the end result?'

'They have given us a promissory note from ECB for £ 60 billion to be distributed pro rata among all loaning banks, with repayment over a 6 year period at 5%. They would rather the banks renegotiated their debts with PRC but they will step in if needs be.'

'What happened with regards to airbus?' asked Harold.

'As I expected, they were a lot less flexible. Eventually we agreed on a 10 year program of gradual fuselage building with EU supervision and EU standards including their 48 hour working directive. Eventually they would build the whole fuselage. Final assembly remains in Toulouse. Non-negotiable. They gave us a free rein with Rolls Royce Aero. They agreed we would need that leverage.'

'Do you think the Chinese will bite?' Harold was quite interested; it was a *very* good deal. They had conceded a lot more than could have been expected.

'I hope so.'

'We always have the nuclear button option' said John.

Helen swung round. 'I thought we agreed it wasn't up for discussion' she hissed.

Edward intervened. 'Wait a second. What is this nuclear button option John?'

John ignored Helen's mutinous looks. He explained the possibility of rescheduling the SAR timetable for Hong Kong by up to twenty-five years. Except for John, everyone in the room looked confused. This type of diplomatic negotiations had been done in the past. But since Wilson's 14 points they had been frowned upon.

Edward broke the silence. 'I'm not sure I want history to remember me as the PM who sold the people of Hong Kong's rights for a plate of lentils' he said loftily.

John raised an eyebrow. 'You can always be remembered as the PM who had the opportunity to stave off the worst ever financial crisis and lost it or as the PM who took hard decisions for the greater good of his people. It's your call.'

Edward thought about this. He knew John was right. It just seemed too sordid for words. He was surprised at John's level of ruthlessness. He'd better watch his back with "noodles". 'OK, this is what we'll do. We now have some very good cards to play. If, and only if, the Chinese make an open threat to push their nuclear button do we push ours. Everyone agreed?'

Helen raised her hand. 'I will only accept if Harold and George endorse it fully and the Chinese agree to keep it secret for five years.'

'Why five years?'

'The PRC should start to move towards a more open society by then. If they don't, we then appeal to the international courts as having been forced to sign under duress. And we don't let them know.'

They all thought about it. It was a good get out clause. One by one they agreed on it. Helen turned to Wilfred: 'we will all need copies of these minutes signed by all present.'

Wilfred nodded. He had already planned to keep a copy to himself. This would increase its political value!

They all walked to the hall. Helen tapped John on the shoulder. 'Can I have a word?'

They walked into the empty cabinet room. 'I thought we agreed Hong Kong was strictly out of bounds!'

'No, Helen. I never agreed to that. I just said I would consider not talking about it. Your strong-arm tactics in Strasbourg have caused me no end of aggravation. I have had the German foreign affairs minister and the Quai d'Orsay chewing my ear all morning. You have pissed off a lot of very powerful people and we have no favours owing any more in Europe.'

'I needed to use those tactics because they wouldn't cooperate!'

'And we'll use the same tactics if the Chinese won't play ball. You twisted their arms and it worked!'

'I never agreed to sell ten million people down the river!'

'But you were quite happy to block everything within the EU indefinitely thus depriving the Poles, the Bulgarians, the Baltic nations and Romania from much needed development funds. Also, sticking to your principles would inflict untold misery on all the British people, some of whom may I remind you, voted you to represent them. Do you think Hong Kong would foot this bill? Like hell they would! China wouldn't let them for starters and even if they did they wouldn't do it. If we offered the guarantee of SAR status for forty-five years we would look like shits and they wouldn't pay. Let's look like shits anyway; shits who defend their country's interests.'

Helen was surprised at these reasons. She hadn't looked at it from that perspective. John was right. Her first duty was to her constituents and her country; the people who paid her wages. 'I'm sorry John. I had never thought at looking at it from that perspective. You're right but I sincerely hope it doesn't come to that.'

John squeezed her arm gently, she didn't flinch. 'I hope so too. The problem with politics is that conditions change very quickly. Do you know Harold Wilson's famous comment?'

'A week is a long time in politics. I know.' She leant slightly and kissed John gently on the cheek. 'Thank you. We'd better leave or people will start wondering.'

Not as much as I am he thought.

That evening Barry checked the last minute rotas for the week-end. He had been chosen for duty at the banquet room. He was pleased for the fact that this showed he had passed muster but this feeling of elation was tempered by the dread of having to confront Pippa when he relayed the news. As he turned round he saw Sir Ian and Psycho smiling at him.

'Well done lad, you were among the least difficult choices.'

'Indeed Barry' said Sir Ian 'maybe there is still some hope for you!'

Barry was irked by Conn's patronising comment. He knew he had been working his socks off and he discovered a hitherto unknown ability to achieve anything he wanted if he applied himself. He felt his time at Buckingham palace was over. He did some quick mental arithmetic. He needed something checking though.

'Am I still in my probationary period Sir Ian?'

Sir Ian was surprised at the question. 'Well yes, I suppose you still are.'

'So my employment status remains unchanged?'

Sir Ian smiled indulgently. 'I think we should review that on Monday.'

'It may take a bit longer Sir Ian. I would like to request my annual leave; ten days.'

'You have only been here for just over three months. Surely it's only eight days?'

'I have been working two extra days this week including the weekend so I would rather have them in lieu if it's all the same.'

Sir Ian opened a drawer and took out a form. 'Fill it in. I'll sign it now and I will confirm it tomorrow.'

Barry filled in the form and handed it over to Sir Ian who folded it and put it in his pocket. Barry bade the two other men farewell and left for home. Sir Ian looked at Patrick.

'That was a very unexpected request Patrick; so sudden.'

"Psycho" shrugged his shoulders. 'Perhaps a few days under my "tender loving care" has been too much of a strain for his system' he joked. 'He has worked hard, I'll give you that.'

Sir Ian remained unconvinced. There had been an element of calculation in this request. Of that much he was sure. Something else was prickling at the back of his mind. Again he couldn't pinpoint it. He went back to his office and analysed Barry's request. He tallied it with the rest of annual leave requests and approved it. He became distracted with a staffing issue at Windsor Castle; Barry's unexpected request merged with a myriad of details he needed to attend to and forgot about it.

For once, Thursday dawned bright and sunny with good weather forecast for the whole day. All the details and plans for the visit were set.

Edward was getting ready for the visit. He was doing some last minute checks on protocol and as well as the profiles of the main representatives of the Chinese delegation. He checked the headlines with irritation. Most of the press were hostile to this visit. There were unveiled accusations that the British government we grovelling to the PRC after the South China Sea incident. He wished he'd had more time to prepare the visit. His press contacts and leverage were nowhere as good as those of Labour. He would definitely have to work on those. He also wished there had been a previous state visit, give him a chance to do a "dry run" with another country where the stakes weren't so high. He checked the timetable yet again. Ma Tsien Zu had left just before midnight from Washington. He wished he knew what his ultimate objective was. The seven hour flight and the time difference meant he would land around noon. The dies were cast.

Meanwhile at Buckingham Palace, the queen was getting ready too. She chose a light blue dress with a linen jacket in a slightly darker tone. A light coat of the exact hue was available should the weather become inclement. Her dresser worked silently; she could sense the queen was deep in thought and was in no mood for light conversation.

The queen, in fact was mentally rehearsing the brief welcome speech. There was no need to review the protocol. After fifty-five year there was no eventuality or variation she hadn't experienced tenfold. She reflected on how things had changed. When she became queen after the death of her dear father, Britain was still a mighty, albeit exhausted, power. China were emerging from a terrible civil war and were, despite her size and her population, a virtual non-entity with an inscrutable leader who had thrown his lot with the communists and was trying to become a regional power. Now Britain no longer ruled the waves, communism was all but dead and China was fast becoming the third world's superpower. Only their leaders remained inscrutable, even Ma Tsien-Zu. She wondered if he had changed a lot, power could damage a man's soul if he wasn't strong enough

EXHALE

Chapter 12

The object of all these deliberations was more than halfway across the Atlantic. He was reflecting on recent events and their consequences. His visit to USA hadn't been successful; anything but. The Americans had rejected any suggestions of joint ventures. He had expected it and as a matter of fact it pleased him. It would give him an excuse in the future to dictate policy in their bilateral relations. He had gone there this time as a matter of political and diplomatic courtesy. His secondary worry was that now the European negotiations needed to a successful conclusion. His main worry, though, was Chung Hing-Lai. The industry minister had "developed" acute gastroenteritis in the last three days of the visit. This had left him, he claimed, with extreme prostration and he needed to return to China to recover. Ma snorted; "extreme prostration" indeed. More like extreme mischief making! Hsien Fang-La had kept him updated. The telephone contacts between Chung and Marshall Wang had been frequent in the last few days. He was planning a serious assault on his authority at the politburo meeting. He had tried to block this "illness" by sending in Dr Woo. Chung had, for once, been one step ahead of him. He had secreted his personal physician in the delegation. This physician had restricted access to Chung and insisted that he fly back immediately. The Americans, wishing to avoid the embarrassment of a dead Chinese dignitary on their home soil, had been far more obliging on providing transport for Chung than in wanting to negotiate. The end result was that Chung would land in Beijing approximately at the same time as he landed in London. No doubt the flight would have improved his general condition and he would experience a "miraculous" recovery by tomorrow. It would be too late to fly to England but not too late to attend the politburo meeting. Son of a turtle! He was aware of the thwarted attempts to arrest his nephew. He wasn't sure if it was due to increased boldness or desperation. He hoped it was the former. Overconfident people were prone to make mistakes.

He got up from his chair in his private office. His back was causing him extreme discomfort. He summoned Dr Woo via the intercom. Shortly there was a knock at the door.

'Enter.'

Dr Woo Chung-King entered the room carrying a briefcase. He was a man in his late 50s who was quite short. Of medium build and a slight paunch his features almost invariably showed a placid expression. He was a firm believer in Chinese traditional medicine, but he was also aware of all the current advances in western medicine. He practiced a skilful blend of both. He still worked regularly at Beijing's top hospital where he would gladly see anyone who requested it. Ma had been unable to convince him to work exclusively for him. Dr Woo had never cared for power and its trappings. He had only agreed to treat Ma because of the state of his back.

'You called for me Tsien-Zu?' He was the only person outside his family and restricted inner circle not to use his formal title.

'Thank you for coming Dr Woo. I'm afraid my back is seizing up again.'

Dr Woo clicked his tongue disapprovingly. 'This is a very heavy schedule. Your back is complaining and instead of listening to it you call me to muffle it.'

'I know. Unfortunately it was necessary. I had no option but to go. Please do your best.'

Dr Woo muttered something under his breath about foolish old bears who should know better as he opened his briefcase. He opened a tub of tiger balm and mixed it with oil of cloves and a small amount of morphine paste. He mixed it up and started rubbing the resulting concoction slowly and expertly on his patients back.

Ma could feel the tension and pain ebbing away after five minutes. Dr Woo was the one person who could keep him going.

'How many red dots in the last day?' They both knew what he was referring to.

'Only two' he replied drowsily. 'I am sticking to a maximum of three a day but try to make do with one or two whenever possible.'

'Good, remember opium can be a very demanding mistress.'

'You needn't remind me.'

'How does it feel?'

'Much better. Still some discomfort but a lot, lot better.'

'I'll give you a session of acupuncture now and a further massage when we reach the embassy.'

'No more opium though.' Ma was very aware of what was contained in the mixture. Dr Woo had explained it at the start of his treatment years ago. He could always recognize the smell, the same way he could smell it in his special cigarettes.

Dr Woo wasn't impressed by his patients attempt at dictating policy. 'If you need it Tsien-Zu, you will have it. We have a deal, remember?'

They both chanted in unison, as if reciting the times table: 'Premier Ma doesn't tell Dr Woo how to practice medicine and Dr Woo doesn't tell premier Ma how to run the country.' They both chuckled. A disconcerting sight for sure especially in Ma's case but there was nobody to witness it.

Dr Woo cleaned Ma's back with a sterile solution and proceeded to expertly insert eight needles along his back. He went outside to wash his hands and let Ma alone with his thoughts. Ma proceeded to recite the list of Chinese emperors. This was a mental exercise which took his mind away from the problems of state and allowed him to relax. He had just recited the last Ching emperor when Dr Woo returned. He removed the acupuncture needles and stored them safely in a case reserved for Ma's exclusive use. He cleaned the back and instructed him to get up.

Ma slid off the bed, legs first and, from a kneeling position, he became upright with the help of his hands.

'How do you feel?'

'Very well Dr Woo, you have worked your magic as usual.'

'Pah! Magic. That's for country yokels.' He was pleased at the compliment nevertheless. 'Have you done your Tai-Chi?'

'No, not yet.'

'No time like the present, especially as you don't have any meetings scheduled.' He walked out of the room into the large rear compartment which was empty at the time. Most people were fast asleep.

Ma followed him obediently. He was always amazed at how he, the supreme ruler in China would always follow the instructions of his doctor.

Woo never profited from his work. He was paid a small retainer and the rest of his income came from his hospital practice. Ma had already secretly bought a lovely traditional house in Hunan for Dr Woo when he retired. It was the least he could do for the only man capable of keeping him going.

As scheduled, the military Boeing 747 landed at Heathrow airport at noon. The queen, Edward and various other dignitaries were waiting on the main concourse. Ma Tsien-Zu walked confidently down the steps, every inch the leader of the PRC. His pain gone and perfectly relaxed he exuded confidence and authority.

The usual routine of brief speeches, national anthems and inspection of troops was dispatched with the minimum fuss and the maximal efficiency. They were all starting to get ready to get into the awaiting cars when Christopher Ward, who had watched events with polite interest, saw a solitary, white haired figure coming down the rear steps of the Chinese plane. He did a double take. He recognised the short slightly paunchy person whose face always had a permanent, placid expression. He looked around; miraculously, Edward was alone with Sylvia waiting for his car. The queen and premier Ma had already departed. He ran towards him and tugged at his coat.

'Edward, you wouldn't believe who I have just seen!'

Edward gave Christopher the alarmed look sane people give to lunatics. 'Who have you seen?'

'Dr Woo Chung-King!' Christopher could barely contain his excitement.

'Who he?'

'Only one of the world's leading acupuncture specialists.' Christopher was disappointed the name didn't register in Edward's memory banks. I met him in 1984 in Beijing, I attended a one month course in

172

acupuncture. He gave some lectures and demonstrations back in 1990. It was incredible. People who had been virtually wheelchair bound could walk with just one stick after a couple of sessions with him.'

'What relevance does this have to this visit?' He was beginning to grow impatient. Christopher could sometimes be very circuitous. This was becoming an exasperating interruption.

'He has a special interest in chronic pain. Ma Tsien-Zu must have some severe chronic condition maybe back pain, which Dr Woo treats.'

'Maybe he just wants the best around him.'

'Not with Dr Woo. He only treats people he genuinely believes need his skills. He is impervious to pressure.'

'Come on now. I think you are speculating.'

'Edward, I have been practising as a GP until I became state secretary. Trust me I know these things. Could I meet him?'

Edward thought about it. 'Sure, why not? Maybe he can tell you something about Ma.'

Christopher have him a very hard look. 'Edward, first and foremost I am a GP. I would NEVER breach patient confidentiality for political reasons.' He had metamorphosed from an ebullient child into an icy cold monster.

'Sorry, I shouldn't have asked.'

'Indeed. Can I still meet him though?'

'I don't see why not.' Edward's car arrived. Sylvia, who had witnessed this exchange in the background, got in first. 'Thank you.' The car left. Almost as soon as the car got started Edward forgot this conversation. He was far more concerned with the success of the visit.

The rest of the day's ceremonies went without a hitch. The military display at Hyde park was superbly executed and, as the weather held, they were able to use the royal carriages to return to Buckingham Palace. Ma Tsien-Zu observed the whole exercise with polite amusement and made sure he made the correct appreciative noises at the right time. The whole exercise, even if it was for his benefit, bored him stiff. The only thing he really looked forward to, as the keen ornithologist that he was, was the visit to the royal aviary at Kew gardens. The rest of the visit left him quite indifferent. He was pleased to meet with the queen again. He had studied her role and her duties with great detail. The more he knew, the more fascinated he became with her. He wasn't infatuated, just amazed and admiring of her constant composure and dedication to a job that was purely ceremonial; she reigned but she didn't rule.

That evening, after his massage (Dr Woo had insisted) he met up with his nephew for a final update before the talks started. Contrary to popular belief, the heads of state do not get involved in much negotiation. This is left to the ministers with their relevant heads of department as well any experts deemed necessary. They are the ones who are really in the know when it comes down to brass tacks. On this occasion, it would be Helen and Ma-Jing-Tao with their respective teams.

'So nephew, what news do you have for me?'

'Nothing much from China. Your concerns were well justified and my protection services did their job admirably. What do you plan to do with Chung? He is now back in China, no doubt stirring opposition against you.'

Ma's eyes narrowed. 'Yes, Chung and Wang will pay for this insult... eventually. I have made plans to clip Chung's wings What is the situation with regards to the share packages?'

'Very good. We are on track to achieving the desired level of control on time. The banks are still hooked on our loans so when the time comes they will have no option but to do our bidding. I am concerned about this Helen Steele woman though.'

'Why is that?'

'She has a very thorough background in business and economics. I did a few checks on her. She appears to be extremely well connected. I had her shadowed.'

'Was it wise?'

'Bearing in mind, it allowed me to find out that she also took a flight yesterday to Strasbourg where the Franco-German summit was taking place, yes it was. Our people can be very discreet too. She returned within twenty-four hours.'

'What do you suspect they know?'

'We know they are aware of the British shares. I suspect they also know about the airbus linked shares.'

'What about the loans? That will eventually be our best leverage.'

'I'm afraid I can't answer that. It is virtually impossible to find out. We do know their financial system is vulnerable at present. They would need around £100 billion to cover the loans at present.'

'Are all these loans exclusively in Britain?'

Jing-Tao checked his notes. 'No, only around £40 billion. The remaining £60 billion is spread around other European banks.'

'£40 billion is a lot by our standards but they could probably cover it.'

'Not at the moment. It would send their economy in a tailspin. The banks would have to recall a lot of bad debts. Bankruptcies would soar. This government is not in a position to afford such a bad start.'

'Very well, this is what we'll aim for.' They talked for a couple of hours more.

At the same time, Helen and Edward were planning for the same meeting tomorrow. Edward was more nervous than Helen.

'So Helen, how do you think it will go tomorrow?'

'Difficult. They hold a lot of trumps but we now hold more than they had anticipated. It hinges essentially on their attitude.'

'Meaning?'

'If they plan to go for the jugular, we'll struggle badly for the next three years. If they are in a cooperative mood we should get by.'

'I understand the industry minister has returned to China, "indisposed".'

'Yes, this leaves to deal with Ma Jing-Tao. At least he has a better understanding of how the western economy works. On the other hand, with Chung, the industry minister, back in China, they may need to push for a good deal in order to secure the undecided members of the politburo's support; especially if they want Ma Jing-Tao to become premier in twenty years.'

'Yes, I can see that will be an additional factor. Do you want me to be there tomorrow?'

'Thanks but no thanks. If you're there then Ma senior will have to be there too. It would complicate things unnecessarily.'

'I see what you mean. You know better than anyone else how

important this negotiation is. The future of our economy depends on a successful outcome.'

'No pressure then' Helen smiled.

'None whatsoever' he smiled back. 'If at any point you need any backup I'll be at the other end of the phone.'

Helen was back in her car. She was checking Jing-Tao's resume which included a photo. He looked like a pleasant youngish man with modern style glasses. She hoped fervently that he was modern in his approach too. Suddenly she remembered a memo about Rolls Royce which was about three months old. She made a quick phone call.

On Friday morning Edward and Ma Tsien-Zu spent an unsatisfactory morning taking in the London sights. The crowds were sparse, even more so thanks to the persistent drizzle. They made polite conversation via the interpreter. Their thoughts, however, were focused on the offices of the DTI. That's where the real action was happening.

Helen and Ma Jing-Tao met face to face for the first time. She was soberly dressed in a business suit. She wore flat shoes. She didn't want to tower over him. Fortunately he was over an inch taller than she was. He was wearing a dark blue lightweight suit.

'Deputy industry minister, I am very pleased to meet you. I am sorry to hear minister Chung is indisposed. I hope he will make a swift recovery.'

Swifter than you think thought Jing-Tao. He nodded gravely. 'I am pleased to meet you too at last Miss Steele. Thank you for your concerns regarding Minister Chung. I am led to believe he is already recovering.' His accent was a slight mixture of English and North American. 'I understand we share a common alma mater.'

'Do we?'

'We both went to Cambridge.'

'So we did, which college did you go to?'

'Magdalene. And you?'

'New Hall, an all girl college. My parents insisted.'

'Why didn't you go to Girton in Oxford?'

'Not brainy or ugly enough' she replied glibly.

Ma Jing-Tao laughed. It is an ongoing joke in Oxford that, as a woman, you have to be uglier than the gargoyles in the college to be considered for Girton. Helen's quick quip had broken the ice. 'I have my doubts on both counts' he replied gallantly.

Helen was taken aback by the compliment. Good heavens! she thought. Everyone keeps making passes at me lately. Menopause is definitely for me!

'Please call me Helen.'

'Please call me Jing-Tao.'

They were both relieved that there was a natural affinity. First impressions can be critical; in this occasion it was positive on both sides. The negotiations wouldn't stall on a personality clash.

Helen gestured towards her office. They both walked in and took a seat on a sofa in the corner. Patsy walked in behind them.

'Would you like something to drink?'

'Coffee, black no sugar.'

'Same here Patsy.'

They made small talk while their drinks arrived. Once they were on the table and Patsy had left Helen looked at him.

'How would you like to play this? We can either have a big conference table with everyone trying to impress each other and us, or we can sit here thrash out the main points and let the juniors deal with the fine detail while we go out for lunch.'

'Jing-Tao smiled. This was a no-nonsense approach he enjoyed. Committees bored him stiff. There weren't too many of those in China, the top man seeks advice from the experts and then will make a quick decision after consulting the two or three senior members of his organisation. He alone carried the can. In the West the committees were designed to share the blame if the plan didn't work. It usually didn't.

'I would rather we did the latter; on one condition.'

'What might that be?'

'You choose the restaurant and I pay.'

'Anything goes?' Helen had raised her eyebrows speculatively.

'Sure.'

'Very well. Let me sort something out. If you don't mind we'll sit at my desk so we can look at various files on my computer.' She showed him a chair at opposite hers at the desk.

While she was out, he stood up and then sat down. She was back in less than a minute and she sat opposite him. She opened a slim folder.

'If you don't mind Jing-Tao I would like to know what you expect to achieve from this visit. I would then like to make our counterproposal and take it from there.'

Jing-Tao reflected briefly on this and nodded. 'Suits me. As no doubt you are aware, the PRC wants to improve the technological standards in our aeronautical industry. We aim to entirely build passenger planes in China.'

'You already do.'

'Come on Helen, forty year old Tupolevs. They are inefficient and expensive to produce.'

'So you would like to build up to date complete airplanes designed with European technology.'

'This is the general plan, yes.'

'Why should we agree to this? Europe has spent a considerable amount of time and money developing these planes.' Come on, she thought, cut the crap and show your cards.

'In normal circumstances this would be correct. However, as you doubtless are aware, we have now got substantial share packages in all the major industries involved in the airbus consortia. We could ask for this at the next AGM.' He tried not to look too smug.

'This request would, of course be supported by major bank shareholders where you also have shares in as well as having lent them major short term loans at 4% interest to the tune of' she made a big show of checking her notes '£ 100 billion.' She paused briefly allowing the latest disclosure to sink in, she could see this had rattled him. 'These loans are on a tthree month rolling basis. You can recall them in part or fully with a two-week notice. Please feel free to stop me if there are any factual inaccuracies.' She added smiling sweetly. 'I am also aware that you know about my unexpected meeting with Angela Merkel and Nicholas Sarkozy three days ago.'

Jing-tao was feeling a lot less smug now. Years of careful secret planning and investment had been brutally exposed with a few choice phrases. He suspected that by now, he didn't hold all the aces. 'How did you find out?' he asked weakly.

'Come on Jing-Tao, we do have our own checking systems. The takeover of the consortia a few weeks ago merely confirmed them. It was unfortunate for you that, having spent a considerable number of years working in finance and banking, I developed an extensive network of contacts on both sides of the Atlantic. They provided me a lot of information far more quickly than if I had gone through the normal channels. When we found out you had arrived earlier than anticipated we decided to monitor all your spooks even more closely. While they followed me on Monday night, they were being tailed themselves.'

Jing-Tao started laughing. 'Enough, enough! This is beginning to sound like a bad James Bond movie: 0017'5% with a licence to check!'

'Indeed, we have checked things and taken some countermeasures.'

'What countermeasures?'

Helen passed a single sheet of paper across the table. This is a promissory note from the chairman of the ECB; he was secretly in Strasbourg too by the way, for £ 60 billion to become available by the end of July. We have already pledged additional money as have other countries. This would cover a most of your loans. The terms wouldn't be as generous but the banks would survive.'

Jing-Tao read the document carefully. This certainly wiped a large chunk of his advantage. 'We still have the shares though.'

'Indeed you do. However, we have alerted all the companies involved as well as all the relevant financial market authorities. You will find it has become much harder to purchase shares.'

'You don't pull your punches do you?'

'No we don't. Now that we have all laid our cards on the table, perhaps we can start negotiating from a revised perspective.'

Jing-Tao nodded and smiled. He had personally expected hand wringing and veiled threats mixed with appeals to cooperation, instead he was facing a formidable opponent. His uncle, on the other hand, had envisaged this alternative possibility last night. Ma senior had felt this was a good thing. For the first time they were being treated seriously, they had forced the entire EU, the world's largest economy, to pool resources and present a united front. This was a major shift in the balance of power. It would look good among the establishment back home.

'Bearing in mind the revised financial position Helen, what are you prepared to offer?'

'Cooperation, in a never before seen scale. This cooperation would bring major benefits to both economies while creating long term protection of everyone's interests.'

This was more like it he thought. 'Please continue.'

'Let's have some clear facts to start with. China is the world's second largest economy after the US. Despite this, your average citizen is worse off than the average Albanian, and they are the poorest country in Europe. Our impression is that premier Ma wants to change this in the long term. Your industry and agriculture are inefficient. There are huge wealth disparities across China. Your CO2 output is excessive, you are considered the worst polluting country at present. We can help you with this, we have the know-how. We have done it in Europe. Our industrial output is among the most efficient, our CO2 emissions, if not actually growing at least are remaining static. We've had very poor countries such as Portugal and Ireland join the EU, not any more so we can help you raise the overall standard of living throughout; concentrating in the poorest regions first and creating a steady homogenous growth eventually.'

Jing-Tao thought long and hard about what she was saying. She was right of course. Some rural areas in China were complete disaster zones, no running water or electricity, endemic malnutrition. It was hard to hear nevertheless. 'What about airplane production?' he said returning to the main point.

'I was just coming to that. We know China's internal flight market is expanding enormously. You have already laid plans for a large number of new or expanded airports. You still need the planes though. These are expensive. What we suggest, and this would be acceptable to all the participants in airbus, is a gradual increase in parts manufacturing. You produce these parts and in exchange we supply you with other parts. Final plane construction remains in Toulouse though. We could create a separate factory within the complex where you could do the assembly using Chinese technicians and engineers. You would agree to a set number of units built per annum. All the construction would be, at least initially, supervised by airbus engineers. Your shares would, of course, entitle you to a part of the profits and you would be invited to be involved in the development of new aircraft.'

'Which part of the aircraft?'

'We could offer a section of the fuselage gradually building up to the whole fuselage. Quality control would remain under our control for at least 5 years until we were satisfied about consistency in the quality. We would have a twenty year agreement on production levels and there after you could increase production of your parts for internal consumption. All export profits and volume of production are controlled by the board.'

'What about the wings?' He knew this was the crucial element.

'Non-negotiable I'm afraid. Airbus have firmly stated they are the critical element in the plane. Production and design remains in our hands.' There was a finality in Helen's tone that made it clear to Jing-Tao there was no point in pursuing this. He nevertheless pushed for it.

'You are still trying to keep us down!'

'No we are not. That's the way airbus operates. If it's good enough for Europe it should be good enough for China. Think about it, this is a good deal, we offer to share future development and current technology. Eventually your engineers will be in a position to develop and build your own planes.'

'Surely not. You wouldn't create the basis for long term unemployment now?'

'It may cause some problems in the future but this will give us breathing space to think of something. We are reasonably resourceful at reinventing ourselves.'

'And then we'll try to copy it!'

'Not necessarily. Once your country is up to date, chances are you will start developing your own technologies. Maybe *we* will be knocking at your door.'

'Maybe you will. What about Rolls Royce?'

'What about it?'

'Rolls Royce is not part of airbus. Aero engines are added according to each airline specification am I right?'

Helen felt slightly cornered. She had hoped that she could gloss over that issue but Jing-Tao was not going to let her. 'I suppose we could work on the same lines as with airbus.'

'I think the rules are different Helen.' He wasn't being threatening but he wasn't going to be pushed around either.

They argued the toss for a couple of hours more. Some of the additional technology and support offered was more than Jing-Tao had anticipated but the aero engines issue remained. Eventually they decided to park it. They wrote together an outline trade and industry agreement proposal and summoned their senior deputies. They gave instructions on the main expected outcomes.

'Right' said Helen, 'time for lunch.'

'Where are we going?'

'It depends on one thing. Are you a vegetarian?'

'No, few Chinese are.'

'In that case I hope you enjoy traditional English food.'

'You're not taking me to the local chippie are you?' He feigned mock horror.

'I was thinking something slightly more upmarket and traditional.'

'In that case, yes, I do enjoy traditional English fare.'

They got into Helen's car. She gave an address to her driver. Eventually they stopped in front of an old fashioned doorway in a narrow street in Covent Garden. Helen looked up. 'We've arrived.'

They both got out. Her bodyguard got out too and the car left.

'Where are we?' He didn't recognise the location even though he had spent many a time in the Chinese quarter nearby.

'This is Rules, London's oldest restaurant. My parents used to take me as a treat quite often. I developed my carnivorous tastes here!'

They walked in. Jing-Tao looked around in amazement. It was like stepping into a 40s movie. The plush red velvet banquettes, the old photographs of long gone celebrities as well as old prints from The Lady, Horse and Hound and the Spectator. A rather decrepit looking Maitre d' approached them. His initial disdainful countenance broke into a smile when he recognised one of his guests. 'Miss Steele! how delightful to see you. It's been a long time.'

'Thank you Mr Jones. I believe I have a reservation for the private dining room for two.'

Mr Jones checked in his reservation book. 'Indeed you do.' He looked up and raised a hand slightly; a young waiter dressed in traditional white shirt, black waistcoat, bow tie and white half apron glided towards them.

'Yes Mister Jones.'

'Robert, kindly escort Miss Steele and her guest to the upstairs dining room.'

'Certainly Mister Jones. This way please Miss Steele.' He turned round, picked up two menus and a wine list and walked past some of the front tables. He turned right and went up a flight of steps. He turned right and opened a door. A table for two had been laid in the room. The pristine white linen cloth was covered with old fashioned table ware. Either side of the table were two comfortable carver chairs.

'Would either of you like an aperitif?'

Helen looked at Jing-Tao, he made a non-committal gesture. 'No thank you.' They both sat down.

Robert presented both menus with a flourish, all part of the mystique of dining at Rules. 'Very well, I will return shortly to take your order.'

'I thought taking you to a Chinese restaurant might be a bit like a busman's holiday, not to mention it might be perceived as an insult.'

'Indeed.'

There was a brief silence as they both studied their menus. After some advice from Helen they settled for roast beef with all the trimmings. They both decided against a starter. It wouldn't do to fall asleep afterwards in the middle of a negotiation! They did agree on a half bottle of Chateaux Margaux, it would have been criminal to have an enjoyable meal without a decent wine to wash it down with.

They chatted amiably about their experiences in Cambridge and the different attitudes to a variety of issues in the period they had been there –Helen was ten years Jing-Tao's senior in graduating from Cambridge-. They ate their meal with great enjoyment and decided to round it with a proper pudding. Helen groaned inwardly at the thought of amount of lengths she would have to swim to burn such a rich meal.

'Speaking of differences through the ages' Helen asked, 'how different is China now compared to say fifteen years ago?'

Jing-Tao gave the loaded question a lot of careful consideration. 'It certainly has changed. The most remarkable evolution has occurred in the major cities. Shanghai is a prime example. Most parts of it are virtually undistinguishable from any western city. Except for the inhabitants of course.'

'What about the countryside, the farmers and peasants?'

'As you pointed out earlier on, there are large pockets of backwardness, deprivation even, but we have identified this already. We hope that some of your suggestions on how to use convergence funds as the EU does will help to reduce the inequality.'

'What about the younger generation the university students the teenagers, are they accepting the current status quo?'

'I'm not sure that I follow.'

'Well, I know Google made a deal with the Chinese government to allow the setting up of their search engine in China, there were strings attached though. Some websites of a more, shall we say political nature, among others were barred automatically. I understand the younger, internet savvy generation didn't take to this kindly.'

'There were some minor protests' Jing-Tao replied guardedly. What was she trying to get at?

'Does that worry you?'

'Not a lot. In China we are more comfortable with the concept of a strong ruler than the westerners are. Some people grumble about this, so what?'

'Do you think you can preserve this situation forever?'

'Probably not. However, we still control most power levers so the status quo will be preserved for many years to come.' He was sounding a bit tetchy now.

Helen decided to probe a bit further. Taking him to Rules and giving him a rich meal had lowered his defences. It was time to explore a possible breach.

'If you were younger, had all the educational advantages you have but weren't a party member with the associated sinecures, how would you feel?'

'Probably frustrated.'

'I understand that you have sensed this and you are allowing smaller state-owned company workers to dictate policy to some extent.'

'Yes' he said curtly. 'Helen, what are you trying to get at?'

'Nothing, just a bit of after dinner chit-chat' she tried to look innocent and affronted but failed.

'Helen' he said gently, 'I thought that from the outset we had decided to cut the bullshit.'

'Sorry, you are right. To be frank, since all this started we have analysed loads of data emanating from China. The changes in the CC of the CPC give us the impression that you are moving slowly towards a more open plural government, allowing the expression of different points of view without retribution. It would be wonderful if it happened. There is always an element of worry with the consequences of an unbalanced person in charge of a country like China.'

Jing-Tao leant forward. 'What I'm about to say stays in this room. Do I have your word?'

'You have my word.' They shook hands on it at Jing-Tao's insistence. He knew that simple gesture would constrain Helen more than any legal agreement. He hadn't spent all his time studying economics, he had also analysed what made people tick.

'If these negotiations are successful, my uncle's position in the politburo will become greatly reinforced. This will allow him to effect major changes in the CC within twelve months, promoting even more open minded party members.'

'We had noticed an increase of these already.'

'After he retires, he would allow his successor to hold open local elections to choose CC members as well as local government officials. They would all have to be party members of course; the difference is that they would come from different wings of the party, without fear of interference from above.'

'Not quite the multiparty democracy we envisaged.'

He looked at her with irritation. 'Helen, we are a very old country with long held traditions and views. The last time we tried democracy it was a disaster which led to warlords and civil war not to mention a savage Japanese occupation as they took advantage of our weakness.'

'You're right, sorry.'

'Hopefully within ten-fifteen years we will create three political parties with defined ideology with the CPC holding the centrist position a right wing and a left wing party. There will be national elections.'

'Not local?'

Jing-tao shook his head, 'never, it would only encourage local party leaders to extend their power base. There will be no more potential warlords. Eventually, if the experience is a success, we will gradually open the political spectrum. There will be no regional parties allowed though.'

'To prevent warlords.' It wasn't a question, more a statement.

'Exactly. Hopefully, in twenty-five years time we will have a normal multiparty democracy.'

'It's a long time.'

'Chinese people are very patient if the wait is worth it.'

'Didn't Leopold Senghor from Senegal do something similar in the 80s?'

'Very good Miss Steele, I *am* officially impressed.'

Robert brought their desserts. They ate in silence. Both were analysing the conversation. Helen was amazed by Jing-Tao's frankness, not as amazed as he'd been. He had fallen into a Chung-style trap but he felt that it would predispose the British government to support China in the time to come.

As agreed, he paid the bill. Before they left, he turned to Helen: 'please remember, this was a strictly confidential conversation. If anything leaks out it would cause untold grief and delay developments for at least twenty years.'

'You have my word.' This time *she* offered her hand which he shook relieved.

They got into the car and travelled in silence back to the DTI. Once there they met with the joint working committee (their meal had consisted of some unappetizing curled up sandwiches; the DTI accountants didn't believe in lavish spending on entertainment!). Their outlined plan had only needed very minor adjustments from the point of view of finance and timetables. There was only one major sticking point: Rolls Royce. The British delegation weren't prepared to give full control of production; the Chinese weren't going to resign themselves to being yet another cog in the production line. Helen and Jing-Tao co-chaired the rest of the meeting. They concentrated on finalising the agreement with the exception of the aero engines. A codicil was added reluctantly by both parts stating that this issue should be subject to a further review in two years time.

Thet evening, Ma Jing-Tao met with his uncle and the senior members of the Chinese delegation. They all studied the redrafted document carefully. Eventually Ma Tsien-Zu gave his veredict.

'Not a bad result deputy industry minister. We have achieved a large number of objectives without needing any confrontation. I would have preferred a shorter schedule.'

'We managed to reduce it by twelve months premier Ma.'

'It's a shame we have not obtained full ownership of aeronautical technology now. At least we should have pressed for the Rolls Royce engines.'

'It was the only major sticking point. The British were very inflexible about it. The Rolls Royce aero engines are linked to Spitfires and Concorde. They became very...emotional about it; a matter of national pride. I felt it prudent not to push the matter today and use that concession to extract more favourable timetables.'

'I see. Could we not use our financial muscle?'

'Bearing in mind they now have major financial backing from the EU, it could create a major economic war. I wasn't sure we had enough resources to follow it through, especially if the USA became involved.'

'Yes, they do like to poke their noses every where. I'm meeting tomorrow with their prime minister, maybe I can convince him.'

Helen, Edward, Harold and John were poring over the same document.

'This looks good Helen' said Edward, 'you fought your corner very well.' There was sincere admiration in his voice.

'Thank you.' She felt exhausted. It had been a very long day. Ma-Jing-Tao's revelations had made her very ambivalent about the negotiation. Few people realised she had a very idealistic streak. She felt the possibility of establishing democracy in China could be worth sharing Rolls Royce. She knew, though, this could only be approved at cabinet level or by Edward and his cabal. She still hoped this would suffice to further Ma-TsienZu's plans. 'There's still a major sticking point though.'

'Yes, Rolls Royce. Losing that would cost us dear. I'm meeting with Ma tomorrow. No doubt he'll chew my ear on the issue' he smiled.

'He has his agenda.'

'Don't we all. Listen, no disrespect but you looked positively knackered. You must get a good night's sleep before tomorrow.'

'You're right'. She yawned 'excuse me.'

They all left. On her way home, Helen made a note in his diary to make an important phone call tomorrow.

Chapter 13

By Saturday morning, Buckingham Palace was a veritable beehive of activity. All available staff had been rounded up and put on extended shifts. There wasn't a single corner or crevice which hadn't been scrupulously cleaned and inspected. Everything sparkled or glistened. The weather was overcast and the muggy atmosphere didn't help so by lunchtime tempers were beginning to fray and sniping and snapping were in the order of the day.

Barry was enjoying a shortened cigarette break in the now familiar courtyard. He was trying to get some fresh air but the weather wasn't obliging. He felt hot and sweaty and would have gladly traded all the cigarettes of the day in exchange for a shower now. He was in his shirtsleeves, sitting on the steps into the kitchen; a cigarette in one hand, a can of fizzy drink in the other. Melanie was sitting next to him looking no better. They had both been given a later start since they were on night duty but after three hours hard graft, they were as tired as the earlier starting staff; and they still had to work late at the state banquet.

'Is it always like this quota?'

'Piss off you tosser! I've told you a thousand times not to call me that' she replied irritably. Melanie was particularly tetchy today; she had period pains and felt bloated and irritable. The muggy weather combined with the repetitive hard work and constant scrutiny was beginning to get on her nerves.

'Sorry Mel.' He too was irritable but felt a row would do them no good. 'Is it always like this?'

'What do you mean?'

'Everybody is flogged to death for a dinner.'

'I have to admit it is more intense that usual. The bosses are all on edge. I even saw Lord Carruthers poking his nose about earlier; something I've never seen before.'

'SMITH! HATTON!! WHAT THE HELL DO YOU THINK YOU'RE DOING?'

Their musings had been interrupted by the towering figure of "Psycho". They both jumped to attention even if in Barry's case the effect was spoiled by the cigarette dangling from the corner of his mouth!

Melanie spoke. 'I'm very sorry Mr O'Malley but we were given a short break.'

'All breaks have been cancelled until teatime. And pull that fucking cigarette out of your mouth you fucker! The smoking ban starts this midnight so you'd bloody well start getting used to it NOW!'

Never had been "Psycho's" nickname more deserved. His shaven head was shining with perspiration, a rivulet of sweat coursed down his left temple and the corners of his mouth were flecked with white spittle. His face, an unhealthy shade of puce was contorted in an expression of pure evil malevolence. The eye patch merely added more horror to the whole tableaux; anybody crossing him today would regret it for the rest of their lives. His rage abated a couple of notches. 'Everyone on duty tonight has to go to the banquet hall. We're rehearsing again.' He waited for any expressions of discontent; there were none. Mel and Barry knew any protests would give them the life expectancy of a snowflake in hell!

'As you say Mr O'Malley.' Barry extinguished his cigarette and carefully disposed of it.

All the evening staff trooped into the banqueting hall. They rehearsed thrice under "Psycho's" beady eye. After three rehearsals he pronounced himself satisfied which was just as well since most of the staff were about to collapse with heat exhaustion in that cauldron of a room. They returned to the servant's common room. On a large table there were two large metal tanks with cold beer and soft drinks. Nobody touched them until instructed to do so by a more genial "Psycho"

'Help yourselves, only one beer though, we don't want you pissed and tipping the soup over the guests do we? He thought the team deserved it. The whole rehearsal had gone without a hitch. They had worked seamlessly as a team without a problem. There would be no problems tonight. He left them to have some R + R and went to Conn's office to update him.

'Good afternoon Patrick. Any problems?' Sir Ian was checking the final details at his desk.

'None that I know of Sir Ian. We have just completed the last rehearsals and everything went without a hitch. I thought we'd let the night shift have a good rest before the evening starts, a shower and all that.'

'It sounds like a good idea.'

'Sir Ian?'

He looked up from his papers. 'Yes Patrick?'

'Should we tell them how important this visit is?'

Sir Ian had been wondering about this very issue earlier on. 'No, I think they already are under enough pressure. It would only add to their natural nervousness.'

'Very well' he turned round to leave.

'Patrick, I know you have performed a miracle of training; you have managed to get a bunch of raw staff ready in record time. Everyone at the Lord Chancellor's committee is very grateful.'

Patrick beamed with pleasure. 'Thank you very much Sir Ian.' He paused for a second but Sir Ian had buried himself in the paperwork again. 'I best be leaving then.'

'Good bye.'

Sir Ian went through the paperwork and staff schedules once more. Everything seemed to be in order. And yet, and yet, there was something gnawing at the back of his mind. Some minute detail which might turn out to be important later. He sighed and gave up. Perhaps he was nervous because this was his last gig, a very big one. His successor had just been appointed. He was due to start in August as he was serving his notice. Fortunately, with the queen in Balmoral, business would be slack and he would have time to adjust to the new role.

Edward and Ma Tsien-Zu had spent a rather boring day in Portsmouth. It had only improved after an improvised detour to a bird sanctuary nearby. That had been the highlight of his visit so far. They returned by helicopter and they were now enjoying a late luncheon at number 10. The interpreter was there too.

(For the sake of narrative fluidity, let's pretend the conversation proceeded uninterrupted. Thank you readers for suspending your disbelief!)

'I have read the proposed treaty Miss Steele and Ma Jing-Tao have drafted. It appears to be quite reasonable except for one point.'

Edward braced himself. 'What would that be?'

'We are still restricted to building parts; under supervision. We aren't involved in building an essential component from the beginning to the end.'

'I appreciate your point of view Premier Ma; however, airbus planes are built this way. Different countries build the various parts which are finally assembled in France. We are committed to letting you build the whole plane in the Toulouse plant within five years. You are very much aware that learning to build planes which are consistently safe and reliable is not something you learn in a two week training course. This is an arrangement which took our European partners and ourselves a long time to agree upon.'

'Indeed, but what about the engines? They aren't part of the plane. They are retrofitted according to each airline's specification. We are entitled to build these engines to supply our planes. Between these four walls; I am the first to acknowledge that at present we do not posses sufficient expertise, but we are fast learners. A quota system like the airbus one could be implemented.'

'Your points are valid but hard for us to concede. The airbus agreement supposes a sacrifice for the country. We had to make major political and financial concessions in order to get an international agreement regarding this offer. Moreover, Rolls Royce aero carries very emotional connotations in this country. As a government we wouldn't be able to survive such a concession; the next government may not be as accommodating as we are.' There was a hint of threat hanging at the end of those words.

'I see, maybe we could discuss this on Monday.'

'Indeed we could but I find it difficult to see how circumstances would change in such a short period of time.'

The meal finished amicably enough. There were no hard feelings. Both men were pressing their suit as hard as they could. At the end, they both bid farewell until dinner time.

It was later in the evening. The queen was applying the final touches to her evening dress. She examined herself in a full-length mirror and nodded approvingly. She felt extremely tired. Her day had been crammed with engagements. She had also rehearsed her after dinner speech. Her eighty-one years weighed heavily for once. All she really wanted was to slide under her bed covers with a mug of hot cocoa and let sleep sweetly overcome her. 'Come on' she said to herself. 'You knew perfectly well what you were getting yourself into when you accepted the job.' There was a knock at the door; the corgis remained silent; they knew who it was.

Prince Phillip walked in, wearing a full Admiral of the Fleet uniform. It had been considered appropriate, after the naval incident, that he attired himself like this. He could convey a discreet further apology wearing the correct regalia. He wasn't happy about it but his wife was his immediate superior so he was prepared to obey his orders. The queen looked at him admiringly; he still looked so handsome after all these years.

'Hi Lillibet, you look grand as usual' he said gruffly.

'Hello Phillip, you look dashing as ever.' She came close and flicked a small piece of lint from his uniform.

He kissed her gently on the cheek and, as if it were their first date, gallantly offered her his arm. 'Once more into the breach my friends, once more!' He could sense his wife's tiredness and was prepared to offer her all his support. They walked slowly down the staircase where most of the other dignitaries as well as the press photographers had assembled.

Ma Tsien-Zu was alone in a car on his way to the palace. He was becoming increasingly angry. There had been an inexplicable delay in leaving the embassy and he was running late. He rapped the partition glass and ordered his driver to go faster. He hated unpunctuality. He was also feeling uncomfortable in his white tie eveningwear. The Mao jacket did have its advantages but it was not an alternative. He noticed his right shoelace was undone and bent over to tie it up. As he did this, the car lurched as it hit a speed bump well over the recommended pace. He almost fell onto the floor. He avoided this by grabbing on to the door handle. As he did this he jarred his back. He felt a massive spasm of pain course down his spine. He barely managed to contain a howl of pain. The security officer in the front seat turned round to ask if everything was OK. Ma replied curtly that it was and advised the driver to watch for speed bumps. God almighty! His back was killing him. He opened his cigarette case and extracted a red-dotted one. He lowered the window and lit up. He inhaled deeply, allowing the drug to act. After a few seconds the severe spasm had abated slightly. He smoked fast, trying to get the morphine levels up as quickly as possible. As the car advanced down the Mall he did some gentle back stretching exercises while sitting down. These had been advised to him by Dr Woo hence his reluctance to have passengers in the back seat with him. The driver asked through the intercom:

'Is everything all right premier Ma?'

'Yes, everything is fine. Concentrate on your driving' he replied brusquely. He lowered the window further to air himself better. It wouldn't do if he arrived reeking of opium laced cigarette smoke!

'We're nearly there premier Ma.' A few hundred yards away, Buckingham palace glowed in the late evening light. It was an impressive view even for someone as blasé as Ma.

The limousine drew to a halt, immediately his door was opened by a bowing footman. He managed to get out without too much pain and, accompanied by Sir Hugh, walked stiffly up the stairs towards the main hall where the queen and other guests awaited him.

As he walked through the door he was guided by Sir Hugh towards the queen and prince Phillip. They proceeded to meet the more distinguished guest with the queen performing the introductions.

Christopher Ward and his wife were watching the whole procedure with undisguised interest. It was their first formal visit to the palace after all. He noticed Ma's stiff gait and the intermittent clenching of the jaw. He had managed to meet Dr Woo and spent a most enjoyable evening discussing the latest advances in chronic pain management with traditional Chinese medicine. Dr Woo had discussed Ma's case, it was a given that confidentiality would be observed at all times. Eventually they were introduced to Ma Tsien-Zu. He murmured some platitude; he was more interested in watching the "patient". He noticed his pupils were extremely narrow and wondered if he had taken any opiates. As soon as the party moved he approached the Lord Chamberlain.

'Lord Carruthers.'

'Yes Dr Ward?' They had met once when the whole government had been introduced to the queen.

'I have a strong suspicion that premier Ma is in severe discomfort. I think his back is giving him a lot of pain.'

Lord Carruthers looked at the guest of honour; he couldn't help noticing his somewhat stiff gait . 'I wasn't aware of this.'

'I think it would make his life a lot easier if his chair were raised one or two inches. It would make his sitting down and standing up easier.'

'This could be difficult. I don't mean to be rude Dr Ward but are you sure of this?' He wasn't being condescending, merely cautious.

'Trust me my lord; I am a GP with a special interest in chronic back pain. This man *is* in a lot of pain.'

'I'll see what I can do.' He drew a footman's attention and explained the situation. After a few moments he managed to inform the queen who merely nodded.

Half an hour later, the guests were invited to the banqueting hall. Ma Tsien-Zu walked with the queen while prince Phillip walked with the Chinese ambassador's wife. Ma-Jing-Tao walked with them. The queen whispered to Ma senior. 'I understand you have some back discomfort. We have made some alterations to the height of your chair.' She didn't offer any painkillers, it would have been an unbelievable solecism.

When they reached their allocated seats, Ma looked at his. It had a couple of cushions hastily tied to the back of the chair. He sat down after the queen; it was better than he had anticipated, even if it meant he was sitting taller than most people. He turned to the queen. 'Thank you very much' he said in heavily accented English.

The meal proceeded smoothly. Due to the late start, it was a very light meal: Vichyssoise followed by poached salmon and new potatoes salad (both from the queen's estate) and Tournedos Rossini with a rocket salad. Dessert was a raspberry fool. There was lovely chilled Chablis for starters and a good 2001 Rioja for the meat. Barry was serving at the lower end of the table. He didn't stray from his allocated route and yet, because it was a smallish, (by Buckingham palace standards) state banquet, he managed to take some pictures with his special ring.

Once the pudding plates had been removed the queen stood up for the traditional welcome speech. There was nothing controversial and she included references to the Olympics which were due in Beijing next year as well as the tenth anniversary of the handover of Hong Kong. She also reminisced briefly about her first meeting with Ma Tsien-Zu over twenty years ago. This raised a few smiles as some of the old hands remembered one of prince Phillip's most widely broadcast politically incorrect gaffes.

Ma stood up with some difficulty. Aided by his translator he replied with similar diplomatic platitudes adding a wish that the queen visit him next year for the Beijing Olympics adding that it was not good when two friends didn't see each other for over twenty years! As he sat down he felt another spasm of pain. The effect of the morphine cigarette was wearing off. He was beginning to regret his request for an informal chat.

Barry was about to leave the banqueting hall when a tap on his shoulder made him turn. "Psycho" glowered at him. 'You're still on duty' he murmured.

'No I'm no.' Barry murmured back. He was tired and in an argumentative mood. He was due to meet with Pippa and her friends at a night bar as a compromise for his no-show for dinner. It had taken him a long time to convince her and now his carefully laid down plans were coming down in flames.

'You are now. Jeremy's only gone and twisted his ankle the stupid sod. He was pencilled in to attend to the queen's after dinner party. You'll have to do. Cheer up! We'll pay you for the extra time.'

Barry was secretly delighted; this was a unique opportunity to take some close-up photos of the queen and her guest. Maybe they might become more relaxed and say or do something worth reporting. He put on his best sulky face; 'Oh all right, I'll do it.'

'That's the spirit.'

'He entered the small antechamber known as the Blue room. It was ready to receive the guests. He took some photographs to adjust for light and distance. He checked them on his mobile phone; picture perfect! There was also an email in his blackberry from Pippa demanding he tell her of his whereabouts. He decided to ignore it. He had some far bigger fish to fry.

Five minutes later the queen walked into the Blue room. Ma-Tsien-Zu walked by her. They were followed by Prince Phillip and Sylvia Faulkner, who was enjoying herself enormously and Edward, Christopher, Ma Jing-Tao and Sir Hugh, bringing up the rest of the party.

Ma senior sat with some difficulty that was apparent to the other guests. His back spasms, like the contractions of labour were becoming more frequent and intense. He was dreading the time when he would have to get up. His eyes took in the décor of the room, not a patch on the imperial palace he thought. His gaze rested on the coffee table where a big porcelain square ashtray lay. This ashtray was there because of tradition. King George VI had been an inveterate heavy smoker; it killed him in the end. He had used the Blue room as a smoking place before and after state banquets. Princess Margaret, another heavy nicotine addict had used the room too, for exactly the same purpose. In Buckingham palace's finest tradition it was now a given that there would always be an ashtray on the coffee table in the Blue room. Ma Tsien-Zu took his cigarette case out and looked enquiringly, at the queen. Ma Jing-Tao took the cue and with elaborate courtesy asked the queen:

'If it pleases your majesty, premier Ma would like to smoke his traditional postprandial cigarette. He does know it is bad for his health though!' The last comment was light hearted, intended to defuse any potential conflict. He knew his uncle was in pain and what he needed was urgent relief.

The queen nodded. 'Please do premier Ma.' She thought nothing of it. All her life heavy smokers had surrounded her; she didn't smoke herself, nor for that matter, did any of her children, but she was aware of the obligations of any hostess to make their guests comfortable, especially this one.

Ma selected his last red dotted cigarette. He offered the others to his fellow guests but nobody took him up. He lit up with a mixture of contentment and relief. He inhaled deeply and held the smoke in for as long as he could. He exhaled. Within seconds the morphine started to exert its effects. That alone eased his anxiety and therefore his pain. He instructed his nephew in a mutter to arrange for Dr Woo to be ready for him in when they returned.

At this point, two things happened: the clock in the mantelpiece started to strike the quarters followed by twelve gongs, there was a knock at the door too. Barry was next to it and he opened it. It was Archie, carrying a tray laden with a coffee pot and milk jugs. Archie smiled as the last chime sounded. 'Whoopee' he murmured with a smile, 'it's after midnight on a Sunday, double pay time!'

Behind Archie, Barry could see "Psycho" glowering. Barry looked at them and then turned round to look at the small party sitting round the table. A few seconds ago he had looked enviously as Ma inhaled. Now he saw a man smoking a cigarette, in a public space, inside Buckingham palace, on July the 1st. The start of the smoking ban! Yippee and hurray! He had just hit the jackpot. He grabbed the tray from a slightly surprised Archie and moved fast towards the table. As he walked he ensured his ring was positioned correctly. He deposited the tray and bowed. Ma obligingly exhaled as he gave a little cough and the picture was taken. He then moved towards a side table where coffee cups were on another tray. He walked back and was joined by a mystified Archie. He managed a couple of photographs with Ma holding the cigarette in his hand smiling. He and Archie served coffee and milk as the guests wished. He walked back and as he withdrew he managed to take a photo of the whole group, with a smiling Ma Tsien-Zu in the middle, breaking the law. Both footmen resumed their positions either side of the door. Barry turned to Archie and muttered 'I really need to go to the bog.'

From the corner of his mouth Archie replied: 'there's a loo on the opposite side of the banqueting hall. It's hidden behind some curtains. Hurry up!'

Barry slid quietly outside and closed the door very gently. He rushed across the room towards the toilet. Several maids and footmen looked on with surprise. He reached the door and let himself in. Mercifully it was empty. He locked the door from the inside and rang Jock.

'What do you want?'

'Jock, I never thought I'd say this but: stop the press!' He derived some childish satisfaction from uttering this cliché!

'Are you nuts? We're about to roll, we're late as it is!'

'Jock, believe me, this is worth it. I have the scoop of the decade.'

'Yeah, right!'

'I've got a photograph of premier Ma, from the PRC smoking a cigarette in the Blue room of Buckingham palace!'

'So bloody what!'

Barry couldn't believe Jock could sometimes be so obtuse. 'Jock, it's now July the 1st, the smoking ban started a few minutes ago.'

'But it doesn't apply to private residences you moron!' Jock didn't want to look like a fool, he was salivating with excitement but needed complete reassurance that it wouldn't backfire.

'Only the Royal Apartments in the first floor count as private residence. The whole of the ground floor is a public working space. Before you ask Jock, yes, I'm positive this is the case.'

'Wait a second.'

Barry could hear Jock barking instructions on the other phone. He always spent Saturday evening in the Daily Herald as it prepared for the Sunday edition.

'Right, send them to me.'

Barry seized the moment. 'What about my request?'

'What request?'

'My moving to the international or national section of the paper? This will blow my cover.'

'Yeah, all right.'

'I need written confirmation, send an e-mail to my blackberry.'

Barry knew what a slippery customer Jock could be.

'You bastard, send me the fucking photographs!'

'Indeed I will, after I have an e-mail!'

There was a clang as Jock put the phone down. He could hear him typing and in less than a minute his blackberry buzzed. He checked the incoming mail, Jock had promised a three month probationary period in the national desk. This was good enough for him. He located Jock's e-mail in his phone and sent two pictures, he kept three others for insurance, he would try and flog them tomorrow. 'I do want joint authorship by the way, your word will suffice.'

'Agreed. Get your ass over here ASAP.'

Suddenly there was a bang at the toilet door. Barry pocketed his phone and his blackberry and then he flushed the chain before opening the door. "Psycho" glared at him.

'Where the hell have you been?'

'Sorry Mr O'Malley, he rubbed his stomach, gippy tummy.'

'I don't care! Get back in there now,'

Barry rushed back. He slid in quietly, his short absence unnoticed; he smiled at Archie and winked. He nodded back. Barry walked again towards the table and poured some more coffee while managing to take a couple more photographs just as Ma exhaled as he extinguished his cigarette.

Christopher smelled the cigarette smoke, it was quite unpleasant but he remembered smelling it before; he couldn't for the life of him remember where. Meanwhile, the conversation was flowing smoothly enough. They had started by reminiscing about the queen's first visit to China, Ma then asked why did everyone wear red flowers in November. He already knew the answer but it kept the conversation flowing.

'Oh you mean red poppy day' said the queen.

Poppies that was it! He was smoking opium, morphine to be precise. Christopher remembered where he had smelled that scent before. It was while working in Toxteth as a GP, many years ago. One of his patients was a hopeless heroin addict. All his veins were shot so he resorted to smoking it. He was a poor wretch, pleasant enough and always polite even when he tried to nick his prescription pad! He had eventually died of AIDS and malnutrition.

'.. so on November the 11th we always present a wreath of red poppies at the cenotaph. It is a very moving ceremony, one of my favourites even if it always fills me with sadness' the queen concluded.

The conversation moved on to next year's Olympic Games and China and Britain's perspectives. There was some gentle banter and Ma Tsien-Zu reiterated his invitation for the queen to visit them. After all, he said, princess Zara had a good chance of representing her country in the equestrian competition. What grandmother would miss the chance to see this live? This caused general merriment. Ma checked his watch; it was gone half past midnight. His back felt a lot less painful and tiredness was beginning to overcome him. He suspected the queen was very tired too.

'With her majesty's permission, I would like to retire. It has been a long day and I am feeling a bit tired.' He spoke in English for the first time. He felt it was the least courtesy he could convey.

The queen smiled and nodded. 'Certainly Premier Ma. May I congratulate you on your English? I didn't know you could speak it so well!'

Ma merely smiled and nodded. Around him people looked puzzled. This was unexpected! Ma Jing-Tao was astonished in fact. It was unprecedented for his uncle to show his cards this way, this could only be for the queen's benefit. Silly old fool!

They all left the Blue room, leaving Archie and Barry to tidy up. Psycho walked in.

'You' he said pointing at Barry, 'never, ever leave a footman alone with guests!'

'We had just served coffee' Barry protested.

'I don't care, you know the rules, if you don't like them, there's the door!'

Barry had been given another golden opportunity, he seized it yet again. 'You know what Mr O'Malley? I think I just might do that. He pulled a bit of paper and a pen and started writing. He gave it to "Psycho" 'There you have it, my resignation. Because I am still on probation as you doubtless remember, my notice period is only two weeks which coincide with my annual leave. I was due to re-start on July the 15th but not any more. Bye Archie, it was nice meeting you.' He left the room quickly before anybody had time to react.

Patrick read the note. It was signed and dated and stated that it had been witnessed by Archie. He shook his head. 'And he showed such promise.' He shrugged his shoulders and went to Sir Ian's office. He knocked at the door but there was nobody there. He walked in, left it on the desk and walked out.

Barry left the palace having hastily changed into mufti. He managed to hail a passing cab and went to the offices of the Daily Herald. There was chaos in there as his scoop had sent all schedules awry. He joined Jock in his office as he was completing a vitriolic editorial regarding the breach of the ban. He put into it all the bile and resentment accumulated for fifty years. He poured scorn on the royal family and their cavalier attitude towards the rules of the land, Ma didn't get off lightly either, described as so arrogant and full of self importance that he chose to ignore the rules of a country where he was a guest. The editor in chief of the Sunday Herald had been brushed aside; he wasn't as strong minded as Norman and meekly handed over the reins to Jock. Barry received congratulations for the scoop. He checked his name was on the story and made a couple of additions to it. By the time Dr Woo had finished massaging his patient, everything was set and the presses started rolling, inexorably.

STUB OUT

Chapter 14

Norman Sewell was out for his early morning constitutional. He did this religiously every Sunday morning. Afterwards he would sit down and read two or three broadsheets as well as the Sunday Herald while he drank a cafetiere of good coffee and some buttered crumpets. Today, his morning wasn't going to be as sedate. He walked into his local newsagent. Mr Garcia, the Spanish owner, who knew him well, gave him a funny look as he passed the pile of newspapers. He walked back home and flicked the kettle on. As it started to boil he checked on the main headlines. The Sunday Herald was the last newspaper on the pile. He became rooted on the spot. "Puffingham Palace" screamed the headline; beneath it was a photograph of Ma Tsien-Zu smiling as he smoked a cigarette. There was a digital time and date on the bottom right hand corner of the photograph which read: 01.07.07 00:01. He was appalled at the headline; it was the kind of thing the News of the World would have been proud of but not the Sunday Herald. He opened the paper and read the main story. He went to the editorial. He couldn't believe what he read. The anger, the vitriol! This had Jock's fingerprints all over. He suspected the chief editor had been brushed aside. He checked his watch, it was half-past seven. There was no point in ringing Jock but Helen needed to be made aware. He pulled out his mobile and rang her.

'Hello?' The voice at the end of the line sounded sleepy.

'Helen, it's Norman here. You guys are up to your necks in brown slurry and the tide is rising!

Helen was now wide awake. 'What are you on about?'

Norman explained the headline of the Herald. 'I hasten to add Helen; I have absolutely nothing to do with this. I don't have any input in the Sunday edition.'

There was a pause at the end of the line. 'Thanks for warning me Norman I think we'd better do some damage limitation.' She hung up.

An hour later she had Joined Edward, John and Sir Norman at number 10. There were several copies of the newspaper. They were all reading it with extreme concentration. Not in their worst nightmares could they have conceived such a catastrophic case scenario. Edward broke the silence first.

'Any reaction from the Chinese?'

'I don't think many of them take the Herald' replied John. 'We need to inform them of course.'

'Of course. I have managed to secure a brief telephone interview with Andrew Marr in his Sunday morning program, hopefully we can defuse the situation a bit.'

Wilfred poked his head round the door. I'm terribly sorry to interrupt but Andrew Marr is on line one.' He looked edgy.

Edward picked up the phone. He tried to sound as jovial as possible. 'Good morning Andrew, thanks for taking some time to speak with me. I'm sure you've read all the papers this morning, including the Sunday Herald.' There was a pause. 'Yes, I'm afraid premier Ma did smoke a cigarette. It had just gone midnight as the time on the photograph shows and with all the excitement of the state visit and the lateness of the hour we forgot to point out the new legal situation.' Another pause. 'Well, as far as I can see it is the result of an unfortunate chain of events and I feel that allowances should be made in this case on two counts. Firstly, it happened on the stroke of midnight and secondly, I don't think it is fair of premier Ma to be aware of every single change of the law the moment they happen. There was a final pause. 'Yes of course you can quote me Andrew. Thank you and good luck with the program.' He hung up. 'That was strange' he said, 'I couldn't help feeling Andrew Marr sounded very excited, almost hyper. Right, if you'll excuse me I had better warn Ma Tsien-Zu about this. I would rather speak to him in private.' The other persons took the hint and went into the cabinet room where they waited for Edward to come back. They were joined by Christopher who had read the newspaper and, having spoken with Wilfred, made his way to the prime minister's house.

Ten minutes later Edward walked into the room. 'Right' he said 'I've spoken with Ma Tsien-Zu and explained the situation. Hopefully they will watch Andrew's program and it will all blow away.' He noticed Christopher. 'Hi Chris, a bit of a mess no? Hopefully my talk with Andrew will defuse the situation.' He noticed Christopher's uncharacteristically gloomy expression. 'What's the matter?'

Christopher hesitated, he knew he was verging on breaching patient confidentiality. 'I'm afraid there's more to the story than you realise.'

'Please explain.'

'You remember I mentioned that Ma might have some sort of chronic back problem?

'Yes you did, when you noticed his personal physician at the airport. Did you get to meet him?'

'I did, but that's beyond the point now. Did you notice how stiffly he walked yesterday?

'Now that you mention it, yes, I did.'

'I suspect he was under a lot of pain. That cigarette he smoked wasn't pure for pleasure; it was heavily laced with morphine, to ease he pain. At the end of the evening he had pinpoint pupils and I have smelled that kind of stuff before when I worked as a GP. One of my patients was a drug addict and he couldn't inject so he smoked.'

'This isn't happening.'

'I'm afraid it is.'

'Is it legal?'

Christopher nodded, 'quite, in fact morphine is widely used for pain relief. As a matter of fact we even use heroin for it, few countries do though. Smoking it is unusual but it makes sense, it gets distributed very quickly across the body.'

There was a knock at the door. Wilfred walked in. 'Andrew Marr's program is about to start. I have set a TV in your office.'

'Excellent' said Edward, his good humour restored.

They all trooped back into his office where the starting titles had just finished. Andrew Marr was looking more ironic than ever. There was a guest with him but the camera wasn't showing who it was.

'Good Morning. Today's events are clearly dominated by this headline.' He held up a copy of the Sunday Herald. 'I have just spoken with Edward Faulkner, the embattled recently elected prime minister who said, and I quote "this was the end of an unfortunate chain of events and I don't think it's fair of premier Ma to be aware of every single change in the laws the moment they happen" unquote.' He raised an eyebrow and spoke again. 'This appears to be a fairly reasonable point of view. Perhaps we should ask the minister in charge of implementing this new law what her opinion is.' The camera panned across and, sitting there, with an expression of righteous indignation was Francine Weekes.

'Ke-rist on a stick' said Edward.

Christopher was tempted to tell Edward 'I told you so' but felt his life wouldn't be worth living if he did, so he decided to keep his mouth shut.

Andrew Marr continued; 'so Mrs Weekes, what do you think of this headline?'

'Good morning Andrew. I think it is very disappointing that the head of state China broke the law as soon as it came into effect.'

'It is more than likely that he didn't know, isn't it?'

'My dear Andrew, if I were the guest of the Chinese government I would certainly make sure that I knew about the laws of their country. As a matter of fact it had been widely advertised and premier Ma had with him the head of the government as well as the Northern Ireland Secretary. Mind you' she added with a condescending smile 'he is an ex-smoker himself so he was probably wishing he could have joined premier Ma.'

'Fucking bitch' muttered Christopher.

'Maybe but their minds were occupied with the state visit and it had just gone midnight, surely they could be forgiven for allowing this to slip their minds.'

Francine sighed like a Barbara Cartland heroine. 'Health is a precious gift, I cannot think of anything more important than that. We are pushing this forward as another step towards improving the health of the nation.'

Andrew turned to the camera. 'There you have it ladies and gentlemen. The smoking ban law is breached within seconds of it starting, by the Chinese premier. On the one hand the prime minister feels that, given the circumstances, some allowances should be made, on the other, his health secretary, on a sacred mission to improve the nation's health, feels that no-one is above the laws of the land. Who is right? That's for you to decide'.

Edward switched the television off. He was trembling with rage. 'Has this fucking bitch taken leave of her senses? Doesn't she realise how important this visit is and how catastrophic it would be to cause any kind of offence? God knows we have said it enough times.' He was now pacing round the room like a caged tiger.

John decided to say what was in everyone else's mind. 'What do we do now with the Chinese? If they watched the program we're not going to come out smelling of roses are we?'

'No we aren't. I'll have to speak with Ma this afternoon as soon as possible. We're also having an emergency cabinet meeting at five today. Wilfred, where's the press contacts diary?'

Wilfred rushed in, shoving Sir Norman aside. As he did the diary fell down; he didn't stop to pick it up 'Yes Edward what do you want me to do?' He looked on edge.

'For starters apologise to Sir Norman for shoving him.'

Wilfred looked disdainfully at Sir Norman. 'Sorry' he snapped. He recognised the object in Sir Norman's hands. 'What are you doing with the diary?'

Sir Norman was looking at the schedule for the day. A cruel smile crossed his lips. 'Oh it's quite all right Mr Wilkes, I suppose with all the excitement of today you keep forgetting things; manners, letting the prime minister know that Francine Weekes was scheduled to appear in Mr Marr's program, probably forget your head next.' Or rather lose it thought Sir Norman to himself as he passed over to Edward the press contacts diary open on today's page. This book contained details of all scheduled press contacts with government ministers. It allowed the press secretary to ensure no double bookings occurred and also to ensure the party line was toed. Francine's name was the only one for July the 1st.

Edward looked at it. Wilfred's unmistakeable handwriting had jotted down all the details. He looked up again and locked onto Wilfred who was now looking positively green. 'Why didn't you let me know?

'I..I forgot' he muttered.

'Did you forget, or did Mrs Wilkes asked you to forget, in exchange for certain favours?' Sir Norman had made the question. 'Perhaps a safe parliamentary seat at the next by-election, in Derbyshire North? Which, as, it happens, is contiguous to Mrs Weekes's who, of course, does hold some leverage in the local selection committees and I understand the current incumbent is planning to retire in the new year. Mrs Weekes didn't want anyone stealing her thunder today but unfortunately the prime minister rang Mr Marr himself so it got out of control. Feel free to interrupt me the moment I am deviating from the facts Mr Wilkes' he added placidly.

Wilfred hung his head down. He had been exposed and there was no recourse. 'I'll hand in my resignation now sir.'

John moved swiftly to shield Wilfred. He could sense murder in Edward's eyes and they needed a charge of assault against him like they needed a hole in the head. He looked at his friend in the eye and shook his head. He bent over and whispered in his ear, 'there is a time and a place "squiffy", this isn't it.'

Edward calmed down, he knew John was right. He needed to start planning. He walked up and down his office and looked at Sir Norman. 'I need to meet with premier Ma this afternoon. We also need an emergency cabinet meeting at five o'clock no excuses every one must attend. After that I will need to meet with the queen let's say eight o'clock. I know it's outside your remit but I would be grateful if you could oblige. Also advise premier Ma that I may need to speak with him again later in the evening. Please let me know when the times are confirmed ASAP.'

Sir Norman bowed slightly and went out.

'Are you letting Francine come into this meeting?' Helen sounded dubitative.

'Oh yes. Most definitely.'

Helen hesitated before she gave the next piece of information. 'I had a call from Wolfgang yesterday. They have discovered some serious budgetary problems and they are cutting the pledged funding from £60 to £ 40 billion. I checked with the Spanish, they're sticking to their pledge thank God.'

'We won't let the Chinese know about this one. We don't want to add more grist to their mill.'

'I agree.' She went back home to work on her figures while Edward pondered on how to best present things to Ma.

In Beijing, Chung Hing-Lai was hosting a meeting of party hardliners. Marshall Wang was due to fly in early in the morning. The manoeuvres had actually been cut short so he could add weight to the assault on Ma. They were planning on Monday's politburo strategy. They were very aware that they had to strike now, if Ma bought the negotiations to fruition, his position would be unassailable and further reforms, the end of their way of life, and worse, their privileges, would come to be. Chung had, for a long time, been his most obdurate opponent. The "birthday" party with the added-on meeting had spurred him into action. He had been completely outmanoeuvred and humiliated; this was an insult and a loss of face he could not tolerate (especially after Ma had the effrontery of sending minutes of the "meeting"). He also knew this was the best opportunity, with some of the heavyweight reformers with Ma and the bulk of the diehards in Beijing, the odds had shortened considerably. His private secretary, one who shared his views, walked into the room without knocking. Chung frowned.

'Profuse apologies for the interruption minister Chung. I have just received this from Britain. I have taken the liberty of translating the relevant parts.' He deposited two faxed sheets corresponding to the first and second pages of the Daily Herald. Ma was clearly identifiable, smoking a cigarette.

Chung read the relevant parts. He looked up quizzically. 'Why are the British press treating our "esteemed" premier Ma like a criminal and demanding his arrest?'

His private secretary, who could read English well and had obtained additional information, briefly explained the ban timetable as well as the events at Buckingham palace.

Comprehension finally dawned on Chung's expression and he gave a broad grin. He looked at his audience around the table. 'Comrades I think we should discuss these grave events.'

211

The queen was reading the Daily Herald. Sir Hugh had been tasked with the unenviable task of breaking the news. Her expression betrayed no emotion. She put the paper down and looked at Sir Hugh. 'Do we know how did this photograph reach the paper?'

'We believe it was a junior footman called Barry Smith; he and Archie Jones were the only two footmen on duty in that room. He handed in his notice as soon as he finished work.'

'I take it we cannot appeal to the confidentiality clause in his contract.'

'You are absolutely correct Ma'am. There was a breach of the law and, like any "good" citizen; it was his duty to report it.'

'It's nice to see that a sense of civic duty still prevails in the country!' The queen could be ironic to the point of sarcasm.

'So it would appear. The prime minister has requested an urgent audience with you around eight o'clock if this is convenient. He is meeting with premier Ma after lunch.'

The queen thought about it. 'Yes Sir Hugh, I think we can make it. Can you locate my son, the Earl of Wessex; I need to speak with him before lunch.'

'Very well Ma'am.'

Ma Jing-Tao was reading the Daily Herald to his uncle. Ma Tsien-Zu's face was expressionless.

'So, from respected leader of the PRC I have now been demoted to common criminal.'

'I don't think it's as bad as that.'

'You may not, but Chung and Wang will. They will be conveying that message at the politburo meeting in about twelve hours time.'

Jing-Tao went very pale.

'You had forgotten hadn't you? With the time difference of twelve hours they have read about this and now they will use it as an excuse to destroy any attempts at reform. By midnight tonight all we have worked towards could be in ruins. I had better speak with Hsien Fang-La and implement the contingency plan. '

'It's now gone midnight in Beijing!'

212

'Fang-la is an insomniac. He won't mind. Give me your mobile. I don't want to use the embassy lines. Too much monitoring. Chung could find out.'

'Now you are being too suspicious.' He handed over his mobile phone anyway. You didn't argue with Ma when he was feeling cornered.

'How do you think they got wind of this?'

'We don't know for sure.'

'Believe me, I have my sources and Chung already knows.' Leave me now please, I need to speak with Fang-La, alone. We will accept Mr Faulkner's invitation for a talk this afternoon. '

Early in the afternoon, all schedules forgotten, Edward was talking with Ma Tsien-Zu at number 10. Ma Jing-Tao was there acting as an interpreter.

'I cannot emphasise enough how sorry my self and the government are about this silly incident which arose from an unfortunate chain of events.'

'Yes' Ma said via his nephew, 'chains of unfortunate or tragic events seem to crop up with remarkable frequency whenever "our two great countries" embark into any joint activity.' He took a sip of his tea while he started at him.

Edward swallowed hard, the memory of three dead fishermen and a wrecked fishing vessel loomed large. 'It goes without saying that there will be no legal repercussions; the matter will be closed. You are protected by diplomatic immunity any way.'

'Do I? Your health secretary appears to think otherwise.'

'She didn't consult with me, she made an unfortunate comment.'

'I thought free speech was enshrined in your constitution?'

'It is indeed but discretion, when choosing our words, must prevail.' This meeting wasn't going well at all. Edward felt like a mouse being toyed with by a very inscrutable cat!

'I think you should know what is going to happen in China in the next six hours. It will have a major bearing on events here.'

'If you feel it is necessary' said Edward unhappily.

'It is, very much so. Tonight at 10pm UK time the politburo will meet as scheduled. Afts soon as the preliminaries have been dealt with,

Chung Hing-Lai and Marshall Wang will show the assembly today's headline. It will trigger a tirade of abuse and criticism of my reforms and the paltry returns they have achieved. My visit to the USA wasn't very successful and this visit's moderately positive results will be completely overshadowed by the insult to the Chinese government I embody. If I want to survive politically I will need to launch an all out assault on Rolls Royce as well as triggering a financial meltdown in Europe and believe me Mr Faulkner, I will do it. There is a lot more at stake than you could imagine and I will let no-one, and I mean no-one to get in my way. Are we understood?' Edward noticed the eyes had become flinty hard as he leant over to emphasise his point.

'We do have back-up you know.' He tried to bluff. His position was even weaker now.

'Do you mean the £40 billion, reduced from £60 billion the ECB have promised?'

Edward's face paled visibly, he felt sick.

Ma stuck the knife in; this was no time for compassion. 'Yes Mr Faulkner, our secret service may not have the glamour of MI-6 but it is quite effective nevertheless.'

Edward swallowed hard again. 'Do you have any suggestions as to how we can avert this? Would an official apology help?' He was now beginning to clutch at straws.

'Come on Mr Faulkner! Talk is cheap. This would be the second apology in less than a month! Don't you think Chung and Wang won't seize upon that? They have been waiting for an opportunity like this to come their way for a long time. They will not let it pass. Their views are different from mine very dogmatic and they are less… flexible. Given the current circumstances, they might be able to convince more people than usual that I should no longer direct matters.'

'Surely the trade agreement shows considerable gains and a shift in China's weight in the global economy.'

'Yes, a shift in weight indeed. The parts are bigger but they are still parts! The hardliners would accuse us of yielding to economic neo-colonialism. Quite ironic as we celebrate the 10th anniversary of the conditional devolution of Hong Kong don't you think?'

Edward thought about the last sentence. 'Could we meet in your embassy at ten in the evening? I need to discuss this with my cabinet.' 'You like to cut things fine.' He checked his watch. 'Very good, ten o'clock it is. I would like to leave now.' He gave an ironic smile. 'I want to smoke a cigarette; it wouldn't do if I broke the same law twice in one day would it?' He stood up and he and Jing-Tao left.

Edward felt deflated the last barb had been unnecessary but he knew he wasn't in a position to rebuke it.

Some time later the cabinet went into session as scheduled. Francine was conspicuously present, her attitude defiant.

Edward abstained from any preliminary niceties and dived in directly. 'This is the situation. The Chinese are going to perceive this as an unforgivable insult to their government. The Hardliners will use it as an excuse to either oust Ma or to increase their powerbase so as to render him toothless in his reform aspirations. The only way Ma can prevent this is to go for our economic jugular with everything they've got. They have also found out about the 30% reduction in the ECB rescue funds. In short, we're up to our necks in brown slurry and the tide is rising.'

John asked 'how did Ma sound?'

'It was a mixture of amusement at the way we had painted ourselves into a corner and annoyance at having to screw us to save his neck. He definitely has most trump cards and a need to use them.'

'It looks like we have now reached a nuclear button situation' John said softly.

'Were not going to war are we?' asked Rufus alarmed. He knew the Chinese would pulverise them.

'No Rufus, this is where behave like fucking whores and sell our pussy to the highest bidder.'

'There's no need for that kind of language' Francine said disapprovingly.

Edward gave her a look of pure hatred and clenched his fists but said nothing.

'What was your gut feeling about what he really wanted?' asked Helen.

Edward repeated the conversation as well as he could remember

(Wilfred was no longer there to take notes of course!) and Helen jotted down a few things. 'Just give me two ticks' she said as the pen flew across the paper.

There was a silence while everyone waited for Helen to put yet another rabbit out of her hat.

'As far as I can see it, the Chinese want two things: the end of the SAR status for Hong Kong and the complete manufacture of Rolls Royce aero engines in China.'

There were some murmurs of protest, mostly from Francine. Her constituency was Derby South, if RR moved she would never be able to show her face again. Her majority was quite slender; she would get slaughtered at the next general election.

'Guys, guys.' Helen raised her hands. 'There is a way.'

'How?' asked Edward. 'If we withdraw our guarantee to maintain Hong Kong's SAR status we're going to look like complete bastards. If we let the Chinese build Rolls Royce Aero in China we lose a vital industry and the good faith of the EU and airbus.'

'We could always give them a bit of both' Helen said with a smile.

'You'll have to be a bit more explicit.'

'I learned through one of my contacts that Rolls Royce Aero is developing a new jet engine. They have calculated, that it should be ready in about three years, maybe four. Apparently it will knock the spots of the competition especially as it uses fewer parts and consumes 15% less fuel with the resulting drop in emissions. We allow the Chinese to build the current engine with production limited to internal consumption and an additional 5% production for export for the next five years and unlimited production thereafter. By the time the contract has expired the new engine will have been out in the market and we'll be one step ahead yet again. Also we sell them part of the tooling, at inflated prices, to fund and, possibly even accelerate, research into the new engine.

'What about Hong Kong?' John was fascinated at the combination of devious and straightforward. She was *very* good!

'Currently Hong Kong's SAR status is guaranteed for a further forty-five years. We offer to reduce the guarantee by twenty years; by that time, if John's calculations are correct, China will all but be a fully fledged multiparty democracy' she abstained from mentioning how much she already knew 'and the need for the SAR status would become obsolete. We would keep this part of the treaty secret for five years until Ma retired.'

'I can't help but feel we're betraying the people of Hong Kong to preserve our own interests' said Christopher.

'It could be seen like that but we will have to explain the situation quietly to them closer to the time. By then, some changes will be happening in China and they will see no point in kicking up a fuss. More importantly, if we all agree, Ma's position becomes greatly reinforced; with Marshall Wang on the way out Chung will become extremely weak. He will probably get sacked within six months we all win and Bob's your uncle.'

There was a brief pause. In an unheard of move, Edward stood up and started clapping, John and Christopher followed suit. Within seconds the whole cabinet, with the exception of Francine, who remained defiantly seated, gave Helen a standing ovation. Helen sat there blushing. Never before had she had never received such a ringing endorsement by her peers. Eventually the clapping died and everybody, bar one, sat down again. Edward resumed control.

'OK, all that remains is to offer a public apology and exoneration to premier Ma.'

'Why?' asked Francine. She knew only too well this would undermine her very public statement of this morning.

'Because, my "dear" Francine' Edward hissed 'we insulted a very important guest. You are right in that laws are there to be respected and upheld but, if a new law comes into being and my guests aren't aware of it, it is my duty to inform them. If I don't, I'm as guilty as they are as you very kindly pointed out this morning. We have just had to lower our trousers and allow ourselves to be buggered like never before. We've only just managed to hang on to Rolls Royce Aero, not thanks to you though. We will apologise and hope for the best.'

Francine sank momentarily into her seat, stunned by the venom in Edward's tone. She looked around the table. People were either avoiding eye contact or looking at her with hard eyes. Only Helen appeared oblivious, scribbling at her pad. It was true, she had never stopped thinking or working, even at school. She wished, once more she'd possessed Helen's capacity for relentless pursuit of excellence. Wordlessly she collected her papers and walked out of the room. As soon as the door closed behind her she rushed to the toilet and started retching. She sobbed as she did so. She may still stay in office for a while but her career like the vomit coming out of her had just gone down the pan.

In the early hours of the evening, Edward went to Buckingham palace. As he walked down the corridor with Sir Hugh he was surprised to see a bunch of scruffy looking men and women carrying heavy aluminium boxes and laying rolls of heavy duty cabling outside the queen's office. Sir Hugh dispensed with the usual ceremony as he ushered Edward into the queen's office. She was busy talking to her youngest son, Edward Wessex. She saw Edward and ended the conversation with her son who bowed as he left. Edward bowed too as he approached the queen.

'Please take a seat Mr Faulkner.'

At least she hadn't gone back to calling him prime minister he thought with relief. 'Good evening Ma'am.'

She looked at him, her face like a mask, the eyes unblinking. 'We appear to have a problem Mr Faulkner, a serious one. I have no doubt you have been watching the news. It appears that I have allowed a new law to be broken. I believe the legal term is aiding and abetting.'

'Ma'am, I can assure you that your government doesn't see it in this way at all.'

'Be that as it may, the facts are there for everyone to judge. I can only assume that the Chinese government is far from pleased.'

'This is true Ma'am. In fact it premier ma assures me it has actually put him in a very difficult position with the politburo. If his enemies are successful it would represent a serious setback for political reform in China. The alternative would mean serious economic difficulties in Britain and the western world for many years to come as he uses all his financial leverage to salvage his position.'

'Not good then. Do you have an alternative course of action?'

Edward explained the special measures the cabinet had just approved.

'I am not sure this will endear us to the people of Hong Kong.'
She was thinking of her position as head of the Commonwealth.

'Probably not but this part of the treaty remains secret for five years; all being well changes in the political map of China will make it more palatable.'

'So all that remains now is to cope from the fallout from the press.'

'Quite. If they are anything like the television reports we could be in trouble.'

'One does not like Buckingham palace to be on the front pages for the wrong reasons.'

'I know and I will be issuing a formal apology tomorrow.'

The queen looked surprised. 'Why should you do that?'

'Because your government, of which I am the chief representative, implemented a law and in doing so caused embarrassment to yourself, in your residence, and to your guest, premier Ma.' Surely she wasn't being deliberately obtuse?

The queen pulled her glasses off and inspected them. She pulled a small handkerchief and cleaned a minute speck of dust. She put her glasses back on. 'Mr Faulkner, you have correctly identified yourself as the chief representative of *my* government and the incident happened to *my* guest in *my* official residence. Your apology will not be necessary.' She looked over his shoulder. 'Sir Hugh, would you kindly invite my son and his team back into my office?'

'Certainly Ma'am.'

The door opened and all the scruffy people started walking in, setting up lights, electric connections and cameras.

'I'm sorry but I don't understand Ma'am.'

'Mr Faulkner, a lot of things happened ten years ago.'

'I don't follow.'

'Chief among these things, was the tragic death of Diana Princess of Wales in Paris. At that time I behaved like a grandmother, my chief concern was to protect my grandchildren: Princes William and Harry from the glare of the press. I misread the mood of the nation, their grief. I paid for that mistake. It will not happen again!'

A make up girl approached the queen. She nodded. Edward retreated. As he did he noticed Reginald Compton, the Lord Chancellor walking in. He came close and winked. 'Sorry old chap, I was under strict orders to keep quiet.'

The film director shouted: 'All set?' There was a general chorus of agreement. The lighting director had finished his checks, the assistant director ordered silence and gave the final countdown: 'three, two, one action!'

The queen was sitting on a gilded chair without a desk in front of her. She was sitting upright and her legs, uncrossed, were perfectly lined and angled to the left. Her right hand was on her left lap with the right hand on top. She was wearing her traditional light blue dress and black court shoes. On her left upper chest was a discreet (but very valuable!) diamond brooch. She gave an impression of control and majesty that fifty-five years on the job had helped hone to perfection. She started to speak.

'My fellow citizens, thank you for allowing me into your homes this evening. As you are aware, there were certain events early this morning at Buckingham palace. My honoured guest, premier Ma Tsien-Zu of the People's Republic of China inadvertently transgressed a law just as it came into being. It is my duty to obey any law which has been passed by the members of parliament as representatives of the nation. It is also my duty as a host to make my guests stay as comfortable as possible. In following the latter, I forgot to remind my guest of my obligations towards the former. Forgetfulness is no excuse however. It was a mistake, my mistake, and as a result, a law was transgressed. This law is clear and the penalties for not adhering to it are clear too. I have contacted the Lord Chancellor: Mr Reginald Compton, as well as the Attorney General Mr Henry Ferguson. I have given them two envelopes. One is to pay my fine as the person responsible for the premises where the transgression occurred, the other is to pay my guest's fine for his actions, however unintentional. Both the Lord Chancellor and the Attorney General have confirmed in writing that the law has been upheld.'

She paused briefly to allow the meaning of the last words to sink in. Reginald looked at Edward and nodded as he showed him three envelopes.

The queen continued. 'I hope this will satisfy everyone that no-one is above the law and that I, the head of state, more than anyone else abides by it. You have my solemn promise that this law will never be transgressed again in my presence. Thank you and good evening.'

'Aaaand cut!'

The director, cameraman and Edward Wessex crowded around the monitor; checking for light, sound and position. Eventually they declared themselves satisfied. Edward went to inform his mother that the take had been successful. The director walked up with a laptop and showed the results to the queen who simply nodded, he then made four quick copies of the brief message onto CD-roms and gave them to his assistants who left the room quickly.

Edward turned to Reginald in amazement. 'Can she actually do that?'

Reginald nodded vigorously, 'Oh yes, rather. She is a citizen like everyone else and even if she rarely uses it, she is entitled to freedom of speech and to present her views for wider distribution. There are copies for ITV, BBC Sky and the Chinese embassy. I thought it was rather clever the way she acknowledged the incident without apologising once.'

'I feel compelled, for the second time ever, to give a standing ovation'

Reginald gave him a look of commiseration. 'I sincerely hope not! As far as she's concerned she has just done her duty with a bit more fireworks than usual. She would think it was rather rum if you did.' Reginald was very old fashioned in his speech.

The queen was sitting at her chair looking out of the window towards the Mall when Edward approached her.

She turned round, having caught Edward's reflection in the window. 'Yes Mr Faulkner.'

'Ma'am, at the risk of sounding sycophantic, that was the most brilliant exercise of damage limitation I have ever had the privilege of witnessing in my entire life.' His tone reflected pure admiration.

The queen thought about this for a moment and then gave a lovely smile. 'Why thank you Mr Faulkner. Age does have its drawbacks but it provides one with a certain amount of experience which can sometimes be put to good use. I felt you could do with a little bit of help. I respect how well you and your cabinet have handled a very tricky situation, especially in the last twelve hours. You had to deal with a very experienced politician who got to the top under much harder circumstances than you did. His experience tells him that this is an extremely good deal, a lot more than he had expected. His prestige will increase and I have no doubt he will be considered one of the great statesmen of the 21st century, if he watches himself. You won't look at your best at present, but eventually facts will reveal you achieved a good result for your country against insurmountable odds. People will eventually realise this, trust me.' She paused and smiled again, 'and you will never refer to this conversation again.'

Edward had never heard such a ringing endorsement from such an authoritative source. It was something he would secretly treasure in the years to come.

About an hour later, Edward John and Helen met with the two Mas in the Chinese ambassador's office. The queen's unexpected TV message, which had already been broadcast in BBC News 24 and Sky news, had sent the news desks into overdrive. This was a veritable bombshell! Ma had seen the message beforehand, his nephew had already written the subtitles in Chinese with the help of an English telecom engineer. BBC, ITV and Channels 4 and 5 were fitting in special slots in the news or their schedules to broadcast it by ten o'clock. Edward outlined the new proposals. Ma Jing-Tao studied them briefly and then he had a brief conversation with his uncle. He turned round to Edward.

'We feel this is a far better proposal. We could start producing aero engines at the beginning of 2009. We should have the five years production agreement start then.'

'In that case' intervened John 'the new timetable for the handover of Hong Kong should start then too.'

The two Mas conferred briefly. 'This is acceptable.'

Helen was giving mental whoops of delight. The Chinese had just given Rolls Royce a further eighteen months of grace.

'Very well' said Edward 'in that case, both Helen and Mr Ma Jing-Tao will finalise the agreement by tomorrow afternoon. We will need the signature of the chairman of airbus industries there too.'

Ma Tsien-Zu nodded in agreement.

'How did you mange to convince the queen to deliver that speech?' enquired Ma Jing-Tao.

'I didn't' replied Edward, 'she took the decision unprompted'

Ma Tsien-Zu sighed. 'You are very lucky to have her' he said in English.

'Indeed we are' premier Ma, 'Indeed we are.'

Ma senior conferred briefly with his nephew who turned round. 'We have to terminate this conversation. There are other matters requiring premier Ma's urgent attention. The only thing that would make this visit a complete triumph would be to nail down the son of a turtle who published the photographs and caused so much mischief.'

Helen broke into a wicked smile. 'But you can, premier Ma. I will tell you how to. If you agree to extend Hong Kong's SAR status by a further three years and accept some minor financial losses, I can hand you Jock Robertson's head on a silver platter and it won't even look like revenge.'

'How could this be done?"

'Allow me to explain.'

Five minutes later after a hasty translation Ma Tsien-Zu nodded with a big smile. Ma Jing-Tao was smiling too. 'Miss Steele, you just got yourself a deal.'

Chapter 15

Chung Hing-Lai was in an exultant mood. He had woken up very early and checked the latest reports on the British TV and radio. Ma was finished. He wouldn't be able to survive the loss of face of being branded a law-breaker. Even their health secretary had slagged him off! It may also be a good time to remind the assembled members of his less than glorious father. Yes, things were looking good even if Wang hadn't been able to make it. Apparently his plane had broken with an engine failure and he had made an emergency landing in southern Mongolia. No matter, more glory for him! He had been in the conference hall since nine o'clock and was satisfied to see it was filling up steadily and people were reading the translated copy of the Daily Herald. He had summoned as many members of the CC as he possible could; it wasn't a formal party conference but he had decided to take the risk of inviting as many people as possible to watch Ma's defenestration.

The meeting commenced at ten o'clock on the dot and once the preliminaries had been dealt with, Chung took the floor.

'Comrades, as you can see, the British have heaped further insults upon our great country. It isn't even two weeks since their Royal Navy killed three of our hard working fishermen and disregarded their lives as unimportant, they are now accusing comrade Ma' –he didn't use his formal title of premier, he needed to diminish him from the outset- 'of being a law-breaker. They change laws in the last minute and use them to try and humiliate us. The People's Republic of China! We have the power to crush them and what does comrade Ma do? Nothing! He stays hidden in the Chinese embassy and meekly allows insults to be poured upon us. Yes, comrades, when they insult Ma, they insult us!

They still treat our country as a bunch of backward yokels, fit only to produce cheap trinkets like these.' He produced a small plastic promotional toy from a fast food company. 'For too long we have been doing their bidding and putting up with their insults. Over the last few years we have acquired financial leverage second to none.' He conveniently omitted Ma's conception of the whole scheme. 'With it we could order, yes, order them to give us their technology, we could study it and we could improve upon it; we could, if that lame duck Ma exercised his full rights.' Chung was, of course, not being 100% factually accurate but he was "working up" the audience now, getting them into a hysterical frenzy by gradually increasing the seriousness of his accusations allowing almost truths to be followed by half lies. Eventually he would launch an outright attack and demand the removal of his rival; his audience, he expected, would be so frenzied they would do anything he asked. As he carried on with his tirade he didn't notice Hsien Fang-La picking up his mobile phone that had started to buzz and starting to speak with someone at the other end of the line.

'Comrade Chung' Hsien said, 'there have been recent developments in Britain.'

Chung turned round to face this interruption. As he did some curtains were drawn to reveal a 100-inch screen behind him which started to flicker. 'Yes, Hsien Fang-La, there have been terrible developments. Yesterday there was only one newspaper, today all the press will be attacking us. Making us the laughing stock of the world; and that traitor Ma...!

'What have I done now Chung?' Ma's voice, sounding placid and bored at the same time, boomed across the loud speakers in the hall, his face showing on the large screen in the hall. A web cam above it had been returning images to England via a secure link for some time now. He had frightened everybody with his sudden image, almost like a god. He had counted upon this. Chung had gone very pale, his expression of hatred replaced by one of fear. He hadn't anticipated this. Ma carried on talking. 'Contrary to comrade Chung's assertions I have been improving China's status as a worldwide power.' He proceeded to outline the treaty he was about to sign with Edward and the rest of the EU countries. He omitted the Hong Kong element of the treaty.

He felt it would be flippant to do so over the internet. Also he had agreed on secrecy regarding disclosure of the agreement. He left the best until the end. 'Allow me to show you something comrades.' The screen flickered briefly and the queen appeared, apologising without apologising. Many people could understand English but just in case Chinese subtitles were running below. The message ended and Ma's face reappeared on the screen. He allowed a brief moment of reflection, letting the message sink in.

'My dear comrades, I am sorry I cannot be with you today but as you can see I have achieved a lot in the last few days. I am asking you now, what would you like, a long complex financial war involving the EU and the USA which would set us back many years and open a chasm of suspicion between the East and the West as comrade Chung demands or, a new era of cooperation and prosperity with China's international status enhanced without any strife as I, your Premier, suggests?' Ma could also rabble rouse like the best as Chung was discovering to his horror.

'MA,! MA,! MA!' The roar in the hall was deafening, Ma raised his hands. 'Thank you comrades. We will have a show of hands. Those in favour of my motion vote in favour now please.' A veritable forest of hands rose. 'And now those against.' His eyes narrowed slightly, his mouth became a straight line; in the large screen the effect was quite intimidating. Only Chung and his sons raised their hands. 'Very well, I consider this treaty approved by the representatives of the PRC.' In saying this, Ma had skilfully introduced a useful precedent of democracy, albeit in an unorthodox way. His attention now focused on Chung. Time to deal with this cockroach in the old fashioned way. 'Chung Hing-Lai' he boomed. 'You have levelled accusations of cowardice and treason against me. You have unlawfully attempted to subvert the party for your personal gain by inviting CC members to a politburo meeting. I will not tolerate this not should any member who understands the importance to sticking to correct procedure. I am ordering your arrest. Is there anyone here today that will speak for you?' Nobody spoke. Years of party control paid handsome dividends today especially when the members took on board Ma's comment of their being at the wrong place at the wrong time. 'Interior minister Hsien Fang-La, arrest this man!' Three police officers walked in the hall and seized Chung. He allowed himself to be handcuffed. He was a broken man before the order came but Ma was taking no chances with Wang still controlling the army. 'Comrades, I propose a further meeting in two weeks time when we can formally endorse this treaty as well as put Chung to trial. Good bye.'

'A thousand years for premier Ma!' shouted a delegate. This was followed by cheering which continued even after the screen went dark.

Back in London Ma turned to his nephew. 'That was very productive. It's nice to know technology can be used to our advantage.' He paused briefly. 'Before you ask, no, you will not be industry minister.' He raised a hand to forestall any protest. There was none coming. 'You will become deput Interior minister. Hsien's deputy will become industry minister while you learn about control; how and when to use it and, more importantly, when not to.'

Jing-Tao thought about this. It made sense. A further promotion would be counterproductive, but a sideways move into a crucial ministry with Hsien, a rising star, as his mentor and supporter was a far better move. He bowed. 'I agree uncle, you are right as usual.'

On Monday the newspapers front pages were devoted to the queen's unexpected televised speech. They were all praising the queen's courage to admit a mistake had occurred (by common unspoken consensus, the breach of the smoking ban had been demoted to a simple mistake; Sir Hugh had earned his salary last night!). There were also favourable comparisons between the palace's torpidity in 1997 and the quick reactions of 2007. All in all, the queen's image had become reinforced; a useful by product.

The only discordant note had been the Daily Herald. Jock had pushed his editorial line against Norman's advice. It made them look petulant still demanding for a full judicial process despite the joint statement from the Lord Chancellor and the Attorney General (which they omitted printing) stating the queen's actions as legal and in keeping with the law and declaring the matter closed. Norman had rung Helen in the evening to warn her about their slant on the story emphasising Jock's overruling.

Edward had issued a statement from number 10 where he praised the queen for her actions and pledged the government's support. Meanwhile, Sir Norman had discreetly approached Francine. He explained what had happened to Wilfred and advised her, in no uncertain terms, about the consequences of not toeing the line. A quick scan through the headlines confirmed to her she was beaten.

Helen and Jing-Tao spent most of Monday morning working on the final detail of the treaty. They also kept a very close eye on the stock exchange. True to their word, the Chinese had offloaded a 5% of their RR and BAe shares on the market. They were putting no lower limit on the value and the shares plummeted with out any of the "experts" being able to understand the reason for this. A lot of time was spent liaising between Berlin, Madrid and Paris ensuring no more toes were tread upon unnecessarily. Ma Jing-Tao met with his uncle to discuss the treaty.

'This is very good, Jing-Tao. I have to say their mistakes landed all we wanted on a plate and more.'

'You mean Hong Kong?'

'I mean Hong Kong. I had hoped for permission to build and develop Rolls Royce aero engines as well as an agreement on parts of the airbus. The British were obviously desperate. I have to admit Chung made my bargaining position easier. The last thing they wanted was some mediocre megalomaniac in charge.'

'I noticed the meeting was far better attended than usual. It looked more like a CC meeting.'

'Yes, another underhand trick of Chung's. As soon as we left for America he changed the scope of the meeting and invited as many CC members as possible.'

'But any decisions taken would have been invalid surely?'

'There were enough members of the politburo to ensure the decision was, technically, constitutionally correct. He could have pulled it off had I not anticipated it.'

Jing-Tao was impressed. He could think two or three steps ahead, his uncle thought twenty steps ahead. 'Can I ask you what did you do?'

Tsien-Zu smiled benignly. 'It was quite simple. Hsien-Fang-La had all of Chung's calls monitored. When he finally knew what Chung was planning he called the local chiefs of police and ensured the best known party hardliners were unavoidably "detained" locally. He allowed a few lightweights to slip through so Chung didn't suspect we were on top of the game.'

'What about Marshall Wang? I noticed he wasn't there.'

'Such a shame his plane had a technical failure and was forced to land miles away from the nearest railway line and all the cars in the air base had one or another mechanical failure! Marshall Wu has definitely earned his promotion to head of the armed forces in September.'

'And yet he isn't one of the keenest modernisers.'

'I agree, but he will be happy to appoint some if he receives the appropriate encouragement.'

Jing-Tao thought about all this. He couldn't help feeling there was a certain sordid tinge to the whole thing. 'Father'

Ma's ears pricked. Jing-Tao only called him that when he wanted absolute honesty in an answer. He found it hard not to tell the truth under those circumstances. 'Yes son?'

'Are you still planning to allow things to move forward as you explained to me?' There was a certain element of pleading in his question.

'Why do you ask?'

'All this manoeuvring, and strong-arm tactics, the lies the deceit. Is it worth your reputation?'

Ma Tsien-Zu had thought about this too, but in different terms. He cared for what history would think about him, but he cared more about not tearing China apart by allowing the disaggregating forces within it to flourish. Chung had very nearly succeeded in ousting him; but it would have caused phenomenal civil unrest, perhaps an uprising. He understood Chinese society was evolving fast, Helen Steele understood it too. It was a question of allowing gradual reform: enough to keep the impatient happy but not so much that the recalcitrant protested. He looked at Jing-Tao. 'In answer to your first question: yes, I still plan to allow things to move forward, but at a pace myself, the CPC and society feel comfortable with. The answer to the second question: why do you care?'

'Perhaps I have lived in the west for too long and I feel that some of the tactics we use are no longer acceptable.'

'You have to remember that we are different societies. Our values and traditions often are poles apart. I am not sure I want the Chinese to think like the Europeans. I hope I can make them understand and the advantages of some of their traditions and values; democracy is the one which springs to mind. Others I do not see the point of. Some things need doing, it is better if I do them and that your hands are clean.'

Jing-Tao could see the sense in this but it still pained him what would people think of Ma Tsien-Zu. 'Is Hsien going to be your successor?'

'Probably, I need him to move around a bit in the various ministries; see how he handles the different problems and how adept he is at promoting the right people. He will stay as an interior minister for a while; I need him to teach you a lot as I explained. We will talk more once we are back home.'

This signalled the end of the conversation; Jing-Tao took the hint and left.

Helen, John, Edward and Harold were poring over the same document. They knew they had given away a lot more than they had wanted but probably less than they had anticipated. The most important thing was they had laid the basis of greater cooperation between Britain and mainland Europe. George W Bush had spoken with Edward and made some discreet objections but, as his country had rejected cooperation with China, even he knew that he didn't have a leg to stand on. The "special relationship" between UK and USA had begun to show its shortcomings.

Jock had been in his office most of the day checking on the stock exchange. He was horrified to see how his investment was taking a nosedive. By the end of the day he knew he was ruined and the Daily Herald was almost bankrupt. It was at this time when his secretary knocked at his door.

'Yes?' he said weakly, the fire and aggression gone.

'Some officers from Scotland Yard to see you Mr Robertson.' Her tone was equally subdued. Two men and a woman walked into Jock's office without waiting to be invited.

'Are you Mr Jock Robertson?' the first man enquired.

'Yes, it's me.'

'I am Detective Superintendent Jack Marland from Scotland Yard. I have a warrant for your arrest on charges of illegal misuse of the Daily Herald pension fund for personal profit. You have the right to remain silent but it will harm your defence if you rely in court something you did not reveal during questioning.' He showed Jock the paperwork. The female officer put handcuffs on Jock. Such was his state of shock he didn't protest.

The police escorted Jock through the newsroom. There was an amazed silence. Norman watched briefly and started writing down possible headlines. He knew Jock would go down for a long time. Helen had warned him all his conversations were being taped by GCHQ in Cirencester. He felt a surge of relief. He clapped his hands once. 'Right guys, it's still business as usual. We have got a paper to write!'

On Tuesday morning Edward and Ma signed the treaty. The press were present en masse. Norman Sewell, that most observant of journalists, would have noticed Helen wasn't present. In fact neither of them were there. They were both sitting in Helen's office at the DTI together with Harold Butler, representatives of Natwest –the main loan holders for the Daily Herald- and representatives for the three major shareholders of the Herald group. Patsy was taking the minutes.

Helen summarised the final resolutions. 'To recap gentlemen, we will help finance a recovery plan. The government will underwrite the pension fund losses as well as discreetly providing additional income through institutional advertising at the Daily Herald. Natwest will agree to renegotiate the loans of the Herald group into a single loan to be repaid over the next twenty years with a fixed 4% interest over the next five years and floating to whatever the market rate is by the end of June 2012. The board will appoint a new managing director to replace Mr Robertson within the next six months. Does anyone have any objections?'

Nobody said a word. Natwest had agreed to these generous terms after Helen had "diplomatically" warned them she would let the Chinese recall 50% of the loans instantly unless they agreed. The main shareholders were relieved the group wouldn't go under. Norman was just glad people wouldn't suffer in the long term.

Harold interrupted the silence. 'What about Mr Barry Smith, the undercover reporter at the palace. Will there be sanctions against him?'

Helen and Norman looked at each other and smiled. 'Mr Sewell and the government have reached an agreement regarding Mr Smith.'

On Tuesday evening, the return dinner was held at the Chinese embassy. It started a lot earlier than usual due to Ma's schedule. He was due to arrive in Moscow early the following morning so his plane would leave just before midnight. It was a formal affair as usual, with the usual speeches at the end. In a break of tradition the queen and Ma went to the airport together. There was no interpreter present at his specific request. They chatted about trivialities most of the trip. As they were approaching Heathrow Ma turned to the queen.

'I wanted to let you know how much I admired the courage of your gesture on Sunday evening. You did me, and the PRC, a far greater service than you can imagine. The only way I can think of repaying you is by ensuring we pass a law banning smoking in all public buildings as well as our embassies.'

The queen smiled. 'I think it is a wonderful gesture premier Ma.'

Barry Smith thanked the waiter in the Havana Palace as he served him the first mojito of the evening. He had been sent there to research into the state of Cuban society and the impact Fidel Castro's terminal health decline was having on them. Norman and Helen had been felt it would be prudent that he should disappear below the radar screen for a while. He worked hard at his report during the early hours of the morning, walking around Havana and nosing around with the help of an interpreter. He had also ventured into the countryside and some smaller cities. He was slowly picking up Spanish and was feeling increasingly comfortable in using it with the local talent. Pippa had dumped him for not showing up at Clar's pre-engagement party. The fact that he had just hit the scoop of the decade made no difference to her. An almighty row ensued and Barry collected his meagre possessions from her flat and decamped to his grandparents until Norman gave him his new assignment. He was going to work for the international news desk but he should try and hone his skills by doing some research journalism in Cuba; so far he'd managed the great scoop of interviewing Nati Revuelta, Fidel Castro's former lover as well as having an informal chat with Raul Castro's private secretary. All the information would come in handy when he returned to Britain. He lit up a Cohiba Robusto; he had acquired a taste for them in the last few weeks. He inhaled and then blew out and while he admired the shape and trajectory of a perfect ring of smoke.